OPHELIA RAVENWARD
THE DAUGHTER OF DEADWOOD

Allen Isom

DEDICATION

For the pain I've felt in the name of love.
For the pain I've caused in kind.
For the ones whose love I carry still,
And the ones I've left behind.

Each heartache; a small sting of death.
Each embrace; the great joy of living.

CONTENTS

ACKNOWLEGEMENTS

I'd like to thank my mother-in-law, Laura. She suggested
I write a series. I only wanted to write horror, but here we are.
This series has quickly become my favorite idea to date.
So thank you for the support and the suggestion.

I'd also like to think my family for their continued support
for my writing. It means the world

Lastly, what few fans I know of, thanks for kind words.
I don't know that I'd care this much if you didn't.

SOMINOR

Deadwood Manor
Knightridge Manor
Duskwatch
Stillriver Kingdom
Endless Waste
Marsh Hollow

Evergreen
Spellevue
Silverleaf
Citadel
Windy
Willow
Springhill
Roche
Village
Roche Manor
Iroveil
Kingdom
Bloodmoore
Manor

Ursalapod

- Similar to a common bear in appearance and temperament.

- Can reach sizes of 2-18 meters in height.

- Most commonly found in forested regions, but mostly among coastal treelines.

- Hearing is sharp, but not overly so

- Additional eyes provide wide field of view

- Diet consists mainly of small prey. Though, "small" is relative

- Opportunistic feeders. They prefer meat but will also forage for berries.

  ~ 4 fur covered tentacles are lined with jagged teeth
     ~ Used to rend the flesh of their prey before eating

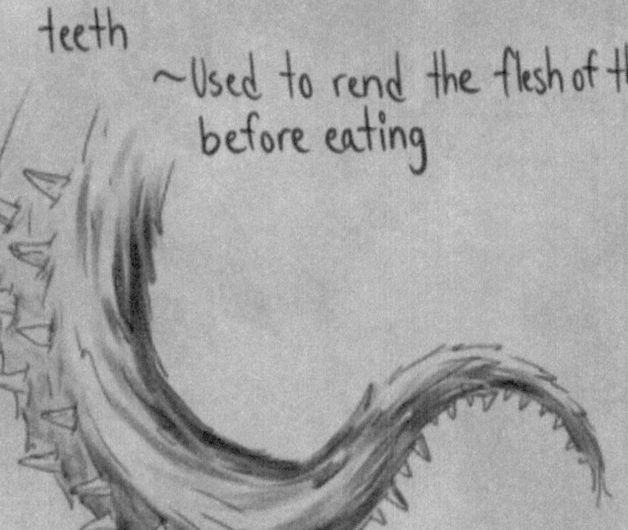

THE GIRL WITH NO NAME

In the middle of the Deadwoods, in the middle of a pouring rain, a young girl came crawling out from the middle of a hole. She was soaking wet, winded, and hadn't the slightest recollection as to how she had ended up in that hole to begin with, or even what her name might have been, if ever she had one. More peculiar still, as she tumbled out of the hole and onto the soggy ground, was the fact that when she turned back to examine the hole, there was nothing there except for mud and sticks. She wondered, among the uproar of new thoughts, if she might have imagined it entirely.

Among the dead trees, the ravens cawed in mounting cries that seemed to herald her arrival as either cause for celebration or dire warning. Either way the ravens had meant it, she preferred they keep quiet. She preferred they give her a moment to sort through her racing thoughts, working frantically to make sense of the vacant corners and missing memories that seemed to occupy her ever-reeling mind with nothing. The forest began to twirl, and the rains that fell on every inch of her exposed skin felt like freezing needles, while the rest found refuge in the thirsty fibers of her thick, gray cloak. It grew heavier with each new drop it drank.

When first she had climbed out of the hole, her breath had come in hard, heaving gulps and her heartbeat matched it, but that was no longer the case. Her heavy breaths turned shallow and quick, struggling to keep up with the panicked fluttering in her chest. She fell to her knees, into shallow pools of frigid mud, wrapped her trembling arms around herself, and rocked forward.

She screamed.

She screamed until her heart stopped racing and her mind stopped racing. She screamed until her muscles were seized by it, and her breath came out in little more than a trickle. Lightning cut through the darkness, followed close by thunder. The ravens fell silent, and in the silence, a not-too-distant shriek clawed its way through the rains.

Her breathing stopped, as did her racing heart, if only for a beat. Her body trembled under the cold rain, arrested by dread. Around her, the ravens resumed their irritating cawing and stirred once more, slowly at first, fidgeting about along the dead branches, and then more frantic as the girl tentatively turned her head to catch a glimpse of what might have made the unnerving sound. The beating of rain on the soggy ground and the flutter of restless ravens were the only things she could hear, but through the misty veil of rain, among the densely packed trees, she saw something stir.

Between the twisted trunks, a shadow shambled unnaturally. She didn't know what it was or how it should have been moving, but how it *was* moving made her uneasy. She slowly stood and the commotion among the ravens swelled. The thing stopped; its body as rigid as the trees that surrounded it. The girl could scarcely make out the shape, save for branches that grew from what she assumed to be its head. The head jerked. It looked right at her.

The ravens cawed.

The girl ran.

She ran as quickly as her freezing cold feet would allow her, her steps uneven on the soaked ground. Stones pounded at her feet and roots scratched at her ankles. The ravens followed alongside her. Behind, where she dared not to look, she could hear the ragged breath and splashing steps of her pursuer. The ravens fluttered in front of her, and their cawing felt angry. She lost her footing and screamed as she fell forward into a puddle.

Amidst fluttering wings and raucous caws, she clambered to her feet. Behind her, the cry of that *thing* came screeching through the chaos. The ravens left her with only one direction to run, she veered left and sprinted away. The ravens took to the trees once again, trailing along her right.

Her thick cloak, which felt heavier with each step, had become ensnared on the dead branches, reaching out like skeletal hands desperate to stop her, each snapping free, too weak to hold her as she ran. Until one didn't snap at all.

The stubborn branch held firm, sending her tumbling to the ground. The ravens flew past her, cawed at one another, and then circled back. The girl rolled onto her back and sat up. The thing that was chasing her was still there, among the trees, charging.

Lightning lit the night.

The beast had four legs, antlers, and eyes that reflected the sudden flash of light, as though shining from the beast itself. A word came into her mind.

Buck.

She wasn't sure how she knew, perhaps in the same way she knew that the birds were ravens and the trees were trees, but the word came to her much like lighting from the storm; illuminating up the turbulent darkness in her mind.

Ravens poured in around her, their wings a flurry of blackened feathers. She screamed in terror, closed her eyes, and held her head. It wasn't until she heard the disturbing sound of the buck mixed with the fluttering of ravens that she opened her eyes again. Ravens pecked at the buck in a barrage of attacks. It reared up on its hind legs and swung its broken antlers wildly, while batting away with its hooves. She kept staring until another bolt of lightning and a clap of thunder finally freed the girl from her paralysis.

As if the lighting had struck her directly, she sprung to her feet and fled. The ravens raced to catch up, leaving the disoriented buck behind. To her left this time, the ravens flowed along through the trees like a dark river. It was then, like the suddenness of the lightning, that another thought snapped into her head.

Are they helping me? she wondered, not daring to look back.

Further and further, she pushed herself through the dark, dead woods that seemed to never break. A labyrinth of twisted shapes and shadows surrounded her without end. Her legs quivered and her heart pounded. Despite the cold, wet air, her chest burned more with each breath. She kept going until she could no longer hear the buck behind her, then let herself come to a rest. The ravens cawed in protest. She didn't care. She was tired and, as far as she could tell, the danger had passed. It was only her, the ravens, and the rain left in these woods.

The tree against which she braced herself was filled with ravens, while those that could not fit took their leave. In that moment of stillness, among the persistent rain, she looked up, still not sure what to make of them. She thought to ask them what they wanted, why they were following her. She wanted to know what they seemed to know already. Where was she? How did she get in that hole? Did they know who she was?

Pointless.

Ravens couldn't speak, she knew that. It was then she realized that she knew quite a bit more about the frightening world she'd found herself thrust into than she initially thought. Though her first memories were of her crawling out of that hole, there hid within her a deep knowledge just beyond her reach. She couldn't explain it; she didn't understand it, but she felt it. And though she couldn't begin to describe what lay beyond this graveyard of trees, she knew a great world existed just out of her reach.

The ravens stirred.

The girl pushed herself off the tree and sharpened her senses, filtering out the heavy rains and the mounting cries of the birds. The sound of rapid splashing approached from the dark. From where she had just come.

She turned sharply to face it, the ravens flocked between her and the sound with little warning. They batted her with their wings and cawed angrily, as if screaming, *Why are you still here?*

A bolt of lightning revealed why. Beyond the unkindness, the buck had found her and locked its lifeless gaze upon her once again. The thunder crashed in, as if the very storm was urging her to take flight with the ravens that had already begun to flee.

She did.

The buck closed in with little effort, disregarding any attempts the ravens made to impede its nocturnal hunt. Exhaustion weighed further upon the girl, her breath consumed, muscles faltering, and her heart threatening to burst.

A glimmer of hope arose within her.

Just as despair had threatened to engulf her, she glimpsed a break amidst the trees ahead. A surge of energy coursed through her body. Her numb feet splashed through puddles, she leaped over errant roots, and pushed herself harder as the edge of the woods drew nearer with each arduous step. Even the skies above seemed to rejoice upon her approach to the forest's end, as the rains eased and the moonlight trickled through small gaps in the clouds above. A sliver of a smile formed on her face. Just as it did, she felt something graze her back.

She screamed as she pushed herself to run faster, instinctively glancing back over her shoulder. Relief filled her terrified heart as she witnessed the buck tumbling across the increasingly sparse forest floor, likely ensnared by one of the many roots she had skillfully dodged. The ravens burst forth from the woods ahead of her and, within seconds, she joined them.

She nearly tripped over her own wearied steps as she put the tree line behind her. Any hint of a smile that might have graced her face only moments before had all but vanished. Greeting her now were row upon row of headstones. Without hesitation, she searched for a place to take refuge.

Across the graveyard sat a large structure.

Manor, was the name her mind placed with it. It was tall and beautiful; hauntingly so.

Among the headstones, ravens had found perch, most of them sitting idly atop a mausoleum. It struck in her a familiar chord. Like the manor, it was not frightening but not entirely comforting. A pale glow was cast over the night as clouds parted and the full might of the bright moon shone through. Its light revealed her surroundings with a new clarity, during which her attention was drawn back to the manor. In the large window facing her, she could make out three faces shrouded in darkness. They were looking at her, and she wondered whether they might be friend or foe. Before she could decide, the buck's haunting cry ripped through the trees.

She chose the ravens.

She chose the mausoleum. The gate to which had been left open..

As she entered the stone structure, she couldn't help but notice the word engraved above the doorway, lit clearly by the pale moonlight, its large, ornate letters carved neatly into the stone.

Ophelia. She read it as easily as she crossed the threshold. She made sure to carefully close the gate behind her. To her dismay, the latch appeared to be broken.

The air inside was just as cold as outside, and the musty smell of stone, dirt, and rain came with it. The floor, however, was dry. A small thing for which she found herself immensely grateful. The tomb felt nearly inviting. In the center of it was a rectangular stone that was capped with a decorative slab. Ornate filigree swept around its borders, and in the center was the stone an image of a woman. She knew it was a grave, but the thought of what lay within did not bother her at all. Instead, a great sorrow came bubbling up from somewhere deep within her, as though she were mourning someone she knew dearly. Someone she couldn't remember.

Ophelia. The name came to her again. It felt warm, like home.

She hid behind the stone sarcophagus and let the name swirl around in her mind. It swept through the empty corners for a connection, a memory, something to make sense of the hidden meaning in it that stirred feelings within her. There was nothing. Nothing but silence.

Silence. Where are the ravens?

The ravens had gone silent. Eerily so. The only sounds to be heard outside of her own breath were the gentle dripping remains of a rain come and gone and the faint stirring of soggy grass under hoof.

The buck. Her eyes widened.

It crept toward the mausoleum's entrance, and with it came the sound of rapidly moving breaths. The decaying animal was searching for her scent. The girl held her breath as though it was the only thing of value in her possession. As though the beast, just a short distance from her, was coming to steal it away. The only thought that brought her comfort was the gate between them.

A sudden gust of wind blew it open.

No.

And just a few moments later, the sound of a hard hoof on harder stone reverberated throughout the small room as the buck entered, and sent a shiver rolling through the girl's body.

She tensed, desperately trying to still herself, but she only trembled more. Her slow, shallow breaths slipped out shaky. To her, they sounded as loud as the thunder. She hoped that wasn't true.

Another step by the undead buck, followed by another one of its shrill, gurgling cries. She jumped, then clasped her hands over her mouth. It stepped forward, around to the left of the stone island, it's hooves lightly tapping on the stone floor. Tears formed in her eyes with the thought that she would meet her end so soon after only having just begun.

SOMEONE'S IN THE CEMETERY

Lady Nikollette A'Mysteriouse spent most nights falling asleep in her study, which over the decades had become a home all its own, nestled within the walls of Deadwood Manor. Her dreams were often filled with visions of monsters, magic, and tragedy. Tonight was no different, apart from one tiny detail. This time when she was awoken by a soft cry, she was surprised to find it was not her own. This time, the cry came in the form of the distant cawing of ravens through a pouring rain. At first, as she shook free the remaining slumber, she considered that it might have just been a howling wind. After all, what would ravens be doing out in a storm like this? But when she looked out the window, the rain fell heavy and true. Not a single hint of wind to be found.

On the desk before her sat a half-drunken cup of moonblossom tea whose steam had long ceased rising. Its iridescent, pale blue color had vanished with the heat. Lady Nikollette stood up from her chair, in no way eager to stand. The vestiges of slumber, and perhaps the tea, left her knees feeling weak. She steadied herself on her desk for the first few steps until she found her footing. She had begun to feel the unwelcome tug of age more often as of late. As she approached forty, she hadn't thought that she would start to feel it so deeply, but a youth filled with fighting monsters and wielding magic had clearly taken its toll.

"Weaving magic comes at a cost," her father had always told her.

She understood that more with each day as she yearned for the same willpower and energy that youth had once bestowed upon her in abundance.

The window was streaked with rain and peering through it was akin to looking through the backside of a waterfall. The first thing she saw was her own reflection. Her normally tight bun had unraveled itself somewhat, giving way to stray strands of hair that shot out in various directions. She pressed her gold, wire-frame glasses back up her nose before they could slide off entirely, and then she worked her hands over her white blouse to straighten out the wrinkles as best she could. The bottom of her blouse had come slightly untucked from her long, black skirt, so she carefully tucked it all back into place. Finally, she straightened the looking glass necklace that had found itself caught on some of the lace around her collar. Once satisfied with her appearance, she looked through her reflection into the night. A rain this heavy hadn't fallen for some time.

"Ominous portent?" she asked aloud. "Or just a storm?"

Through the thick curtain of water, she could make out the shadows and shapes that made up the family cemetery. She smiled and wished them a well-deserved rest, and though she'd only met a handful of them in her youth, she cherished them all dearly. Then her smile slipped away at the intrusive reminder from the back of her mind that *all those graves are empty.*

Her eyes lingered on the hollow graves, and she found herself wishing – as she often did – that there was some way to find their remains and return them to their rightful places of rest. On the surface, she understood that doing so would mean very little to the graves themselves, or even the remains, but to her, it would mean the world. It would mean she still had family close by. Deep down, she knew she would never find them. They had been lost long ago. Taken.

She was alone. The last remaining member of her family. A bloodline that would end on the hallowed grounds of Deadwood Manor. She wished the Deadwoods that surrounded the manor were still green and full of life, as they had been when she was a girl. That this house could still be called Greenwood Manor.

Far in the distance, muffled by the rain, a new sound found its way to Nikollette. Following close behind the sound was a bolt of lightning and the crash of thunder. She couldn't be certain that the sound wasn't part of the storm, but to her, it sounded like a voice. Like it was coming from deep within the Deadwoods.

"No, that can't be." The whispered words, meant to soothe her troubled mind, did nothing of the sort. In her gut, she knew what it was she had heard, no matter how much reason tried to convince her otherwise. It was then that what looked like – through the wavy streaks of rain – a small unkindness of ravens came flying out of the tree line.

In a storm like this, Lady Nikollette couldn't believe ravens would ever bother to take flight. The chaotic black blurs came to rest atop her mother's mausoleum. They twitched in the rain and fidgeted restlessly back and forth. Their refusal to take refuge from the storm confounded her even more.

"Ominous portent indeed," she murmured.

Empty.

The thought found her again. She wished she had had more time to know her mother. Fourteen years was hardly enough for a child. Over the years since, Nikollette had wondered: if her mother and aunt had still been alive, could perhaps all of this been avoided? Perhaps the Deadwoods would have still been green. Perhaps Father would have still been there to guide her. *Perhaps*, she thought. *What use is perhaps?*

A rapping on the door of her study, soft and considerate, pulled her attention from the ravens.

"Yes, come in, Mr. Bishop."

First to appear was a wild tuft of black hair, followed by the rest of the lanky, wide-eyed boy. His glasses hung at the edge of his nose, exposing the blackened eyes beneath the illusion of normal eyes the magical spectacles provided. He pushed them up and apologized. "Sorry to disturb you. How did you know it was me?"

"You don't have to wear those when you are in this house," Nikollette reminded him as she turned back to the window. "You don't need to hide from anyone here."

"Sorry," Barnaby apologized again and then took off his glasses, folded them, and hung them from the topmost button of his pajama shirt. "I just have gotten so used to wearing them. I suppose I forgot."

"No need to apologize. I guessed you might have heard that sound through the storm."

"Who wouldn't have? It was as loud as the rain."

"It was actually quite a faint scream." Nikollette looked down at him over the top of her wireframe glasses. "Not all of us are gifted with such keen senses as you, my young friend."

"I'm not sure gifted is the way I would describe it, but yes, sorry. I forget sometimes."

"Apologies for nothing make apologies mean nothing."

"Right." Barnaby shook his head and moved on. "So, do you know what the trouble is?"

Nikollette was silent for a moment, and then she lifted her hand and pointed out the window. "Do you see that unkindness perched atop my mother's mausoleum?"

"I do." Even through the wall of water running down the glass, and even in the dead of night, it took Barnaby no time to zero in on the birds. "What are they doing out in the rain?"

"I couldn't say," Nikollette responded. "Would you believe me if I told you they flew out from the Deadwoods before perching there?"

"Flew? In this weather?"

Barnaby went silent. Nikollette looked at him from the corner of her eye, careful not to turn her head and possibly interrupt his train of thought.

"Maybe another animal died in the woods, and the rustling of its corpse frightened the ravens enough to send them flying?"

"Perhaps," Lady Nikollette responded. "That was also my first thought. That is, until I realized the ravens could have simply flown to a new tree or even higher up in whatever tree they might have already been perched."

"That's a fair point," Barnaby added. His brow scrunched up and his eyes narrowed. "Rather ominous, wouldn't you say?"

"I would." Nikollette smiled.

The two of them stood side-by-side without a word for minutes. A crash of thunder tore through the silence. Another scream from the Deadwoods came right on its heels.

This time clearer, closer.

"Should I wake Amarine?" Barnaby asked.

"No, let the girl sleep." Nikollette waved off his concern. She saw his frustration.

"What if there's danger?" he asked, raising his voice with a sense of urgency. Nikollette suspected this might be his indirect way of waking up Amarine. "Only dead things come out of those woods. She should be ready with us."

"I understand your concern. Truly, I do." Nikollette placed a gentle hand on his shoulder and closed her eyes. She drew in a slow, audible breath and then let it out. Barnaby, whether he meant to or not, did the same. "But I can't imagine there is anything in the Deadwoods that we cannot handle ourselves."

Nikollette let go of him and returned her gaze to the window. "Besides, you know how hard it is to wake up Amarine. By the time you have woken her up, the trouble will have arrived, been met, and been promptly dismissed with little consequence."

Barnaby smiled and Nikollette added, "Hardly seems like a thing to bother the tired girl's rest over. Wouldn't you agree?"

"Maybe," Barnaby reluctantly admitted.

Another cry came through the trees, and it seemed as though it was carried on the wings of the ravens. A second unkindness, this one more formidable in size, came bursting through the tree line. The dark shape of the cawing mass flowed through the rain as a single entity, highlighted by another strike of lightning and another clap of thunder.

"More?" Barnaby asked. "Why are there so many?"

Lady Nikollette hushed him, her gaze never wandering from the events unfolding just across the cemetery. Still, she could not make out what danger might be lurking beyond the tangle of dead trees, the dead of night, and the veil of rain.

"If that one didn't wake Amarine, I'm not sure what will," she whispered.

Together, they watched the ravens congregate on top of the mausoleum. Those that could not squeeze themselves into place found headstones nearby upon which to perch. Footsteps came pounding into the study from behind them. They turned to see Amarine, in her pajamas and rubbing her tired eyes. Her white hair was a tangled mess that nearly stood on end as though she had been struck by lightning herself. In that moment, the rain outside seemed to soften, as though Amarine's very presence was enough to lighten even the most stubborn skies. The view from their window became clearer.

"What's with all the noise?" Amarine asked at the tail end of her yawn.

"It's the Deadwoods." Barney turned to look at her. "There's something in the Deadwoods."

"Someone," Lady Nikollette corrected without looking away from the window.

"Someone?" Amarine asked as she plodded toward the large study window. "Why would someone be in the Deadwoods?"

"That *is* the question," Nikollette answered.

Their conversation came to an abrupt end as another scream pierced the night. A torrent of ravens erupted violently from the tangle of trees. They swirled chaotically; their cawing filled the air with discord as they searched and shoved for a place to perch among the others. A figure followed, emerging from the tree line with a stumble.

"Who is that?" Amarine nearly shouted, her sleepy eyes widening. "Why were they in the Deadwoods?"

"Hush," Nikollette whispered. "Be still. To date, nothing good has ever come out of those decrepit woods."

A parting of the clouds above brought clarity to the stormy night, revealing to the trio at the window that the mysterious figure was no more than a young girl. A frightened expression was etched across her face, and her soaking, tattered robes rose and fell with each labored breath. Moonlight illuminated her pallid skin as she frantically searched her new surroundings, no doubt seeking refuge. Her gaze darted from the mausoleum, where the ravens perched and cawed, to their very window.

"Can she see us?" Amarine asked.

"Not likely. The study is nearly as dark as the cemetery." Though Nikollette didn't quite believe that to be the case.

Over the girl's shoulder, something no one in the manor could either see or hear stole her terrified attention.

"What was that?" Barnaby asked, straightening up, "It sounds like an animal."

The mysterious girl gave the manor one final look and then ran for the mausoleum. The unkindness that had amassed didn't so much as flinch as she ran past but simply turned their heads and watched. Nikollette had never seen so many ravens sit so still and silent in her lifetime.

"What's wrong with the ravens?" Barnaby whispered, "Why aren't they moving?"

"Strange," Amarine added. "I hadn't even noticed."

All at once, the ravens took flight, a cloud of black rising and blocking out the moonlight before vanishing into the night. Immediately after their departure, a buck came staggering out of the Deadwoods, from the exact spot where the girl had appeared. Its antlers sat askew, one of which was snapped in half and swinging loose. Ribs jutted out from a gaping hole in its torso, and moss hung from its decaying body. Its cry, painfully screaming from its half-skeletal face, sounded like an uneasy mix between that of a living buck and the bubbling squelch of some dying thing choking on its own blood.

"You've got to help that girl," Amarine pleaded as she tugged on Lady Nikollette's blouse without looking away from the horror before her.

The buck sniffed at the ground and then the air. It wandered, staggering through the cemetery, drawing nearer the mausoleum with each twitching step.

"Yes, I think you're right. You two go to your rooms."

With that, Lady Nikollette turned sharply, plucked a book from her desk, and marched out of the study.

Terror rolled through the girl's body. She could hear the buck searching for her scent just around the corner of the sarcophagus. Her heart sank, as the decayed snout of that wretched beast came sliding into view.

This was it.

"Excuse me," the girl heard a voice command. She could hear two quick hoof taps as the buck turned to face it. The mysterious voice continued, "You are not supposed to be here."

The buck howled, and a roll of thunder came from the now-distant storm. The already dark tomb, lit softly by moonlight, grew darker as sparse clouds came filling back in. The girl turned and pushed herself up onto her knees to get a peek at what was unfolding outside.

Outside the mausoleum stood a woman. She held in her right arm, propped up against her torso, a narrow book that was currently flipped open. Her left hand held a quill, which darted about as she scrawled something on the parchment. The buck lowered its head, aiming its broken antlers at the woman, and then launched itself at her full speed. The clouds above flashed with light and growled with a low thunder. The woman did not seem worried. The girl wanted nothing more than to call out, warn her somehow.

As the buck closed in, the woman tore the paper free, and tossed it in the direction of the buck with seemingly little worry at all. The sheet of parchment landed gracefully on the wet grass, and from this distance, the girl could just make out the symbol drawn on it. A moment later, the buck's hoof stepped right on top of the paper. The girl felt a tingle along her arms and neck.

A loud crash.

An explosion of dirt and grass.

A steaming trail of ash and cinder.

The clouds parted immediately after. The girl could feel a distinct hum in the air and a jolt of something running through her body. The woman closed her notebook, tucked her quill back into the cover,and let it drop to her side where it hung from a strap of leather that cut across her chest and over her shoulder. She took a moment to wipe debris off her long skirt and white shirt and then ran her palms over her hair and brushed a couple of strands out of her face, all before looking directly into the mausoleum. The girl ducked.

"You can come out now," the woman called. "You'll find no danger remains."

The girl didn't budge.

"Come now." Again the woman spoke, this time more gently. "It is perfectly safe."

The girl stood up slowly and drew in a deep breath.

"There you are. Come on out. You must be freezing. You'll get sick if we don't get you taken care of."

Cautiously, the girl stepped around the stone sarcophagus and made her way to the exit. The woman stepped just as slowly toward her.

"I cannot imagine how terrifying that must have been for you. What is your name, young lady?"

Her name? She still didn't know. There was only one name should could recall. One she had read only recently. It was the name that came leaping from her mouth without thought.

"Ophelia," she said softly.

"Ophelia," the woman repeated inquisitively. A smile stretched across the woman's face, and Ophelia saw her eyes quickly dart to the top of the mausoleum entrance and then back to hers. "My name is Nikollette A'Mysteriouse. It is nice to meet you, young Ophelia. Why don't you come inside with me? We can give you some clean clothes, a warm shower, and a safe place to rest your head until morning. Only if that is okay with you, of course."

Ophelia thought about it for a moment. This woman must have been one of the faces lingering in the dark of the window. Ophelia looked at the window again. Inside stood the two other faces, still watching. They were younger than the woman. Sahe could now see that they were smiling. Ophelia turned back to Nikollette.

"Thank you. That would be very kind."

"Kind? No. Simply the proper thing to do. Come. Follow me."

Nikollette turned and marched through the soggy cemetery. Ophelia could see the heels of her boots sinking into the soft ground, yet she walked with such poise, while Ophelia struggled with each sinking step of her tingling feet.

She couldn't wait to feel warmth.

WELCOME TO DEADWOOD MANOR

Deadwood Manor sat in the center of a clearing surrounded by the dead forest Nikollette referred to simply as "the Deadwoods." There appeared to be only a single dirt road leading in or out of the grounds. Nikollette explained to Ophelia, as they walked toward the front door, that once upon a time the residence had been called Greenwood Manor, and the surrounding forest had been named in a similar fashion. When Ophelia asked what had happened to the forest, Nikollette casually answered that it was a long story best left for another time. Ophelia did not press the matter any further.

On one side of the manor, from where they had just walked, sat a moderately-sized cemetery, where Nikollette explained all her family had, at one point or another, been buried. While walking around to the front door, Ophelia saw a fountain without water. Dirt filled its bowl and a stone figure, broken off at the waist, stood upon the arid ground. The road leading in and out circled the old water fixture and a carriage sat adjacent. Ophelia could see a short wall of flowering hedges just past the manor's main entrance, on the other side of the house. She craned her neck, attempting to steal a better look.

"The garden," Lady Nikollette explained as they walked up the front porch. "Not well tended these days. More a wild mess of flowers and vines than a garden. But out back, there is a large, open meadow where we train."

"Train?" Ophelia asked; puzzled.

"It's a bit of a larger conversation, like the woods, that I'm all too happy to have later. First, you ought to clean up." She gave the door a gentle push, letting it swing open, gesturing with her hands for Ophelia to lead the way. "Welcome to Deadwood Manor, Ophelia."

The heavy-looking wooden door opened with an effortless grace and not a sound. A wall of warmth fell over Ophelia and brought with it a scent that caused her body to ripple with relaxation. It was as inviting a place as she could ever hope to encounter. Familiar in a way she could not begin to explain.

The foyer was tall and open yet still cozy. It towered above her, running the entire height of the manor, and from its domed ceiling hung beautifully crafted, cylindrical lights that burst to life as the door opened, casting a warm yellow over the open space. It was as if they too were inviting her in. As though she was an old, familiar face that the manor itself had awoken excitedly in the middle of the night to greet with a smile.

At the opposite end ran a wide staircase that led up to the landing above. The banisters that ran along either side looked as fluid as a flowing stream, twisting along and curling up at their ends. Ophelia stepped onto the wooden floor as she crossed the threshold in awe and marveled at the intricate, geometric patterns that fit into one another seamlessly in alternating shades of rich browns and subtle reds.

"It's beautiful," Ophelia's remarked.

"Yes," Nikollette responded from behind her, shutting the door. "Even now, after all my years, I continue to find myself taken aback by its majesty. I'm not sure how my family managed to build such a work of art, but I'm eternally grateful that they did."

Ophelia turned back around to face Nikollette. "Are the others your children?"

"The others?"

"Yes." Ophelia suddenly felt uneasy. "Or was I mistaken? In the window, watching."

"Ah, I wondered if you'd seen them." Nikollette smiled and nodded. "Though I do consider them family, they are not my children, not really. They are my wards, and they do live here. You'll meet them in the morning, but for now, let's get you taken care of. Besides…" Nikollette raised her voice as though she were no longer talking to Ophelia. "…those two ought to be sleeping. I wouldn't want to wake them at this hour."

In the distance above them, Ophelia could hear the gentle sound of feet running across the second floor, followed by two doors shutting, one after the other. She smiled at Nikollette. Nikollette smiled back.

Turning and walking across the foyer, Nikollette waved at Ophelia to follow. Ophelia did, staying close beside her.

Ophelia was led down a corridor behind the grand staircase, where painted portraits adorned the walls, all of the people she could only presume were Nikollette's family. She passed one of a woman with dark hair and beautiful, sleepy, green eyes. The name beneath read "Ophelia." Ophelia said nothing. Instead, she looked down at her pale feet as they popped in and out from beneath her tattered gray cloak. The name belonged to someone else. She had stolen it.

Then Nikollette stopped. Ophelia nearly collided with the kind woman but managed to stop herself just shy of it. She jumped back and looked up at Nikollette.

"Sorry." The apology came out on instinct.

"No apology necessary, except perhaps on my end. I would have done well to give you some warning that we've arrived."

Lady Nikollette stood before a door. It was a green door that was rounded at its top. The intricately engraved wood almost looked alive, with a forest scene between two trees that ran from roots at the bottom to lush leaves toward the top. Ophelia wondered if that is what the forest around the manor once looked like.

"The Greenwoods," Nikollette said as though reading Ophelia's mind. "This is my study. Come and find me once you are done with your shower. This way."

Nikollette continued to the end of the corridor and then turned right. Immediately, she stopped at another door. This one was hardly remarkable. When Nikollette opened it, Ophelia could see right away that it was a bathroom. She could see it in her mind as well as she could with her eyes.

"Do you know how to work a shower?" Nikollette asked.

Ophelia nodded with a confused look on her face. Her response came out as a question. "Yes, I do?"

"Memories are a funny thing. Don't think about it too much. For now…" Nikollette opened a cabinet door beside the bathroom from which she produced a towel and a garment. "…here is a towel and some clean pajamas that ought to fit you nicely. You'll have proper clothes available to you in the morning."

Ophelia smiled and took the linens from Nikollette. "Thank you."

"Of course. Just remember to come see me in the study when you're through."

Ophelia nodded and watched as Nikollette disappeared back around the corner. The bathroom tiles were cold on her bare feet, but she was excited to get cleaned up. She looked at herself in the mirror. Her face was spattered with mud. Her short black hair was flat, wet, and tangled, and her green, sleepy eyes looked as though they might just shut right then and there. She turned on the shower, held out her hand, and shivered in delight as it warmed up and ran over her cold hand.

Ophelia found the door to the study even more enchanting seeing it again. She ran her hand against it and imagined that whoever had carved it must have done so with painstaking love and care. Upon first glance, she thought the green color might have been painted, but looking at it now, it appeared as though the green color was as much a part of the wood as the grains that ran down it.

"You can come in," Nikollette's muffled voice sang from inside the study. "It isn't locked."

Ophelia's face burned as she jerked her hand from the door, and she imagined she looked as red as flame. Cold brass knob gripped tight, she took a deep breath and let the heat on her face dissipate before entering.

"Have a seat, dear." Nikollette, sitting behind a desk, gestured to the empty chair across from her, a high-backed chair like Nikollette's, and like most of the other things Ophelia had encountered in the manor, these chairs were bathed in beautiful filigree and ornate carvings. "Feeling better? You look quite cozy."

Ophelia sat in the chair, running her hands over the sleeves of her warm pajamas. She smiled. "Yes, thank you. Much better."

"So, Ophelia, how is it that you came to find yourself in the middle of the Deadwoods on such a dreadful night?"

"I don't know." Ophelia was quick to answer, having spent her time since last seeing Nikollette trying desperately to figure it out. To uncover anything that might give her any clue as to who she was. She came up empty. "I can't remember."

Nikollette thought for a moment.

Then she asked, "Do you know where you live? Where you came from?"

"No." Ophelia grew anxious. "I can't really remember anything."

Tears began to form in Ophelia's tired gaze. She wiped them clear and turned her head, looking out the same window she had only a few moments ago been looking into.

"Only your name then?"

"What?"

"Your name," Nikollette repeated. "You only remember your name? Ophelia. You would have no way of knowing this, but Ophelia was my mother's name."

"Well…" Ophelia wrapped her arms around herself, avoiding eye contact with Nikollette. "That's not my name. I took it from the mausoleum. I'm sorry. You can have it back."

"I see." Nikollette smiled. "Keep it. It suits you. Besides, who has ever heard of giving back a name? It is hardly something that one can take in the first place, just as I'm hardly the only Nikollette to have ever lived."

Ophelia looked up to see the kind woman smiling at her. There was something about Nikollette that made Ophelia feel at home. The same feeling she had had when she first read the name Ophelia on the mausoleum.

"Tell you what…" Nikollette leaned forward. "I could try to use magic to see what it is you've forgotten, but I'd like to get permission first before I go poking around in a life that isn't mine to be poking around in."

"Will it hurt?"

"Well, it won't involve any more lightning bolts, if that's what you are asking, no."

Ophelia smiled, followed by a brief giggle. "Okay then. Do I need to do anything?"

"No, nothing at all," Nikollette assured her and then leaned back in her seat and held up a small pendant that hung around her neck from a silver chain. It was a circle of glass, with a tiny chip at one edge, held in place by a silver frame. "Do you see this?"

Ophelia nodded.

"It's a sort of magical item, a talisman called the Looking Glass, and it can reveal to me all sorts of hidden truths about all sorts of things. I don't use it often on people, especially without their permission, because that would be quite rude, don't you think?"

Ophelia nodded again.

"I mostly use it on magical creatures or other inanimate objects that might possess magical properties. It's very helpful and saves me a fair amount of trouble from time to time. Magic can prove to be dangerous if you don't possess the knowledge behind it. However, that is something we can discuss later and in greater detail. For now, I just need you to sit there. There is nothing dangerous about this particular magic."

Ophelia straightened herself up in her chair and swallowed the lump that had formed in her throat. Even though Nikollette had said it wouldn't be dangerous, she could hardly put out of her mind the image of that beastly buck or the electric sensation that ran through the air. Such power.

Before she could summon the courage to change her mind, Nikollette lifted the circular piece of glass up to her eye.

Within seconds, tears ran down Nikollette's face, but before they could inch their way any further, she lowered the looking glass and wiped them away.

"What's wrong?" Ophelia asked. "What did you see?"

Nikollette smiled, a sad sort of smile, and sniffled a little before waving her hand. "I saw you," she finally said. "I saw you in the Deadwoods, and I saw you here."

"Nothing else?"

Nikollette looked away.

"Then why are you crying?"

Nikollette stood up slowly and then walked around her desk without a word. When she arrived in front of Ophelia, she knelt in front of her and grabbed her hand. Her grip was both soft and firm all at once.

"I'm crying because, in all my years, the Looking Glass has shown me many things, and it has answered many questions. It has illuminated the darkest of mysteries, and it has lifted many a veil, but now…" She paused, looking deep into Ophelia's eyes, as though she was looking for something inside of her. "Now it has left me with more questions than answers. Who you are, I'm afraid, shall remain a mystery. For now, at least. I'm sorry, Ophelia. Truly."

Ophelia was overcome with an almost instinctual urge to comfort Nikollette. It wasn't her fault the Looking Glass couldn't reveal anything helpful. She had forgotten nearly everything, so there was likely nothing of value to find. It wasn't her fault that Ophelia had just shown up in front of her home. Nikollette was doing the best she could for a girl she knew nothing about and had never met. For that, Ophelia was grateful.

"It's okay," Ophelia finally choked out, placing her free hand on top of Nikollette's. "You tried your best. At least I'm not out in the cold anymore. You've done plenty."

Nikollette nodded, smiled, then stood up and ran her hands over her skirt and blouse, straightening them while taking in a sharp breath through her sniffling nose. She forced a smile through her sadness and it quickly grew into something genuine. Like some subtle magic.

"Come then." She held out her hand. Her voice wavered ever so slightly before righting itself into a more joyous tone. "How about I show you to your room so you can get some rest? Tomorrow, we can discuss more about what it is you wish to do, and you can meet my wards. I know they are eager to meet you."

Ophelia smiled at Nikollette's warmth and the prospect of meeting the others and then asked, as she took Nikollette's hand and stood, "How many others?"

"Just the two," she answered. "Two is all we are allowed to teach at any given time. They are both about your age, based on the looks of you. I don't suppose you would know how old you are?"

Ophelia thought for a moment and then shook her head.

"Well, let's just say you're sixteen. You look sixteen."

Ophelia smiled. "Sixteen it is then."

When Ophelia entered the bedroom, her heart set aflutter. The sight, the smell, the feel of it triggered a cascade of unexpected reactions in an instant. Well-worn scenes depicting lush forests alive with pixies adorned the top half of the walls with magic buried deep in the lively imagery. Below, dark wood paneling gleamed in the candlelight, as if it too were alive and pulsing with magic.

A single window sat opposite the door. Beneath it, a cushioned bench, and beyond it hung the moon. Beside the window, to the right, a wardrobe stood tall and proud, with ornate carvings covering the doors and a deep, rich wood finish. Its brass handles formed a woven pattern that coiled in and over itself, like a sleeping serpent wrapped around a gem that sparked with a mischievous glint. To the left of the window, the bed.

The bed stood out, enveloped in an aura of grandeur, its towering headboard reaching high into the air, adorned with intricate carvings of magical creatures and delicate filigree. The bedspread was a rich burgundy silk, trimmed with delicate lace and embroidered with golden threads. The massive four-poster frame was made of dark, polished wood. At the top, a plush canopy of silken curtains hung and seemed to billow gently in a breeze that wasn't there.

"I hope you find it comfortable. It has been years since I've slept here, decades really, but I do recall it being quite the sleep." As Nikollette spoke, she looked around the room, as if she were visiting a place that had been lost to time and memory.

Ophelia sat at the foot of the bed and gave it a bounce. "It's wonderful. Thank you."

Nikollette turned abruptly to face her, like she had forgotten she had a guest there with her. "Yes, good. Oh!" She then twirled toward the wardrobe, resting a hand on the door but not opening it. "Any clothes you need tomorrow, you'll find in here. If they aren't to your liking, let me know and we'll sort it out then. Is there anything else you need?"

"No." Ophelia shook her head. "Thank you."

"Okay then." Nikollette took three quick steps to the door, turned, and added, "I'll leave you be. If you need anything, just find me in the study. Otherwise, I'll see you in the morning."

She stepped back, out the door, and closed it. The room went dark, lit only by the pale moon as Nikollette's footsteps faded into the night and down the hall. Ophelia climbed under the covers, laid her heavy head upon a large pillow, and slipped sweetly into slumber.

THE DEFENSELESS HEART OF RENÉE ROCHÉ

Renée sank into the mud, a glue that had ensnared her and refused to let go. The mudstalker closed in on her with no difficulty at all. Its hard, segmented body slid through the thick mud like a serpent through grass. White eyes blinked along each segment in sequence, hard eyelids clicking like the gears of a clock running double time, counting down what seconds of life she had left. Though she had seen drawings of mudstalkers and heard tell of their incomparable speed, she had never actually seen one, and she wasn't sure she'd ever get the chance again.

Not that she wanted to.

There was nothing either sword or arrow could do to save her, no matter how skilled the hand that wielded them.

This was the end.

She would be consumed with nary a second thought from the

detestable neverbeast. She would slide right down its gaping maw — *perfect size for a human body*, she thought — as easily as it slid through the mud. She'd struggle for as long as there was breath in her body, which she didn't imagine would be long, before its twisting movements would snap her bones and its corrosive bile break her down into nothing. Then the creature would turn its many hungry eyes to the other townsfolk in Roché Village.

If the swords of what few soldiers that patrolled the area could not manage to pierce the hide of this unimaginable terror, then what hope was there for anyone else? She closed her eyes, wanting no longer to peer into the terror that waited in its open mouth. She readied her body and waited for its final strike, hoping only that it would strike quick and true, that she might slip into unconsciousness before should could experience any pain.

"It's there!" a man's voice called out.

"I see it," another replied.

Renée opened her eyes just as the neverbeast lifted itself out of the mud, thrusting toward her in a final strike. Not a moment later, the once-muddy ground hardened itself and rose, forming a wall between herself and the flesh-hungry creature. The wall shook on impact, sending clumps of dry dirt into Renée's lap. Renée leaned to the side; curiosity pulling her. Around the dirt wall, she found a man kneeling just beyond her reach with his fingers in the mud. He turned to face her.

"Lady Roché," he laughed, his smile paralyzing. "I've heard much, though I don't believe we've ever met. I'm Marcel."

It was all happening so fast. There was only one thing she could think to say at that moment. Only one thing that *needed* to be said.

"Look out!"

Marcel jumped back reflexively as the mudstalker lunged. A quick stumble, and he caught himself, the neverbeast springing past him. His fingers went to work in the mud. He traced a quick series of interlocked squares, never taking his eyes off the beast. It slid with a deadly grace, spinning its body around like a whip, until its hungry mouth was once again aimed at Renée. However, before it could strike, Marcel said, with a confident calm, "Got you."

He pressed down into the muddy symbols. They melted beneath the pressure of his forceful hands with a faint glow. The mud around the beast hardened instantly, trapping it in place. It flailed fruitlessly, eyes blinking erratically. Once the danger had been contained, Renée looked to Marcel and instantly found herself lost in his eyes. Their sharp, silver gaze seemed to pierce the world from between the strands of loose, black hair that hung haphazardly, refusing to remain tucked behind his ears. His face was framed by a chiseled jaw which held a victorious smirk.

Another man walked over with nary a care in the world.

"Took you long enough, brother," the man said as he came around to the front of the mudstalker. "Now, let's see. That is an awfully big worm in such an awfully humble village."

Renée found herself taken aback by the casual weight of his words. He didn't seem afraid whatsoever.

"Well, Bastien"—Marcel placed his muddy hands on his brother's shoulder—"would you like to finish the job, or should I?"

Bastien looked at Renée and smiled. Then he turned back to the writhing mudstalker. "How about you be a gentleman and help the young lady out of the mud? I'll take care of this neverbeast."

Bastien kneeled beside the mudstalker. Marcel held out his hand but took it back immediately upon realizing just how muddy it was. He wiped it clean on his gray pants. "Sorry about that," he said and held it out again, cleaner this time. "May I help you up?"

"Yes," Renée replied, placing her hand in his. "Thank you."

As he stood up, he pulled her out of the mud.

"You know," she remarked, "my hand is already muddy."

"So it is," Marcel replied with a laugh.

She smiled.

Beside them, Bastien continued to trace lines in the mud around the beast, as carefree as a bored child might. When Renée leaned in to catch a glimpse of the symbols, she lost her footing and slipped. Luckily, Marcel was there to catch her.

"Oh my," he laughed as he hooked his arms under hers and pulled her in close. They stood silent for a moment, their faces no more than a gentle breath apart. "Best take care not to lose your feet."

It wasn't her feet she was afraid of losing. Her heart raced faster than it had when faced with the looming death of the mudstalker's gaping mouth. Only, her heart wasn't racing away this time but racing toward.

"All set," Bastien's voice came, booming, scaring the moment away in an instant. Marcel steadied Renée and then let her go. They both looked to Bastien as he asked, "Ready?"

Marcel nodded, "Go right ahead. I cannot wait to see if this actually works. Total transmutation would be quite the feat."

Bastien snorted with a sharp laugh. Then he pressed down on one of the many pentagonal symbols that surrounded the mudstalker. They all lit up, if for only an instant, and just as quickly as the light faded, so did the life from the mudstalker; its writhing body finally brought to rest. Its shape was preserved, but it had transformed into nothing more sinister than a likeness shaped of dirt. Renée couldn't believe her eyes.

"Ha!" Bastien stood, proud of his achievement. "I knew it would work! I told you!"

"Yes, brother." Marcel walked over to Bastien and put a muddy hand on his shoulder. "You continue to amaze me. However, this would certainly prove more useful if it didn't take so long to perform."

"Agreed, but it will still have its uses, I'm sure."

"Most certainly."

Renée watched the two men stand there, talking about what had just transpired as though it were no more a feat than a hunting party letting loose an arrow and felling a deer. She'd never seen anything like it. She'd heard whispers of someone, somewhere in Sominor, doing things beyond what ought to be possible, but now she'd seen it. She'd seen it, and she wanted nothing more than to learn it.

"How did you do that?" The question nearly leaped from her tongue.

It wasn't a particularly illuminating question, she knew that, and she was certain the answer would be entirely more complicated than the two men were prepared to give, but it was the only thing she could think to say. The two men looked at her and smiled, but before they could speak, Renée added, "You *must* teach me."

The brothers exchanged silent looks. Bastien looked unsure, but Marcel shrugged his shoulders and smiled before he answered, speaking more to his own brother than Renée, "I think we might be able to accommodate that. Besides, we can't be everywhere, and doesn't everyone deserve protection, should there exist the means to provide it?"

"I couldn't agree more." Renée beamed. The thought of learning all that she'd just witnessed set her thoughts ablaze, and doing so at the instruction of Marcel had her heart burning in kind.

Andre Roché sat silent. He knew how he felt and knew precisely how irrelevant his feelings were. His wife, Marie, marched across the room in defiant strides, each step a punctuation on the litany of objections pouring from her impassioned lips.

"I don't care what they promised, Renée, you simply can't go. You mustn't. I'm your mother, and it's my job to keep you safe. You'll be risking your life. Throwing it away, even!"

"Mom." Renée, much to Andre's hushed amazement, spoke softly in her insistence. "This is what I want. I'm not a child, even if I'll always be one in your eyes. I love you for that, truly. But this? How can I not go?"

"Monsters and nightmares are not meant for girls to fight. That is a man's duty. A soldier's."

"Keeping safe those we love, those around us? That's everyone's duty. I've made my choice. I'm going."

"Andre." Marie turned to face him with a wild, desperate glare. "Talk some sense into your daughter. Tell her she can't go."

Andre took in a slow breath and closed his eyes. He exhaled as he stood, opened his eyes, and spoke. "As your father, I agree with your mother in that what you aim to do, I feel, is a man's duty."

Marie huffed with a smile, as though the day were won and Renée would stay with them in their family manor.

He continued.

"But, as a man, I see in your eyes that there is no sense to be talked into you. You've been nothing but sensible, and what you aim to do, I know, is nothing but right. What's more, it seems a soldier's place has become increasingly ineffective. If there exists a way to combat the new dangers that have found us, it is all our duty to fight. I know your mind is sharp, I know your body is more than able, and what I feel should have no bearing on the life you choose to live."

When he'd finished, Renée only nodded in acknowledgment of his reluctant blessing, and Marie stewed in it, her face red and tears in her eyes.

"You've killed our daughter," she said firmly before leaving the room.

He hoped, one day, Marie would come around. He knew his daughter would do great things for this world. Great and undeniable things.

Dinner at Greenwood Manor was a welcome one. Renée had ridden to Greenwood from her family manor in the span of a day, with little else to eat except for an apple and a dinner roll. Her appetite nearly arrived before she did.

She sat across from a young girl, Nikollette, whose mother, Ophelia, sat at the end of the table to her immediate left. To her right, Marcel's wife, Antoinette. Marcel sat across from Antoinette, and at the far end, opposite Ophelia, sat Bastien.

It cannot be said that Renée was in any way happy to learn that Marcel was married to another woman. He had shown no indication as such when first they had met. However, when she met Antoinette, she found it difficult to be upset. Antoinette was a small woman, delicate and beautiful. A radiance shone from every soft glance and graceful motion. She was everything Renée had ever wanted to be when she was a girl. Everything she thought a woman should be. Nothing like herself.

Worse still, she was kind.

It was Antoinette that had greeted her at the door. She had welcomed Renée with a warm smile. Offered to take her coat and tend her horse. Both, Renée had said, she would take care of herself.

As they sat, with the food plated before them and the aroma enveloping the room, Renée's stomach turned, begging her to dive in without delay. To fill her belly until she was done, when she could sit back and let the satisfaction of the meal wash over her. Antoinette, however, looked as though she could go without food for as long as it took. She hadn't even caught Antoinette so much as to give the enticing meal a sideways glance. As if it were all for show, nothing but garnish to an evening of conversation and good company.

"I'd tell you to go ahead and eat," Antoinette leaned in and whispered to Renée, "but I'm sure my husband will demand all of our attention first."

Marcel stood.

"See?" Antoinette added with a hint of levity.

He spoke, "I'd like to raise my glass to Renée Roché. May she take to magic as easily as I take to this meal before us. We look forward to having fresh hands at the ready, to push back against whatever nightmare might claw its way out from the Neverwas."

"Hear, hear," everyone at the table responded as they raised their glasses and smiled at Renée.

"Thank you," she replied. "Eager to help."

"You'll be wonderful," Marcel added. "Now, let's eat!"

Finally.

Renée tried to contain herself, even as each bite melted in her mouth, and the soft sound of her delight quietly escaped.

Slowly, she reminded herself.

"So…" she set her fork down and looked around the table. "…does everyone here know magic?"

Utensils ceased their toils, and chewing slowed among the new hush that had washed over them.

"Nikollette is too young," Bastien said, his voice flat.

"And these two lovely ladies refuse to learn," Marcel added with a laugh, a hint of frustration swimming beneath it.

"Excuse the tension. It's a tender subject." Antoinette looked at Renée. "He often confuses disinterest with refusal. For instance, I might say he refuses to cook a meal, and he might argue that he simply isn't interested. But where would you be, love, if I wasn't around to feed you?"

"I'd wither away like a tree with no light. Left to waste under the darkness of my own grief," Marcel was quick to answer, jest in his voice and in his eyes. He added, "As it has ever been, you are my world." He smiled at her and winked.

"It's lucky we've found such brilliant men to love," Ophelia chimed in, a smile glinting through her otherwise sleepy eyes, "and unlucky that brilliant men often feel the world exists entirely of their own interests."

"To be fair," Marcel countered, a heavy shift in his tone, "magic is something everyone should learn. If everyone knew how to wield it, the danger of neverbeasts would be no more severe than an encroaching bear. A skill to learn, to master, to use as freely and simply as any other for the safety and prosperity of all."

It was as though Marcel had reached into the heart and mind of Renée, grabbed hold of her thoughts and feelings, and flicked them free from his tongue as if all his own.

"I agree," she said softly. "If more people in Roché Village had known, none would have died."

"And what of the boredom?" Bastien asked, his demeanor unchanging.

"What of boredom?" Marcel huffed. He gave Renée a look that

said, *here we go.*

"When magic removes the danger, when it hurries along the work without effort, what do you suppose people will do with magic when all it is needed for has been accomplished?"

Not a sound, heads slightly bowed like children before their father. Renée joined them in their reverence. Marcel did not.

"Then people would be free to live the lives they've always dreamed of without the fear of pain and death; whether it be through the bellies of neverbeasts or their own left empty from lack of food."

"Boredom is as much a blessing as it is a blight. Not everyone spends their free time in pursuit of good."

"One can reason with a man; none can with a beast."

"Yet it is men who are most malicious in their violent pursuits."

"Boys," Ophelia cut them off. Her voice rang tired. Clearly a position she had found herself in more than once. Perhaps one time too many. She continued.

"I'm sure our lovely guest would prefer to enjoy the rest of her dinner rather than watch the two of you bicker. She came all this way to learn from you. Let's not have her regret it."

"So sorry," Marcel offered.

"As am I," Bastien added.

"No apologies needed," Renée assured them both. "It'll take more than a disagreement to scare me away."

Perhaps it was the heavy meal that had brought her nightmare about, maybe nerves, but regardless of the cause, Renée was up while the rest of the manor slept soundly. The bed was softer than she was used to so she took to pacing while she waited for the terror to fade and the still of darkness to bring her heart to rest. After what felt like hours, she gave up and snuck downstairs.

The first time she had had this particular nightmare was three nights before she'd arrived. It had come to her every night since. Once was enough. The mud, the screams, every terrible detail replayed without conclusion. No handsome hero to swoop in a save the day and no enchantments to abate the danger. Just mud, and screams, and the look of that woman's twisted face tucked away in the dark throat of that awful beast.

She took a seat in a large room with various chairs and couches positioned around a large hearth. She sat in a chair at a game table beside one of the windows and took in the stars peppered across the sky. Thoughts of her parents came to her with reassuring words from her father and the tears of loss from her mother. It was a worry, Renée knew, that came from a place of love.

"Unable to sleep?" Marcel's whispered words should have startled her, but she felt only an ease come over her.

"Bad dream," she replied, not taking her eyes off the night sky. He sat in the chair opposite her and did the same.

"Not too bad, I hope."

"The mudstalker."

"I see." He took a breath and thought for a moment. "A very bad dream, but one with a happy ending."

"Yes, well, I always seem to wake up before the good part."

"But you're living it now. So I'd say you did wake up *to* the good part. From now on, you always will."

"I fear I'll dream up another." Renée looked at him. Tears hung from her eyes, trembling, "It was my fault. It was my nightmare that brought that terrible beast to life. They died because of me."

"No, they didn't." Marcel looked into her eyes. The silver of his cut through the night like stars themselves. "You had a dream, and it seized upon your heart and mind, where it stole its way into reality. You didn't bring anything about it because it wasn't your choice."

"I can still see that woman's face inside its mouth. Caught in a scream that wouldn't come. The air gone from her. Her eyes darting between my own, begging me to help. The life leaving them in a snap." She looked away, wiping the tears running down her face.

"If you would blame yourself, then you would blame every man, woman, and child in Sominor of the same. But they are not to blame, and neither are you. And unlike them, you have decided to do something about it. For that, you should be proud."

"That does make sense, logically, yet the guilt still weighs."

"That is precisely why I'm happy to have you with us. Even though a thing isn't one's fault, if one can do something, one should. I know you'll make it right, a thousand times over, and I know you'll feel the debt never repaid, but I also know, from the brief time I've had the pleasure of knowing you, that you'll never back down from what is right."

He stood up. With a soft smile he added before walking away, "If I know my brother, he'll have you up at first light. With that said, may slumber find you swiftly, and your dreams be ever sweet. You'll need all the sleep you can get."

Renée only nodded as his footsteps faded through the halls of the slumbering manor.

The dawn light had only just come peeking through the trees as Renée came to the field behind the manor, her eyes heavy but alive with anticipation. At first sight of Marcel, her heart started to hum. Then came the thought of Antoinette to temper it. Like a strange and bittersweet melody danced within her, twirling and leaping with joy at the very thought of him, when, at the same time, it wept softly in a mournful chorus for what could have been and would likely never be. She only hoped the distraction that came with learning magic would be enough of one.

"The first thing you will learn are the three tenants of summoning magic." Bastien paced as he spoke. Marcel sat observing in an iron lawn chair some distance away, near the tree line, as Bastien continued. "Magic requires three things to work. Intent, will, and action. Without intent, there is no purpose for magic to act upon, without any force of will, there is no power to summon it, and without any action behind your intent or your will, there is nothing tangible with which to weave magic into reality. Anyone is *able* to perform magic, but to know *how* is another matter entirely. My brother will demonstrate."

Marcel scribbled on a small sheet of paper, stood, and held it out for Renée to see the neatly arranged triangular shapes. When he dropped it, nothing happened.

"Now, Marcel, if you wouldn't mind doing that again, but with intent and with will."

Marcel nodded and then performed the same action. This time, when the paper landed in the grass, the blades wriggled before giving way to blossoming flowers in a ring around the point of contact, like a ripple in a pond, rolling across the lawn, and it didn't slow to a stop until the flowers bloomed just at Renée's feet.

"That was beautiful." There was a distant awe in her voice as she knelt and plucked a purple heart-blossom from the ground.

"You see, it isn't enough to simply write down a spell or trace it into the mud; there needs to be something else behind it. It's *that* something we will need to develop in you through training. I will train you in all that we have cataloged thus far in our discovery of magic, and my brother will guide you along in practical application."

"You will start with me until I feel you have a good grasp on the theory. Then you will be under his skilled hands as you attempt to put that knowledge to use."

Renée couldn't wait.

The first couple of weeks were not terribly exciting for Renée, aside from what brief moments she spent with Marcel. Most of her lessons consisted of reading and lecturing from Bastien, a kind, warm, and extremely intelligent man, but not the one she'd hoped to spend her time with. He was the older of the two and reminded her very much of her father.

What followed the stale instruction on theory came the first of her practical lessons with Marcel. Anxiety found her in those magical moments. The conflicting feelings threatened to tear her apart. It wasn't long before another noticed her apparent anxiety, though entirely misunderstood it.

Much to her relief.

"Don't let these boys intimidate you," Antoinette remarked as she sat reading at the kitchen table with a cup of tea steaming before her. She lowered her book and looked at Renée, smirking as she spoke. "They may seem impressive right now, but they are still just men."

That isn't exactly why I'm nervous, Renée thought.

"Yes," Renée replied. "I guess it's all just so new and—"

"Magical?"

"Yes, magical."

"Come, have a seat." Antoinette gestured to the seat across from her. Renée couldn't help but admire the deep blue of her eyes that shone like brilliant sapphire and felt as deep as the Endless Ocean. She assumed they were the same age, but Antoinette carried herself with the confidence of a woman who had lived a lifetime.

Renée sat, brimming with discomfort. The woman married to the man she found herself helplessly pulled toward sitting across from her, more beautiful and kinder with each interaction. She wished it possible to hate Antoinette.

"It's so nice to have yet another lady in the house. I've been hoping to get a chance to sit and talk. They've kept you so busy," Antoinette carried on with the conversation.

"Feels like all I've done is read for weeks. It's nice to finally have my nose out of a book."

"I could only imagine," she chuckled. After a short sigh, she asked, "Well, now that you're finally free from the tyranny of parchment, I can finally get to know you. Do you have any brothers or sisters? I've heard of the Roché family but not much except that they are a generous family."

"Yes. At this point, the words have been seared into my mind." Renée responded with the same, cordial chuckle. She continued, "No, no sisters. Just me and my parents. My brother passed when I was a girl."

"Oh, dear. I'm so sorry for your loss."

"It was a long time ago, but thank you."

Renée tried to remember him but, as usual, there was no face to put in that blank space. Not anymore.

"Well, even though Ophelia and I aren't related, we are like sisters. So, if you ever find yourself in need of a sister, know that you now have two right here in this manor."

A sudden laugh escaped Renée. To be sisters with the wife of the man you couldn't get out of your head? How could she have found herself in such an absurd predicament? She stifled the laughter quickly. Antoinette was sincere, and Renée was glad.

"Thank you, Antoinette. That means a lot to me."

"Of course."

Renée asked, "So, why haven't you taken to magic? Your husband is very passionate about it. I'm surprised you aren't as well."

"Yes, well, my dear husband and I may share a deep love for one another, but magic is a pursuit in which I've found little interest. Even as fantastical and as useful as it may be. Ophelia and I are content, but I'm sure that answer isn't terribly satisfying." Antoinette spoke with no animosity or passion. She answered as calmly as one might when asked about their day. It was the truth, plain and simple.

"You're right," Renée nodded, smiling politely at Antoinette. "Not very satisfying at all."

Antoinette laughed.

"Like the sweetest song ever written. Music to my ears." Renée instantly recognized Marcel's voice as he came into the room. "I could listen to it day and night and never tire of such a lovely tune."

He strolled up from behind Renée, walking around the table, and then leaning over Antoinette's shoulder and wrapping his arms around her. He kissed her cheek and squeezed tight.

"Now," Marcel added, standing back up straight and leaving his hands to rest on Antoinette's shoulders, "My darling wife here isn't telling you horrible lies about me, is she?"

"No," Renée answered. "Just getting to know one another."

"Yes," Antoinette added. "I was telling Renée here how nice it is to have yet another lady in the house. If you aren't careful, you boys will find yourselves neck-deep in strong women, with stronger opinions."

Renée chuckled, as did Antoinette.

"I should hope so," Marcel boomed. "I've been more than happy to serve at your pleasure since the day I laid eyes on you, and I'd be devastated if I couldn't for a hundred years more."

Renée felt like she could relate.

"A hundred," Antoinette responded, rather theatrically; a hand on her chest. "I should hope not to live so long."

"Well, if it means I can keep looking into your eyes, I'd settle for eternity." Marcel finished by kissing Antoinette atop her head.

Somewhere in the manor, Nikollette could be heard laughing.

"Any plans for children?" Renée didn't know why she'd asked. She wished it were physically possible to put the words back into her mouth and choke them down, never to be heard again. Luckily, neither Marcel nor Antoinette seemed to mind the question at all, as though they'd been asked more than once.

"Oh, no," Antoinette explained. "Parenthood isn't for us."

"Simply not in the cards," Marcel added. "So we had to settle for being one another's entire reason for being."

He held her tighter, and Renée felt even worse for the question.

After a moment of silent reflection between Antoinette and Marcel, he looked at Renée. "Come. We have more training to do, you and I."

"Looking forward to it," Renée answered, clearing her throat. She looked to Antoinette and added, "I look forward to talking more with you."

"And I you," Antoinette replied. "Perhaps Ophelia and young Nikollette might like to join us next time."

Renée nodded and then took her leave with Marcel. She doubted she could ever see Antoinette as a sister, but a friend was most certainly possible. She poured herself further into the distraction of magic and found herself wondering when the very thing she desired so eagerly to learn had been relegated to nothing more than a way to keep her mind occupied. A helpless shame found her.

Magic had once again been made the focus of her thoughts. A choice she was glad to have made. Better still, at the end of her second week of practical study, two new students had joined her. Diedrich Finch and Victor Gideon.

"A pleasure to meet you," Diedrich said, happy as can be. He seemed very much the jolly sort.

Renée took his hand and shook it, "The pleasure's all mine."

Diedrich looked around and added, "I'm so happy to be here. The silence is a welcome escape from the constant bustle of Stillriver. Though, I admire how well ordered they maintain such a large city, it can often be overwhelming."

"I would imagine," Renée said.

The Kingdom of Still River was nestled on the western edge of Sominor, among the grassy plains dotted with flowers and the glimmering rivers that snaked their way among the rolling hills like life-giving veins. She knew right away they would become good friends.

"And it is a pleasure to meet you as well, Victor," Renée extended a hand for him.

He looked at her hand, but didn't take it. He simply nodded while she uncomfortably let it fall to her side.

He hailed from the Kingdom of Ironveil to the east, hidden among the hardened walls of the Ironhide Mountains. The same mountains that rose just behind Roché Village and her family home. She had visited a few times in her youth, and not once did she find it welcoming. Victor represented it well.

One month later, Illana Fairwind joined them from Silverleaf Citadel, a fortified city in the south. It sits along the edge of the dense vegetation that makes up the Wilds, a largely unexplored forest home to both dangerous animals and neverbeasts alike.

"So wonderful to have another woman to train alongside," Renée had told her when they met, "Not that it should make a difference."

"It shouldn't," Illana replied with a smile, "and yet, all too often, it does."

Renée enjoyed her time training with the three of them. Well, perhaps not Victor, but the things they learned were nothing shy of miraculous.

"Are you sure about this, Ms. Roché? It seems rather dangerous." Bastien stood across from her on the training grounds with an arrow at the ready.
"It does seem rather ill-advised," Dierich added. "Perhaps it would be safer to fire the arrow *near* you, rather than at you."

"Aw, just do it, Bastien," Marcel egged him on with a sliver of a smirk. He looked at Renée. "I'm sure Ms. Roché is more than capable."

His confidence in her made Renée nervous. Beside Marcel stood Diedrich, Illana, and Victor. Opposite them, near the manor, Ophelia, Antoinette, and Nikollette looked on.

"Yes, I'm sure, but this isn't something we taught her, and I don't know if it will work."

"Just do it," Renée shouted at him. "I'm ready."

Bastien nodded, took aim, and let loose the arrow. It flew, fast and true, right toward Renée. In a flourish, her fingers moved in and out of different positions, the leathers bracers on her wrists emitted a swift and sharp light, and the arrow careening toward her stopped, splintered, and then burst to pieces back in the direction it had come from. The arrowhead tumbled through the air and stuck in the ground at Bastien's feet.

"Remarkable," Bastien muttered. He held the bow at his side, dumbfounded as he looked down at the arrowhead near his feet.

Marcel ran to Renée to congratulate her. His laughter boomed and he hoisted her up in the air with a full twirl before setting her down again. "You're a genius! An absolutely mad genius!"

"Thanks." She shied away from his touch and turned the focus to her bracers. The symbols once painted into the hide were now marked only by glowing embers that fizzled out and faded away. All that was left beneath was the leather, just as it had always been. "It was quite simple really."

"How?" Bastien asked as he joined them. "As far as I am aware, the magic can only be cast all at once. The intent, the will, the act, all working in unison."

"Yes, well, that's exactly what got me thinking. Could I put my intent into the symbols beforehand? Could I resummon that intent through sheer force of will? Could I perform a new act to draw the magic out of it? I developed some simple hand gestures to coincide with some of these symbols. I think it might even be possible to cast with only hand gestures, but I question the efficacy. However, I doubt anything more than simple line spells could be woven in such a manner."

"Yes, how very clever." Bastien examined the bracers.

"Yes, she is," Marcel agreed, patting Renée on the back. "Possibly more than any of us."

Renée's heart felt as though it had been bathed in a ray of warm sunshine on a cold winter's day. A moment of true magic swiftly tarnished by the voice of an unlikely friend.

"Show those men how it's done, Renée," Antoinette cheered from the back door.

Renée and Antoinette shared a sincere smile. Ophelia nodded with a hand resting on Nikollette's shoulder. Nikollette gave her an excited round of applause.

The three others joined her.

"It only works once?" Bastien asked. "Can you use the same bracers again?"

"Actually, you can. And the number of uses is determined by the method of imprinting and the durability of the surface it is imprinted upon. I've tested burning them into leather and was able to get two to three uses out of them. Each weaker than the last. I would imagine etching symbols into steel might prove to be even more useful."

"Well, more useful, but rather cumbersome," Bastien countered.

"Sure, but a couple plates of armor might provide some much-needed assistance in the field."

"Perhaps even a sword," Marcel added.

"Yes," Renée replied.

"No," Bastien cut in, stern. "Magic is for defense. Use weapons if you like, but to enhance them with such enchantments would only do more harm than good."

Marcel looked at Renée and rolled his eyes. "Regardless, Renée, you continue to impress us."

"Those hand gestures," Victor asked, "can you show me?"

It was the most Victor had ever spoken to Renée of his own accord since joining. She smiled. "I'd love to."

THE TIDES OF BATTLE

Soaring over the battlefield, with wild eyes set above an untamed snarl, the neverbeast – a skinkweasel to be exact – hurled toward its foe, its clawed fingers poised for the deadliest attack it could summon. The skinkweasel exhaled a fierce roar, spewing forth globs of saliva. Its short, purple fur fluttered erratically against the warm, battle-torn air, and its serpent-like tail flailed close behind.

Moments ago, it had been slithering through a forest, hunting bright leeches. Its empty stomach grumbled; hunger pangs jabbed from within. In a blink, all traces of the forest had vanished, and the bright leeches it had been stalking were nowhere to be found. Instead, a woefully uncomfortable world enveloped its senses, burdening it with an oppressiveness it had never felt. Nevertheless, the skinkweasel remained steadfast in its attack on the creature before it, motivated by forces beyond its comprehension.

A monstrous raven, unlike anything the skinkweasel had ever encountered, awaited its imminent strike. As it drew ever closer to its target, the skinkweasel's minuscule mind whirled with a maelstrom of confusion and doubt. Why couldn't it stop itself? How had it come to be entangled in such a predicament? The thought of its impending demise gripped its racing mind, echoing a terrible realization. "I'm going to die."

The Endless King lorded over the chaotic battlefield. Upon his raven head sat a small crown of bone, a raven's skull affixed front and center. Below, his hordes of Endless flowed around his molting feathers, like skittering insects. The tide of battle was turning in his favor, and soon the Kingdom of Still River – the last of its kind – would be his for the taking. A prize hard won. Its people to live on, endlessly.

He could see its great, white walls in the distance, like some cosmic being had erased part of the horizon, leaving only blank parchment, inviting him to write the final chapter of his illustrious tale. It was then, during his scheming and coveting for a prize not yet won, among the plumes of smoke and the twinkling embers, that he noticed something flying toward him. A small, serpent-like creature, no bigger than a human head. Compared to the Endless King in his raven form, it looked no more threatening than half a worm dug up from the dirt and carelessly tossed in his direction. His head twitched to the side, until one of his eyes had locked onto it. With a snap of his beak, the Endless King swallowed the tiny creature with nary a second thought.

"That was really helpful Victor, thanks," Illana Fairwind shouted to

Victor Gideon from across the battlefield. Surrounding Illana, a ring of black flame, fringed with deep purple light, formed a barrier between herself and the warring hordes. Beyond her circle of flame, more fire followed the movement of her arms. It swirled as though it had a mind all its own, dancing to the songs of war. The flame swept over the Endless army. They reached up to the sky in a twisting column before crashing back down again and spreading through the enemy ranks. A sight, both captivating and terrifying to behold.

Adorned in purple and black leather armor from the tops of her hands to the soles of her feet, Illana moved gracefully as more black flame poured from the Obsidian Flint ring on the index finger of her right hand. The fire surged tirelessly toward the Endless King as she shouted again, with a hint of a smile traipsing through her words, "You think perhaps you could summon something a bit more, I don't know, useful?"

Victor stood safely atop a pile of fallen masonry, another building turned rubble, just outside the battle. His red frock coat rustled in the smoke-stained breeze. He frantically moved his hands into various positions. His fingers appeared tangled, yet moved with precision. On his wrists, symbols etched into steel bracers flickered with light. Broken stone floated up around him and, with a simple gesture at the end of his hand motions, the heavy stones flew into battle. They collided with the Endless, leaving them stunned or trapped beneath the stones' weight. Victor allowed little space in between his deadly volleys, and the exhaustion in his face and body became more evident with each hurled stone. He looked at Illana with a scowl and shouted, exasperated, "You *know* I can only summon one at a time, and you *know* they are summoned at random! If I got to choose the beast that I desired from the Neverwas, this war would have ended before it even had a chance to begin!"

From the battle rose a hundred voices in unison that scolded them both. "Will the two of you quit your bickering and focus? I don't know how much more pain I can take!"

Illana and Victor looked up at Diedrich Finch, who floated above the battle with his eyes closed, perched atop a steel plate engraved with repeating linework that emitted a low, steady glow. Below him, his replicants fought valiantly against the Endless hordes. Their identical blue tailcoats were difficult to miss among the sea of black and gray. They fought face-to-face with the Endless, swords swinging with deadly speed and accuracy. Unfortunately, for every one Diedrich Finch, there were twenty Endless, and for each Diedrich Finch defeated in battle, a new one leaped down from the primary Diedrich above.

Illana felt the searing kiss of her black flames, a stark reminder that her mind had wandered too far. She reclaimed dominion over them with ease. Victor nodded and brought the bestial horn, hung around his neck, back up against his lips and blew.

At the edge of chaos, secure behind a phalanx of conjured, dirt soldiers, young Nikollette A'Mysteriouse stood, transfixed in agony, a hand pressed firm against the side of her stomach. As her father finished scrawling the final symbols into the soil, summoning forth a second row of soldiers, he scooped her back up in his arms with as tender an urgency as one could in the heat of battle. His tired hands shook under Nikollette, no doubt weary from weaving such complex spells. For a moment, her breath was lost in the pain screaming from her side. She closed her eyes tight as he hurried to put distance between them and the carnage unfolding.

"I'm sorry Nikollette," he said, his words as genuine as his love, and a great concern in his expression, "but this fight is one for which you are no longer fit."

Racing over to join them, clad in yellow and black leather armor, ran Spellkeeper Irons. The only remaining Spellkeeper among the ranks of Spellevue. His backpack jumped along with each hurried step, and the various ampules and tools bounced along the black leather bandolier that cut across his chest. Their bright clinking and jingles were a melody out of place among the distant shouts and screams. He looked well-worn, but his eyes still burned with a steadfast sense of duty. Nikollette knew the look.

"What happened to her? She wasn't attacked by the Endless, was she?" he asked with heaving breath.

"No," her father replied as he lowered her gently. The pain came with renewed wrath, and she found her breath in the scream that followed. It tried to leave her again, but she held tight in forced gulps.

"Just breathe, my little shadow," her father spoke as though they were home, as though her injury was nothing more than a scrape. She felt like a little girl, and in that moment of stillness and safety, her breath came rushing back in.

"It looks deep," Spellkeeper Irons observed.

"An errant arrow, unfortunately." Her father lifted the bottom of her shirt to reveal the injury just below her ribs. "One of our own, it seems."

They both looked at it closely and then her father added, while turning back to observe the distant conflict, "An accident I would like to believe, but most likely a soldier turned Endless, though still very much alive." He turned to Spellkeeper Irons. "I need you to keep her safe and heal her as best you can with what remaining regents you have at your disposal. The others need me."

"Wait," Nikollette grunted, her teeth clamped tight to hold back the pain, "I can still help."

"My little shadow," her father replied, "you have done all you can, and it was more than enough."

Nikollette, ever defiant, set about to prove her father wrong. At her side, strapped over her shoulder, she lifted a narrow book and summoned the quill from its cover before flipping it open. Its pages sat blank. The quill shook in her pain-weary grip. She tried her best to etch a spell into the empty page. The ink came in erratic lines so imprecise that, when completed, held within them no magic whatsoever.

Just lines on paper.

"You see," her father explained. "Your body is too weak, and your will has gone. Rest. You are safe here with Irons."

"She's in good hands," Irons replied as he dabbed the wound with a cloth. "It will take time, but she'll be able to walk home by the time

I'm finished here. I can promise you that much."

"I believe you." Her father put a hand on Irons' shoulder and then gave Nikollette a sincere look. "I must leave you now, little shadow, and this is one time you cannot follow."

Before Nikollette could mount a protest, the sound of a distant horn blow called away her father's attention. He left her and Spellkeeper Irons with a nod and returned to the battlefield, taking with him the first row of dirt soldiers.

The haunting cry of Victor's horn tore through the air with enough force to punch a hole in the sky larger than anyone might have expected. What came falling from it was a hulking neverbeast nearly the size of the Endless King's crow form. It crashed down atop an entire battalion of Endless. The ground itself seemed to tremble with fear. Its four fur-covered tentacles flailed erratically, and teeth, where its suckers should have been, cut through the Endless as if they were nothing at all. The four, beady eyes of its wild, bear-like face blinked feverishly as they darted around. It cried out with a confused and heavy-breathed growl that petered out into a whimper.

It sounded frightened.

"Finally," Illana cried in delight. "Something useful!"

She returned to the graceful choreography of her obsidian flames with renewed vigor and furious intent.

"Attack the Endless King! Restrain him," Victor commanded the new neverbeast before he resumed his volley of rubble into the thick of battle. Thanks to the damage caused by the Endless King and his army, it was unlikely Victor would ever run out of ammo, so long as his will held. So long as he could keep his eyes open.

"Warn me next time," the many voices of Diedrich's replicants called out. "You can't possibly know the pain of being crushed, and I pray you never do."

"Warn you?" Victor seemed offended. "The horn *was* the warning! With all those ears on the battlefield, I would have thought at least *one* of you would have heard it."

"Yes, but an ursalapod? And one of this size?"

"Again, you *know* I don't get to pick!"

Illana couldn't help but laugh. "We know, Victor! Get that beast to work, will you?"

Victor nodded and then shouted at the giant ursalapod again, who hadn't yet moved, pointing at the giant raven. "Seize the Endless King, you clumsy beast!"

The ursalapod's expression changed in an instant. The confusion on its face vanished, only to be replaced with fire. A fire it aimed squarely at the towering, decrepit raven. It roared. Spittle rained down on the battle in heaping globs. The ursalapod dug its clawed toes into the ground and charged toward the Endless King, its four furry tentacles flailing at its sides.

"Move your replicants," Victor called up to Diedrich.

"I'm trying!"

"Just wanted to make sure you had enough of a warning this time."

Nikollette wondered, as she lay in the capable hands of Spellkeeper

Irons, if she would survive the day or if her father had been merely expressing to her how he wanted the world to be rather than how it truly was, a terrible habit of his that forced her, at a very young age, to observe the world more closely for herself rather than rely on her father's assessments.

The constant vibration of battle that buzzed along the ground was now punctuated with the steady rumble of the ursalapod's footsteps. She couldn't recall ever seeing one so large. It was easily two floors in height, and though slightly shorter than the Endless King in his current form, it appeared to be significantly more capable.

After all, who would bet on a raven against an ursalapod, all things being equal?

"Pretty incredible, isn't it?" Irons commented as he mixed various flowers and liquids in a small bowl beside Nikollette.

Her body grew colder with each fleeting moment, and the searing pain from her wound was beginning to fade into a dull ache. Even wounded and woozy, she couldn't understand how he could sound so calm, and were it not for her dire condition, she might have marveled at his effortless tranquility. Beyond them, a battle for the fate of their world waged. Four weavers stood defiant against an overwhelming torrent of Endless soldiers. Even still, Nikollette felt it irresponsible of Victor to not immediately dismiss the ursalapod and attempt to summon something less destructive. If he were to lose consciousness, that beast could unleash untold carnage. It was, as far as Nikollette could discern, a sign of desperation. Yet here knelt Irons, as calm as one could possibly be.

"Incredible isn't the word I would use." Her words squeezed themselves out between grunts and heavy breaths. "Terrifying, certainly."

Spellkeeper Irons smiled and then applied the salve he had been brewing to Nikollette's wound, accompanied by whispered words. Fresh pain came shooting through her and elicited aching screams and fresh tears. His chant ended.

"Terrifying *is* incredible, if you simply set aside the fear for just a moment and see a thing for what it is rather than what you feel, a skill I picked up over my time working with your father," he said as he continued to rub the salve over and around the wound. A prickling sensation crawled along her skin. Irons continued, "I am terrified, but I can also appreciate just how incredible all of this is. To witness you all wield magic in the way that you do is nothing short."

Nikollette felt the numbness wash over her and with it, warmth. "I'm so tired," she managed to say as her heavy eyes blinked slowly, "but I can't sleep. I need to help."

"No, you don't," Irons assured her, placing a firm hand on her shoulder before she could even try to sit up. "Let the medicine do its job. You and I would do little else but get in the way."

Nikollette blinked again, but this time she felt as though time had rushed by her in an instant. Irons was no longer looking over her but rather putting his tools away. Behind him, some distance away, she could see a figure shambling toward them. An Endless corpse.

She blinked again.

When her eyelids reluctantly parted, she found Irons wrestling the

Endless corpse. She tried desperately to lift her heavy head, to force her body into action, but it was no use. Amid the battle, the ursalapod struggled to contain the Endless King. His black wings fluttered violently in defiance against the giant neverbeast's tentacles. Illana's black flame, caught in a gust, was sent hurling back toward her. Her screams cut through the orchestra of battle like a discordant note. As her eyes surrendered to darkness, Nikollette could hear her father shouting but couldn't make out the words. Silent screams resounded in her mind as nothingness consumed her senses.

Memories and nightmares. For Lady Nikollette, the two seemed to only grow more indistinguishable as time went on. She'd awoken from her dream with a jump and a cold sweat on her brow. Her heart calmed down as she regained her composure.

She did her best to unravel the dream from which she had just escaped. The nightmare that her mind had woven together from her memories and her fears. A tapestry of terror that formed a litany of images she'd much rather never see again. A terrible magic.

"Memories and nightmares," she whispered and let her eyes close gently. "Memories and nightmares."

She let out a sigh, allowing the thoughts to stew. She knew she wasn't the skinkweasel.

Nightmare.

She also knew she wasn't the Endless King.

Another Nightmare.

Nor did she think she was close enough to really hear Illana,

Diedrich, and Victor. Perhaps she had been.

Uncertain.

Passing out during that battle was a memory. However, when she had asked about it, her father had told her she had passed out in his arms but that her account of events after were fairly accurate. The ursalapod was also a memory. It still came up in passing conversation from time to time to this very day. It was quite the beast.

Magister Irons' – only a Spellkeeper then - diligent care was another memory, but one Magister Irons had stated must have been half a dream. When asked all those years ago about the Endless that attacked him, he had just smiled, chuckled, and then blamed it on the medicine.

A nightmare, she thought, concluding her dissection.

She looked at the brass clock ticking away at the edge of her desk. If they weren't already, Barnaby and Amarine would be up soon. Nikollette only hoped she had woken up before Ophelia. The poor girl had been through enough, and she'd like to be there to help facilitate introductions before leaving her at the mercy of Amarine's excited prattling.

The Magic of Mornings

Ophelia's eyes opened wide, startled awake from a nightmare. She sat up to the rising sun and the passing sound of hurried steps just outside her bedroom door. She had dreamt she was back in the woods, running from that horrid beast, but something had been different. As she ran, she had thought she could sense something, or someone, watching her from deep within the twisted trees. When she had turned around, there stood a man. He had been older, perhaps Lady Nikollette's age and his smile had been welcoming. His eyes; a hypnotic silver.

"Do I know you?" He asked. "You feel familiar."

"I don't know," she had replied.

"Ah," he said after an uncomfortable silence, "You live with Nikollette."

Ophelia had only been able to nod.

"Be wary. She'll not tell you of all the danger ahead." He said this as he walked away, "You'll find she keeps a great many things to herself."

He had stopped and turned, "I, however, will never lie. Especially when death is so very near." Then he had pointed past Ophelia.

When she had turned, the undead buck was charging toward her. The beating of its hooves in time with that of her own racing heart.

Just a nightmare, she thought.

The day could not have been any more different from her dreams. A bright beam of light shone on the floor just beyond the foot of her bed, illuminating the entire room in a rich, comforting glow. As far as she could think, this was the first of daylight she had ever seen. She rubbed her eyes, forcing them to adjust to the day she was soon to meet.

Ophelia dropped herself off the edge of the high bed and, upon landing, wiggled her toes around in the billowing cloud of a rug beneath her while she stretched. After a couple of soft cracks along her back, Ophelia made her way over to the wardrobe, where she remembered Nikollette had told her there would be clothes. Her skin ran warm with a ripple of goosebumps as she entered the vibrant beam of morning sun warm enough to make her freshly woken mind yearn for sleep once again.

Just a couple more minutes. Right here, on the floor, in the sun.

She pushed the thought aside.

The window beckoned her over, and as she approached, she could already make out a mostly blue sky, peppered with remnants of clouds from the storm. Beneath that, she could see distant hills obscured by what seemed to be endless forests of dead trees.

"The Deadwoods," she murmured as she knelt on the cushions of the bench.

The trees twisted and tangled, their branches gnarled, and what remained of their leaves were withered and black, as if they had been scorched by some long snuffed-out fire. The life had drained from them, ages ago, never to return. While she was in the woods, the air had hung thick with foreboding but looking at it from up high, in the reassurance of day, she thought it seemed significantly less so. Between her and the Deadwoods was a field of green grass scattered with scars of well-trod, worn-out bits of bare dirt. Surrounding the area were large, stone statues in various states of decay. The least worn among them was a woman that she thought looked familiar, though it was difficult to tell from such a distance.

"That must be where they train." Ophelia's recollection brought with it the same question: *train for what?*

Magic, she now presumed. However, before she could get her answer she'd need to get dressed.

In the dim light of the moon and candle, the tall wardrobe had seemed more enchanted than it did now in the light of day. The serpentine handles on each door that had seemed to coil and glimmer in the moonlight now looked like nothing more than a woven pattern of worn brass. The jewel at their centers no longer seemed to twinkle either. Just dirty, green-tinted crystals. She gently ran her fingers over them; a slight shock met her touch. She pulled her hand back instantly. Inside, she could just make out a rustling, sweeping sound. The clatter of wood and metal came with it. Then the wardrobe began to shake.

Perplexed, she stood there, glancing around the room as if she might have done something wrong, hoping she hadn't broken anything.

As suddenly as it had started, it stopped.

Through the silence, Ophelia cautiously reached for the wardrobe again. Her hands trembled on approach, and she swallowed her nerves before snatching the brass handles. The doors opened in quite the normal way, revealing quite the normal contents.

Inside sat a pair of nice, black, ankle-high boots. Besides those, a pair of black stockings folded neatly. Above, hanging from the clothes bar, were four garments. A long, black skirt, a white blouse, and a small black coat. She smiled and took the clothes.

Once dressed, she gave herself a quick look in a body-length mirror that stood beside the wardrobe. She felt comfortable, but she couldn't help but notice that she looked remarkably similar to Nikollette.

Now, if only something could be done about my hair, she thought as she combed it as best she could with her fingers. The short black strands, for the most part, settled beside her cheeks. Some of it, regretfully, was a little less willing to compromise. She licked her hand without thinking and matted it down. "It'll have to do for now."

On her way out the door, she stopped in front of the desk that sat in the room opposite the bed. She hadn't noticed it the night before. On the center of the desk sat a long, slender notebook with its spine positioned at the top, out from which came a leather strap. An ornate frame was embossed on the cover. It wasn't flowing or elegant, not like the other accented designs found throughout the house. No, the design on the cover of this book appeared more rigid, geometric, perfectly intentional in every segment of every line. In the center, the image of a quill with a similar design.

She knew that book. She knew that quill.

Curiosity got the better of her and she opened it. The pages were all blank but seemed to hum in a way she couldn't quite describe. More curious still, there appeared to be no evidence that any pages had ever been torn from it. The notebook felt as though it was calling out to her, begging her to pick it up, tempting her to write in its pages, filling the blank space until there was none remaining.

It was a sudden burst of muffled laughter from somewhere beneath her that pulled her attention. Ophelia felt her chest tighten, and she remembered that there were still two others in this house she had yet to meet. She hoped they were nice.

The manor felt different. Its hallways seemed smaller, but its rooms felt larger and carried a soothing stillness. Ophelia was able to find her way back to the stairs, down into the foyer, and followed the voices into the kitchen.

The walls were lined with dark wooden paneling, and the floor was made of large stone tiles. At one end sat an enormous fireplace, with a black iron pot suspended above charred coals from a stout chain. A large wooden table sat in the center of the room, surrounded by chairs with red, cushioned seats. There sat Nikollette and a young boy who looked to be roughly Ophelia's age. He regarded her with a cool gaze and a nervous sort of disinterest.

The daylight bounded in from a long window that ran from beside the fireplace and across the entire length of the wall. It afforded anyone stirring the cauldron or washing something in the sink a lovely view of the back meadow. On another wall sat a large, cream-colored, steel cupboard. Its door was half open and occupied by another person. She didn't say a word, just simply stood in the doorway.

The boy smiled but looked toward the cupboard almost immediately. Nikollette did the same and cleared her throat. Behind the cupboard door, the girl carried on, oblivious to Ophelia's presence.

"…but what I'm most excited about is having a girl in the manor my age. Barnaby, I don't envy you. Looks like you'll be the odd one out."

Nikollette cleared her throat again.

"Not that I have anything nefarious planned," she continued with a slight chuckle. "I'm just sayin' tha—"

The girl leaned back and peered out from the cupboard and across the table, where Ophelia stood silent, smiling.

"Oh." Her smile beamed and her voice nearly sang. "Hello!" She shut the cupboard and brought a glass jug of orange juice to the table, along with a muffin, and proceeded to almost glide over to Ophelia. After setting down her haul, she extended a hand. "I'm Amarine. Amarine Isles. And you must be Ophelia."

"I am. Hi," Ophelia responded, grabbing Amarine's hand. "It's nice to meet you."

"You as well! I could hardly sleep last night knowing you were just down the hall from me. I had so many questions, and I was so eager to say hello. I'm really excited to have you here and I—"

"Amarine." Nikollette interrupted the persistent stream of words that flowed from Amarine's lips. "Why don't you offer Ophelia a seat at the table or perhaps some breakfast?"

"Yes, sorry." Amarine winced through the smile that never seemed to break as she turned back to Ophelia. "I get a little carried away sometimes. Come and sit with us. There's plenty of food."

Ophelia joined the trio at the table, sitting across from Nikollette and the boy, beside Amarine. She said hello to the boy in a meek voice as she sat.

"This is Barnaby," Nikollette finally added, having grown observably impatient at the ever-expanding silence filling the room. She looked at him. "Barnaby, this is Ophelia."

"Sorry." He straightened his posture a little and pushed his glasses up his nose. "Pleasure to meet you. I'm Barnaby Bishop."

Ophelia met his hand halfway across the table and shook it. It was cold, remarkably so. "Ophelia. Hi," she managed to squeak out.

"I'm sure you have plenty of questions," Nikollette chimed in again, "but seeing as how you likely aren't sure exactly what it is you should be asking, might I take the liberty of giving you a brief explanation?"

"That would be very nice, thank you." Ophelia smiled. Amarine slid her muffin to Ophelia, who gave her a quiet thank you, pinched off a small piece, and popped it into her mouth. It was sweet. Amarine never stopped smiling at her. Ophelia could feel it as she tried to remain focused on Nikollette.

"Deadwood Manor." Nikollette waved her arms in a wide, sweeping motion. "My family's home for generations. I won't bore you with its history, so we'll start where you are likely eager to learn. It was my father, Bastien A'Mysteriouse, who discovered magic along with my uncle, Marcel."

Ophelia noticed the mood change.

"Sominor had been, prior to the discovery of magic, a mostly peaceful land, whose only real danger were the laws of nature and the rare encounter with things that were never meant to be. We call them neverbeasts. No one is entirely certain how they came to be in our world. We only know where they came from. Our nightmares.

"A place that never truly was, filled with things that never were. So, the Neverwas is what we came to call this world outside of our own. Slumber bridged the two worlds. Magic was meant to help secure Sominor, but the opposite came to pass. It was a discovery my father lamented often toward the end.

"Soon after the discovery of this power, my father and my uncle learned to wield it. Where swords and arrows failed to meet a challenge, where lives stood at fear or risk of death, magic rose to the occasion. Regrettably, more often, the occasion arose. No one knows what role the use of magic had on the ever-increasing threat from the Neverwas, if any at all, though my father postulated that perhaps magic served as a catalyst in the minds and hearts of people, fueling their dreams and imaginations in a way that nothing had before. Regardless, the threats grew more rapidly than the power in the magic of only two men. So, they trained others. Spellweavers, they came to be called. The threats continued to mount.

"This magic is now taught to a select few. Who receives this training is a decision made in part by the three Eldweavers, the first class of Spellweavers to ever be trained: Diedrich Finch, Illana Fairwind, and Victor Gideon. Once they agree to allow a new weaver into the fold, that person must then undergo a trial to determine if they are indeed worthy enough to weave magic into the threads of reality.

"So, my dear Ophelia, what questions do you have for me? I'm happy to answer what I can right now and happy to answer what I cannot in the days ahead."

She thought for a moment and then asked, "So, there are other houses like this one?"

"Yes. Two others. Knight Ridge Manor, led by Lady Corina Knight, and Bloodmoore Manor, led by Lord Avery Winthrop. Each have two wards of their own."

"Why only two?"

"Well, power has a way of bending the will of those who wield it. So, the Eldweavers decided to restrict training to only those who were deemed necessary. Smaller numbers are easier to manage."

Ophelia nodded along. She wanted to ask if anyone had ever misused magic, but instead shifted her attention to the other two sitting at the table with her.

"Can you two do magic?" Ophelia looked back and forth between Barnaby and Amarine.

Amarine smiled and then eagerly reached for a shaker of salt, dumping some out on the table. "Yes! Watch!"

In the pile of salt Amarin traced lines with her pinky. The design was an arrangement of squares, larger ones arraigned in a line, with smaller ones interconnected along their ends.

"Ready?" Amarine smiled mischievously at Ophelia. "Watch."

Amarine then tapped the center of the design. The salt first vibrated, though the table was still, and then each grain gravitated toward the center of the pile, the symbol erasing itself. From the table, the salt seemed to take root and grow, forming branching limbs that sprouted leaves. Then, as suddenly as it had grown, the salt leaves fell apart, grain by grain, until the entire salt tree was bare. Then the tree itself collapsed into a small pile of nothing more than ordinary salt.

"That was lovely, Amarine," Lady Nikollette expressed.

"Thank you, Lady Nikollette." Amarine bowed her head.

"That really was beautiful," Ophelia couldn't help but reiterate, finding no other way to describe it. She looked at Barnaby next, excited and eager for more. "Can you do that, too?"

"Well, um." Barnaby shifted uncomfortably and pushed his glasses up again, though they hadn't slid down since he last adjusted them. "Yes, but not exactly. I—"

Lady Nikollette saved him the explanation. "Barnaby has a little more difficulty with magic than Amarine. He is what we call divided. Half ghoul, half man. It is his ghoulish half that makes weaving difficult. However, it was his doing that enchanted the glasses he wears and that cold box over there. So, although weaving may take Mr. Bishop more time to accomplish, he can accomplish it nonetheless and quite powerfully so, if I might add. Go ahead and take your glasses off now, Mr. Bishop. Ophelia is likely to see you without them at some point."

He looked uncomfortable, almost upset by Lady Nikollette's request. "Fine."

When Barnaby removed his glasses, the brown eyes that once peered out from behind the glass had gone, replaced by deep obsidian. Ophelia could see herself, along with the reflection of the room, in his eyes. They were captivating. She leaned in.

Barnaby, on the other hand, leaned back, asking, "You aren't afraid?"

"Afraid of what?" Ophelia asked. "I think they look quite lovely."

"Most people are afraid." Barnaby looked away. "I can't say I blame them. Ghouls are terrible creatures."

"What is so terrible about black eyes?"

Barnaby paused at the question. He looked unsure of how to answer it. She had asked the question as she would have any other and became confused by his reaction. An uncomfortable smile forced its way onto his face, and he pushed through the apparent discomfort of the topic well enough to explain.

"Well, that's not all there is to ghouls," he said, standing up and walking toward the cupboard. "They are also very strong."

The cupboard was nearly twice as tall as Barnaby and looked to be about ten times heavier. Still, with seemingly little effort at all, Barnaby lifted the cupboard up, smiled at Ophelia, and then set it down gently.

"See?" He pointed at the cupboard. "Quite strong. But if you also take into consideration their short tempers, incredible speed, taste for living flesh, and the ability to heal so fast that normal weapons make them difficult to defeat, then you might imagine why people would be fearful."

"Oh, I see." Ophelia nodded and then looked him in the eyes with all the kindness she could summon. "Well, I'm not afraid of you."

Barnaby's unusually pale skin turned a purplish pink as he awkwardly took his seat beside Lady Nikollette. Lady Nikollette and Amarine said nothing but shared a smile.

"How did you become divided?" As soon as the question left her mouth, Ophelia regretted it. She could see the change in Barnaby's mood clearly on his soured face. "I'm sorry. I'm not sure if I should have asked."

Barnaby didn't answer. Instead, he excused himself and left the room.

"I didn't mean to—"

"It's not your fault. He'll be fine," Lady Nikollette assured. "He doesn't like to talk about it, but you couldn't have known. Though, I suppose, that is his story to tell when he is ready," Lady Nikollette said, before changing the topic. "More important now is a question for you. Would you like to stay with us while we work to uncover the mystery of your past? I have a feeling you may take well to magic."

Ophelia was surprised and then confused. "I thought you said each house can only have two wards?"

"Yes, well, I do hold some influence with the Eldweavers. I don't like to exercise such influence in the name of fairness, but I believe you to be a worthy exception. Now, before you answer, I must warn you. This life can be difficult, dangerous, and painful at times; often mildly, but occasionally extremely so. I have found, however, that there is little one cannot weather with the right people at their side."

Ophelia looked to Amarine, who was smiling, nodding, and ever so slightly mouthing the word *yes*. Then she looked back at Lady Nikollette, her heart fluttering and her stomach turning excitedly. "Yes. I think I would like that very much. Thank you."

Lady Nikollette nodded, stood up, and then walked to the middle of the kitchen. "Then let me get to it. I trust Amarine to show you around the manor. I'll go speak to the Eldweavers at once." Lady Nikollette produced a silver coin from a pocket hidden in the folds of her long skirt. She smiled playfully and added, "And if you go outside, mind grandfather. He's getting old, and I worry last night's storm might have made the crack running through him worse."

She winked at Ophelia and flipped the coin. It sang beautifully as it spun into the air. Ophelia watched it until it vanished at the apex of its journey. Lady Nikollette had vanished as well.

Amarine nearly leaped from her seat and grabbed Ophelia's hand. "Let's go! I have so much to show you!"

AN UNUSUAL REQUEST

The kitchen melted away as the coin spun through the air. Upon the coin's decent, the halls of Spellevue came pouring down around Nikollette. Her heart raced with the sweeping motion of the shifting reality. Small beads of sweat formed on her brow, and she couldn't help but open her mouth to take in a gasping breath. As quickly as the coin fell, she regained her composure with the grace of a seasoned traveler. She caught the coin without looking. The stained-glass window behind her, above the main entrance, painted her hand in multi-colored rays of light. She tried to remember the last time she'd entered through the front door, an errant thought not worth dwelling on as she walked straight through the entrance hall and into the main chamber, the World's Room. The cool air of Spellevue made short work of drying her glistening skin.

A lovely tune hummed through the space with the beauty of a blue-wing on a summer's afternoon, and upon entering she was greeted by its source. It was the newest Spellkeeper, carrying a stack of books;

Rosalin Starling. As usual, Rosalin presented herself as would a cool spring morning after a gentle rain, as pleasant as could be. Though Nikollette had not spent much time with Rosalin, the girl seemed to possess a natural gravity that made those around her want to fall into its cheerful pull.

"Lady A'Mysteriouse—" she said before being interrupted.

"As I've told you before, Nikollette is fine, dear."

"Apologies, Lady Nikollette."

"Not needed. How are you doing today, Rosalin?"

"I'm doing great. Just trying to keep up with my reading. Magister Irons likes to keep us busy, and I'm only halfway through the archives."

"I'm sure he does." She smiled at Rosalin and then leaned in close. "He wasn't always such a stick in the mud. He used to be fun, you know?"

Rosalin let out a giggle that echoed through the chamber of polished stone with all the ease of a bouncing ball. "Well, as tough as he is, he knows quite a lot. He said I could accompany the weavers on their next encounter. I can't wait!"

"Well, congratulations, dear. That is an exciting time. I'm sure you've studied well all your herbs and tonics?"

"Yes, of course."

"Wonderful. Now, I hate to cut our conversation short, but I need to speak to the Eldweavers. Would you be so kind as to point me in their direction?"

"Where they usually are," Rosalin answered without hesitation. "In the Council Chamber."

"Of course. Thank you."

The two exchanged smiles and went their separate ways. As Nikollette walked across the World's Room, the hard heels of her boots rang out in delicate taps. It was the only sound in the enchanted space. As ever they did with every visit, childhood memories flooded her mind. The stars that lit the room were to blame, glimmering above her. Her eyes glistened, and the subtle hint of a forlorn smile appeared before fading away again. With a single deep breath, she managed to put the flow of memories to rest. The present and the future were too important now for her mind to be cluttered with thoughts of the past. There was much she needed to do and dwindling time in which to get it done.

She entered the Council Chamber with little regard to what the Eldweavers might have been discussing, though she didn't interrupt even if her unexpected appearance caused a noticeable pause in their discussion. She hardly paid it any mind, instead simply taking a seat on a wooden bench just beside the door.

"These encroachments seem to be happening more often. The number of neverbeasts, and their growing variations? Something needs to be done," Eldweaver Gideon spoke, firmly.

"I understand your concern, Victor, but we must always weigh the morality of our actions if we are to maintain the trust and goodwill of the people. Trust is the bedrock of all that we are, and raising an army is hardly conducive of trust," Eldweaver Fairwind responded with the cool, even-handed demeanor she always had. "We should continue to handle each incident as they occur. To go looking for trouble is to find it."

"I am inclined to agree with Illana," Eldweaver Finch added with a smile.

"Of course you are," Eldweaver Gideon snorted. "We'll come to a point when our numbers are too thin to answer every call. How many lives will it take to move you?"

"Listen," Eldweaver Finch continued, making his point, "we don't hunt; we protect. We don't attack; we defend. We simply have too much power to go about wielding it without hesitation. We can't let our desire to do what we feel we must infect our ability to discern what is right from what is not."

"With Diedrich and myself, the tally comes out two to one," Illana concluded before Victor could let even the slightest sound escape his open mouth. So, he shut it. She continued. "We will maintain our defensive stance and only act when called upon."

The three of them stood up from their triangular stone table and nodded silently at one another. Victor was the only one among them who hadn't the decency to summon even a polite smile.

Nikollette stood along with them and, before they could walk away from their seats, she spoke. "Excuse me. If I could have a moment of your time before you go your separate ways. I have a request that needs your urgent consideration."

Illana and Dierich smiled, nodded, and sat back down. Victor let out a short grunt and begrudgingly took his sit along with them.

"Thank you." Nikollette's voice was reverent for the three sitting before her. Though she'd known them for most of her life, she knew when it was time for casual familiarities and when it wasn't. Now, it wasn't. She continued. "Just last night, a young girl, no older than sixteen, found herself fleeing the Deadwoods and coming to a stop in my family cemetery. She didn't know where she had come from aside from a hole in the ground, nor who she was, aside from a name: Ophelia Ravenward."

"The Deadwoods." Illana's normally calm eyes lit up with a flicker of curiosity. "Is she divided? How did she survive?"

"I cannot say if she is divided, but she doesn't appear to be. And as for how she survived? With great difficulty, I can assure you."

"Haven't you seen her through your looking glass?" Victor huffed. "Or did she not grant you permission?"

"She did, and I did," Nikollette said, still calm. Now wasn't the time to get into it with Victor.

"Well," Diedrich pressed, "don't leave us wanting. What did you see? It must have been something for you to come here to ask our council on the matter."

"The looking glass showed me a frightened girl running through the Deadwoods and landing on my doorstep. One who appears to have spontaneously popped into existence."

The Eldweavers exchanged concerned looks. Illana was the first to speak. "A young girl, bearing your mother's name, appeared in the cursed woods on your family's grounds and found her way through a storm to your door?"

"More or less, yes." Nikollette nodded.

"I see." Illana closed her eyes a moment and leaned back in her chair. "So then, why is it you've come to us?"

"I've come to ask if I might take her on as a ward, that she might endure the coming Trial of Talismans."

"What?" Victor shot out of his seat. The wooden chair skittered along the floor as his hand slapped down on the table. "You already have two wards under your care, and you come to ask for more? You, better than anyone, know the rules."

"My father—"

"Your father isn't here. You are as equal as any of us. There are no exceptions in equality."

Nikollette allowed the silence to ruminate as Diedrich and Illana seemed content to watch the exchange. Once Victor had calmed himself and taken his seat, Nikollette resumed speaking.

"*My father* understood the importance of maintaining control over this power he discovered, this power he shared. He also understood that, where fate is concerned, one can hardly exercise control. I believe Ophelia's appearance under these strange circumstances to be a sign. If my looking glass could not paint a clear picture, then perhaps magic has already woven itself throughout her being. If we ignore that, if we cast her out, we may very well do so at our own peril. However, if we take her in, we can guide her along our shared path." Nikollette watched Victor's opposition only grow as she spoke. She added, "I intend on choosing a successor after my wards are deemed fit. I will not be taking on another group, nor will I continue practicing magic."

"What?" Illana raised her voice in what almost sounded like protest.

Victor's usually hard face softened at the news. Diedrich's jovial demeanor suddenly fell flat. Illana pried, "When was this decided?"

"Only recently, and for reasons I'd rather not discuss, but I've made up my mind. I only ask, as my final act, that you let me pass on all I know, all my father knew, to one more soul. Should the trials deem her worthy."

"And what of the others?" Illana asked. "Victor is correct. There can be no exceptions in equality."

"Then give them each the opportunity to bring a third ward into their ranks. Not a guarantee of a third, but a chance. All I'm asking for, begging for, is a chance. Victor is right. We could certainly use the help. We cannot know what the future holds, but the trials can at least lend us the wisdom to know if those we choose deserve the chance to help keep Sominor well-guarded."

The Eldweavers exchanged looks, and then Diedrich answered for them all. "Let us deliberate. We'll call you back when we are done."

Nikollette bowed her head, turned around, and walked out. She stood beside the door, her back to the wall, folded her arms, and closed her eyes. Her heart fluttered.

Slow and controlled; the measure of each breath came in deliberate action. Her body relaxed, and her mind eased. The memory of her mother came to her.

"My darling Nikollette." The sun shone over them both as she looked up at her mother, whose voice floated as softly as the white patches of cloud in the sky above the unfinished Spellevue, her heart racing away with her courage like a hungry dog with a stolen gobbler's leg. Visions of the danger that awaited her through the door of the trials flashed like dire warnings.

Her mother's voice. She focused on her mother's voice.

"Your body? Your mind? You can experience this life at their whim, or you can use them to create the life you deserve. Life, as it always has, starts simply with the breath. So, breathe my darling daughter. When you're ready, walking through that door will be nothing more than another choice. One in an uncountable number of choices that only you can make."

She opened her eyes. Her mother's wisdom turned over in her mind. She didn't find it helpful, not at this moment. This choice? It wasn't hers. Not this time. Nor did it feel like a choice at all. Everything rested on the prevailing of her own words in the hearts of three and on her carrying out all that lay ahead of her.

The words you chose. The thought came in her mother's voice. She softly snorted at the notion.

The door opened. From it, the three Eldweavers stepped out into the corridor to join her. Illana first, followed by Diedrich, and Victor last, not bothering to make eye contact with Nikollette. She remained solemn, but in her heart, she smiled. She already knew the answer.

"We've decided to afford each manor the opportunity to put forth a third. The trials are already planned two weeks from now to accommodate Lord Wainwright's potential second, Constance. We will inform Lord Wainwright and Lady Knight that, should they desire, they may extend an offer to an additional ward. Ensure that Ophelia is ready and aware of the danger she is to face."

"Thank you." Nikollette bowed. She let her smile come peeking out when she lifted her head. "I am in your debt."

"There is no debt," Diedrich chimed in. "Only the chance to let fate decide what happens next."

Victor turned his back and stormed off, muttering, "Fate. We make our own."

Neither Nikollette nor the two remaining Eldweavers dared respond but rather shared knowing glances until Victor turned the corner at the end of the corridor. Diedrich wandered off in the opposite direction with a chuckle. Illana stayed with Nikollette.

"Why did Victor seem so upset?" Nikollette asked, genuinely confused. "More Spellweavers is precisely what he wanted."

"You are correct," Illana answered. "The final vote was unanimous, but Victor didn't want three more weavers. He wanted an army. One in every village, city, and kingdom. Most of our deliberations consisted of him attempting to convince us to just be done with it and allow any who wish to attempt the trial. I imagine he'll continue to be upset about it for some time. You should also know, Victor will be investigating the Deadwoods. So, if you do see him, don't be alarmed. We all feel that such a mysterious occurrence requires further investigation."

"He is more than welcome." Nikollette nodded as she spoke. She had more to say, plenty more, about Victor as a person. None of it good, and none of it serving any purpose in saying, so she kept it to herself.

"So, you really want to leave magic behind?" Illana changed the subject.

Nikollette smiled the way she remembered her father's smile when he was left to break hard news to her gently. "It doesn't feel like a choice. Magic has been a part of most of my life. It has been the source of so many wonderful memories. It has also been the cause of the worst. I've spent years wishing I could change the way things happened but have come to accept that I cannot. I appreciate now the notion that each step we take in life is built upon every step that came before and building toward those yet taken. I know in my heart that it is what I must do, regardless of if I want to."

Tears formed at the corner of Illana's eyes. A soft smile held her high cheeks even higher. She closed her eyes and nodded. "You will be sorely missed, my dear girl."

"Girl." Nikollette shook her head and chuckled as she pulled out her coin. They shared one more smile before she gave it a flick. There was a long journey ahead of her – ahead of them all – and she had to make sure everything moved along as it was meant to.

INTO THE NEVERWAS

When Amarine took her hand, Ophelia wasn't sure what to do. She pulled it back. Though Barnaby hadn't been the most welcoming, in that moment she wished he was still in the kitchen, at least to help steer some attention away from her.

"Sorry," Amarine said with a sudden jolt. "I'm just so excited to show you around."

"It's fine. I just…" Ophelia wasn't sure what to say. Instead, she tilted her head and looked to the place Lady Nikollette had been standing. "What happened to Lady Nikollette?"

"She went to Spellevue. That's where the Eldweavers live."

"Yes, but how?"

"Oh, that is a courier's coin. You picture the place you want to be and then you flip the coin. You'll get one, once you pass the trials."

"If," Barnaby muttered, having only just walked back into the kitchen. He froze when Amarine looked back at him with a scowl. He looked at Ophelia. "Well, umm, it's not that I don't want you to pass the trials, it's just…there is no guarantee anyone will pass. Not everyone passes. That's all."

"Yeah, well, keep your pessimism to yourself next time," Amarine scolded him before turning back to Ophelia. "You'll pass. I know it. You'll get your own coin and your own talisman and everything. Then you can live with us!"

The kitchen fell silent.

"Come on then," Amarine's voice cut through it, and she extended her hand. "Let me show you around."

Ophelia smiled, nodded, and took Amarine's hand. She turned to Barnaby before Amarine could take off. "Are you coming with us?"

Barnaby's pale gray skin again turned a slight shade of purple. He muttered, "No, thanks. I'm quite familiar with the manor."

Amarine giggled. "Let's go. You're making Barnaby blush."

Barnaby shot Amarine a glare before storming back out of the kitchen.

"Is he upset?" Ophelia asked quietly. "Did I do something wrong?"

"Oh, no," Amarine said with an unconcerned wave. "He's just shy. He used to blush whenever I would talk to him. That's just the way he is with new people. Soon he'll feel more comfortable around you. You'll see. He's a nice guy, once he gets to know you. Come on. Let's go."

Amarine led her out of the kitchen and back into the foyer, her excited smile accentuated with a giggle. Once in the grand space of the foyer, Amarine let Ophelia go and twirled around, arms outstretched.

"Isn't it amazing?" Amarine stopped spinning and took a deep breath. "I used to live in a home for the unkept. That's kids without parents. Mine was nice enough, though I'm told most homes aren't. Friendly people in Evergreen. It was cramped though. But this place? This is more space than I ever thought a home could hold."

"It is very lovely," Ophelia answered. "How did you end up here, if you don't mind me asking?"

"Oh, luck mostly." Amarine smiled. "Luck has a lot more to do with things than people like to give it credit for. They found me in the forest, alone – almost dead, I'm told – when I was just about two years old. They put me with the other unkept, and I lived there for most of my life. One day, almost a year ago, I just so happened to be running through the streets of Evergreen. That's the town I'm from, by the way. I'll show you one day. It isn't far. All because my pet cat, Tabitha – she was a tabby – had gone off through a window someone forgot to close. A pet cat, mind you, that I was only allowed to keep because it had a very calm temperament *and* the madam in charge of us had a cat that looked just like it when she was a girl. The same madam who had left us alone that afternoon to go to the market to stock up on necessities. Kids eat quite a bit.

"Being alone, I figured I could go out, fetch Tabitha, and return before she ever knew I was gone. I ran through town as though there were no one in it but me chasing after Tabitha. I wasn't worried or panicked. In fact, I was having a lovely time. That is, until I lost sight of her. Distracted, I bumped into Lady Nikollette. I fell and then bounced right back up. I asked her if she'd seen Tabitha. She said she'd seen me chasing a cat, if that's who I was referring to. I told her it was.

She said she was impressed with how easily I had maneuvered through the streets, that I reminded her of herself when she was a girl. And that's how I ended up here, more or less. See? Luck!"

Ophelia found herself lost in the barrage of words that had poured out of Amarine with an unwavering cadence. It took her a moment to reconcile what she'd just heard with what it all meant. She knew what a town was, and Evergreen felt familiar, in a way. The image of a cat pounced through her thoughts, taking shape as it went.

"I'm sorry," Amarine added as she waited for the silent Ophelia to say something. "It's a lot. I tend to do that. In a home full of unkept, you need to talk fast if you want the chance to say your peace without interruption. I've got plenty to say. If I'm ever going too fast, just tell me to stop. It won't hurt my feelings. I've been trying to work on it."

Ophelia smiled along with Amarine. She nodded. "Okay. I'll do that. Though, it doesn't bother me. I don't have much to say because everything is so new, so it's nice to just listen."

"Sounds like the makings of a perfect friendship." Amarine's smile widened at the proclamation, and her eyes lit up without warning. She nearly shouted, "Let me show you my room!"

Amarine's room was roughly the same size as Ophelia's. The layout was similar as well. The bed wasn't nearly as grand as Ophelia's, however. It looked to be the same size, but the frame was short and far simpler in design. Along the walls hung drawings of creatures that Ophelia didn't recognize. Next to her desk, in the corner of her room, there sat a short box with a large metal horn that seemed to grow from it like a flower. It curled up and out of the box, opening at the end with large, engraved copper petals. In the center of the curved horn, set atop the box on its end, sat a green crystal. Grooves ran in parallel around it, from top to bottom, and a copper rod had its end set within the grooves.

"You like music?"

"What?"

"It's a crystalphone," she explained, walking over to it. "It plays music. See?"

Amarine turned a crank on the side and flipped a switch. The crystal spun slowly and the copper rod ran along the grooves, crawling ever downward with each rotation. The most beautiful song came softly from the copper horn.

"That's pretty."

"Yeah, I love music," Amarine replied with her eyes closed and her head swaying side-to-side with the tempo. She stopped suddenly and looked at Ophelia. "That's why I made these! I forgot to tell you!"

She practically bounced over to Ophelia and ran her fingers beneath one of the sapphire orbs that hung from her ears.

Ophelia took the slightest step back. "What are they?"

"My Singing Sapphires," Amarine exclaimed as she worked to remove one from her ear. "I enchanted them myself. Here."

She handed it to Ophelia.

Ophelia looked at it and then at Amarine. She was handed the earring as though she should know what was so special about it but didn't say anything, not wanting to feel foolish.

"Go on," Amarine encouraged as she put the other orb of her remaining earring into her own ear. "Give it a listen."

Ophelia put the sapphire into her ear slowly. It began to vibrate, then hum, then sing. The song wasn't the same as the one playing on the crystalphone, but it was equally as lovely. This one had an upbeat tempo. Her foot tapped as if acting on its own, and before Ophelia knew it, she was smiling and her head was nodding along.

"It's my favorite song." Amarine had raised her voice and then held out her hand as she removed the sapphire in her own ear and let it dangle from the chain. "It's really helpful for when I use my talisman."

Ophelia gave the earring back and Amarine re-attached it.

"What exactly are talismans? Lady Nikollette's is a looking glass, but it seemed kind of ordinary."

A mischievous sort of smile crept into Amarine's expression. She whispered, "Wanna see?"

Ophelia wasn't so sure now, but she nodded anyway.

"Okay." Amarine pulled at the long, leather string around her neck until something popped out from beneath her shirt. Attached to the end was a small object, covered in red fur peppered with dark red spots. "The Never Paw. It lets me walk through the Neverwas completely undetected. Watch."

Amarine took a deep breath and then vanished in a blink. Ophelia looked around. There was no trace of her. In an instant, Amarine reappeared beside Ophelia with a, "Boo!"

Ophelia jumped.

They both giggled.

"Everyone's talisman is unique. When you pass the trials, you get one. I love mine. I have to hold my breath to use it though. Time moves a little differently in the Neverwas, so I put in my sapphires to time myself. I know exactly what part of the song is when I will start needing to breathe soon. It's a ton of fun. *Loads* of neverbeasts."

Amarine gestured at the drawings on the walls. Ophelia let her eyes follow and asked, "Did you draw these?"

"Yes." Amarine walked over to the one Ophelia had been admiring. "This is a shift-scale. They are serpents that can re-arrange their scales to hide in plain sight. They can look like anything, so you never really know when one is going to come out of nowhere. Though I suppose, when you think about it, all neverbeasts come from nowhere. I mean, the Neverwas is a place, but it's also not a place. If that makes sense. Though, there are many ways of loo—"

"Amarine."

"Yeah?"

"You're doing it again."

"Oh, sorry about that."

The two girls looked at one another in silence before erupting with laughter. Once it died down, Ophelia walked along the room and took in all the different creatures Amarine had drawn.

"Aren't you scared?"

"No," Amarine said, taking a seat at the foot of her bed. "Like I said, they can't see me while I'm in there. I *can* touch them though. I don't often do it because I'm not sure if they can feel me or touch me back, but I have petted a few kitten-pillars. They seem to like it.

Especially if you scratch 'em under the chin."

"Kitten-pillar?"

"That one." Amarine pointed to a drawing above her desk. Ophelia went to look at it more closely. "I miss Tabitha sometimes, so when I see a kitten-pillar, I can't always help myself. I've tried dreaming one up, but dreams aren't usually the sort of thing people can control. They aren't mean, per say, but they are a bit mischievous. Suppose that's what I like about them. They aren't as big as normal cats either. Like they'd been shrunk down to half the size of a normal cat and then stretched out to double the length. They've got four pairs of stubby legs, so they aren't as agile as a normal cat, not on the ground at least."

"They can fly?"

"Oh no, but they can glide. They sort of run through the air once they get off the ground. Pretty nimble, depending on how much room they have to glide around in." Amarine sat up again with a jolt. "Hey!"

Ophelia turned to face her. "Yeah?"

"Want to see the Neverwas? I can take you."

Ophelia thought about it for a moment. "Are you sure it's safe?"

"Sure, as long as you stick with me, you'll be fine."

"Okay," Ophelia agreed with uncertainty.

"Great, but let's do it out back. Not a lot to see inside the manor."

The scent of storm clouds lingered in the air. Though the field was well-maintained, Ophelia couldn't help but notice that the statues that surrounded it looked as though their best days were behind them.

"That's grandpa," Amarine said, pointing at one of the statues.

A layer of moss crawled up the base of the old statue. Its weathered surface made the man look older than Ophelia thought he ought to, but she wasn't sure how old that ought to have been. He did, indeed, have a crack running through him, from his left shoulder and up through his neck on the right. It was as if the storm had tried its best to strike the old man down.

Amarine asked again, "You sure about this?"

Ophelia, with a grimace, "Yes?"

"Okay, hold my hand. Don't let go, and hold your breath on the count of three."

"One…two…three."

Ophelia looked over her shoulder as the world blinked out of existence. Barnaby had just stepped outside and, in that moment, he looked both concerned and frustrated. It was replaced with something much darker. Ophelia felt a sense of unease as the ground beneath their feet began to shift and swirl like an endless sea. The air was thick with a cloying mist that obscured her vision, and strange sounds echoed all around. Though she could see no one else around, Ophelia couldn't help but feel as though she was being watched.

The statues in the field looked more worn and weathered than before, and Grandpa was missing his head. The Deadwoods that surrounded the manor appeared thicker than they should have, and the trees twisted and turned in even more unnatural ways.

The manor no longer felt inviting, but imposing. Its walls looked new in some places, while others looked old and worn. Its sections seemed to shift through various states and locations, as though no one person could quite figure out what the manor was meant to look like, and instead argued over what should go where.

There was a figure in one of the upstairs windows, hiding among the darkness of the empty room. Was that her room? Was he smiling? She watched as it took a step closer to the window; out from the shadows. His silver eyes gave him away. It was the man she had seen in her dream.

Amarine tapped Ophelia's shoulder. Ophelia looked at her and then at the place she was pointing. Coming out of the tree line, a shape appeared, at first slow and then faster as it ran toward the manor. It was large, bigger than them, and had four massive tusks protruding from its head, but it was clear the beast wasn't headed for them.

Ophelia fought every urge to run, if only because Amarine seemed entirely too calm. Just then, something small and quick scurried across the field, only a few feet from where they stood.

Ophelia panicked.

She let her breath out with a scream and ran. She ran without looking. She ran until she bumped into Grandpa, at the base of which she fell. The statue wobbled slightly.

Amarine came back. "What happened?"

She rushed over to help Ophelia to her feet.

In an instant, Barnaby appeared, standing over Ophelia as bits of stone came raining down around her. The bulk of Grandpa's stone face tumbled through the field with heavy thuds before coming to a rest at the edge of the Deadwoods, a singular cement eye staring back at her, somehow disapproving.

"What were you thinking, taking her into the Neverwas?" Anger seared the edges of Barnaby's words.

Ophelia felt embarrassed as Amarine helped her up. "It was just supposed to be a quick visit. I wanted her to see it. It's not a big deal."

"Yeah, well." Barnaby looked furious. "You almost got her killed. You're both lucky I showed up when I did. That stone head of his was likely heavy enough to crack your skull."

Before Amarine could rebut him, and before Ophelia could thank him, Barnaby had stormed off.

THE FEARLESS HEART OF RENÉE ROCHÉ

When Renée, Marcel, and Illana arrived at the edge of Windy Willow township with one of their new recruits, Dominic Irons, they weren't quite sure what to expect. The town had been evacuated days before their arrival. What the townsfolk had only been able to describe to them as a "murderous murmuration" wasn't much to go on. The only other information offered up was that the creatures could flay a man in mere moments.

Renée wasn't a fan of the name "murderous murmuration." She often enjoyed watching the murmurations that flittered along the lake at the bottom of the hill just outside of Roché Village. The way they danced, moving like some living liquid suspended in mid-air. She couldn't imagine anything murderous about a murmuration. Then she saw them.

Small, winged creatures perched along the township's rooftops. At first glance, the beasts appeared to be nothing more than small things with black wings, but as the four of them drew nearer it became clearer just how horrible they were. Each wore an empty human face, like a mask, featureless and stretched over them. Beneath the skin sat skulls, whose teeth grew from their misshapen mouths like daggers of bone. They were no larger than the size of a small melon, but as the murmuration took flight, they spread their wings, revealing their true horror.

When they came within town limits, it was impossible to miss the sound. How terrible, the sound. Their leathery wings beat in an unnatural rhythm, an ominous hum that seemed to echo through the otherwise silent skies and dug itself beneath Renée's skin. Her jaw clenched.

The four of them took refuge in the nearest home and observed from the shadows. Out the window of the small house, looking up at the flock of certain death, they were met with hundreds of empty, expressionless faces staring back at them. The murmuration soared overhead and the sound grew in intensity, building to a crescendo that pulled a quiet whimper from Dominic.

"I don't think I should have come," Dominic's shaking voice managed to sputter out.

"It'll be fine." Renée turned to face him, immediately taking charge. "You stay here; we'll take care of this."

"Right." Marcel backed away from the window, practically having to force himself to look away from the terror in the skies. "You are most certainly not ready for this."

"Okay, good." Dominic sat in a wooden chair at a small dining table; shaking. "What are you going to do? There are so many of them."

"That…" Marcel let the question stir and the silence linger before finishing. "…is an excellent question. Any ideas?"

When he turned to face Illana and Renée, he was initially met with blank stares and shrugging shoulders.

"I think we can fight them if we can split them up," Illana offered and then added, "but they don't seem like they would be too keen on separating."

"Agreed," Renée chimed in. "And picking them off one at a time would leave us vulnerable to the others and most certainly wear us out before we could finish them. There are hundreds of them, and just the thought of casting even twenty spells in a row has me feeling faint."

"Both excellent points," Marcel considered.

"Though," Renée offered up, "there is something I've been thinking about trying lately, but I haven't had the chance. This seems like an opportunity as good as any."

Marcel smiled. "None of your ideas have let me down so far. What's the plan?"

Renée smiled in return. "First, we'll need a distraction."

Renée only caught glimpses of Marcel as he leaped from roof to roof, the symbols etched into the leather of his boots flashing and vanishing with each mid-air step he took. The murmuration crept closer by the second. Their shrieking cries rose and fell with each unpredictable shift of their fluttering mass. They flew with a frenzied energy made even more terrifying by the violent shifting of their dark cloud.

"How is it coming along?" Marcel shouted from across the village. "I'm running out of steps on these boots, you know!"

Renée and Illana worked furiously to etch symbols into the dirt at the town square. Illana finished the large circular pattern, and Renée was putting the finishing touches on the complicated triangular pattern within the ring.

"Are you sure this will wor—" Marcel's voice cut out. Renée saw his foot fall through the air. The fall from the house he'd just leaped from was sudden, but he managed to stick the landing, rolling out of it as though that had always been the plan. He always managed to look like everything he did had been planned.

The murmuration did not hesitate in its movements. Marcel raced toward the town square. "Seems impossible! Dangerous even!"

"It'll work! Just make sure you lead them straight to the center! Then wait for them to strike! It's a straight shot!"

The cries of the murderous murmuration rose as Marcel drew nearer and nearer the others, standing safely out of harm's way. When he finally reached the center of the symbols, he stopped and turned. The murmuration rose before him, like a serpent poised to strike.

Strike, they did.

As a wave of empty faces and razor teeth came crashing down at him, he was pulled, through sheer force of magic, to his left, wrapped in the capable arms of Renée. She smiled, as did he, both their breaths warm on one another's faces.

"Well, hello there," Marcel said.

Illana sprang into action on the opposite side. She knelt, placing her hand at the edge of the circle. Before the murmuration could realize they'd struck nothing more than dirt, the circle flashed. From the dirt, a bubble rose. One larger than any of them had ever seen. It swirled with light and color. The murmuration beat themselves against it. It flexed and bowed but did not break.

"Seems the teacher has become the damsel," Renée said, staring deep into Marcel's eyes.

"Hey!" Illana shouted through beleaguered breaths. "Let's finish this!"

"Right." Renée let go of Marcel. "Excuse me one moment."

She swept her long, flowing skirt aside and lifted a worn leather boot before stomping it into the ground. The triangular pattern within the bubble lit up, and from the dirt erupted a great torrent of flame.

The murmuration fell into chaos, with each monster for themselves as they, and the flame, pounded at the bubble. Their efforts, fruitless. Renée ground her foot into the dirt harder, letting her entire will pour from her being. Her voice roared alongside the raging flames.

"I can't hold it!" Illana's cries competed with the violent rumble of unforgiving fire.

Renée did not let up.

Illana's bubble burst.

The resulting explosion sent each of them flying off their feet. A column of flame reached for the sky, threatening to ignite the very clouds above them, and a rush of air was pulled violently toward it. A moment later, once the fire and smoke had gone, only a thin layer of glass in the shape of a circle remained.

"Whoa," Dominic shouted and came running from the house he had been tucked away in. The others made slow work of finding themselves in the aftermath. He approached Renée, arm extended, "That was incredible! I've never seen anything like it!"

Renée took his hand and climbed to her feet. She brushed the dirt and soot off her purple overcoat, panting. "Honestly"—she surveyed the glassy landscape in front of her— "I wasn't entirely sure it would work, but I had a feeling. Looks like I gave it a bit more than I needed to."

"You think?" Illana sounded irritated as she trekked across the glass. It crumbled beneath her. "That was far too dangerous. You could have burned down the entire town."

Marcel stood up between them. "Illana, you may be right, but that isn't at all what happened. The town is safe, and so are its people."

He turned his head, his face out of Illana's view, and gave Renée a wink and a smile. That smile that always seemed to melt her in place, threatening to crystalize her, just like the dirt, under the heat it cast.

"Now, let's just take the time to properly revel in our victory and return to the townsfolk with the good news." Marcel turned and walked away, wrapping an arm around Dominic as he did. They walked off together. "Mr. Irons, I hope you learned something today." His voice faded as they went.

Illana approached Renée with a stone expression that made Renée feel like a girl again. It was the same disapproving look her mother gave her whenever she made a mistake or acted improperly for a young woman of her stature.

"What?" Renée asked, unable to take the look much longer. "I apologize, all right? I'll be sure to exercise restraint next time."

"He's married, Renée."

"Excuse me?"

"You know precisely what I'm talking about." Illana's eyes locked onto Renée's, unflinching. "So, whatever feelings you harbor, I suggest you temper them. No good could possibly come of it. I suspect you know this already."

"I would nev—"

"Save it. I don't need your assurances. Your actions will suffice."

Illana walked off without another word, while Renée was left to stand there without a word to say. She couldn't argue with Illana, but how was she supposed to contain these feelings?

There is no seal to contain the heart.

The mere thought of it gave her an idea.

The foundations of Spellevue had taken longer to complete than expected, but it was done. The walls had moved a little faster but were far from complete. That day, they all gathered, not to continue construction, but for some reason undisclosed to any of them. Bastien stood before them with a reserved smile. Marcel stood beside him, his usual bright spirit subdued. On the floor, in the center of a hexagonal room they'd been told would be a trial room, there stood a doorway. The door was made of glass. It did not reflect, nor could Renée see through it, but the shimmering glint of it was unmistakable.

Renée, Illana, Dierich, and Victor all stood silent, while whispers floated among the newer recruits, Dominic Irons, Alice Comstock, Carmine Halifax, and Delia Bloodmoore. Behind them, Antoinette, Ophelia, and a young Nikollette stood and watched. Renée turned and stole a quick glance and secret wave at Nikollette. Her new earrings, circular in shape and filled with smaller circles linked together, wiggled with the sharp turn of her head and bumped against her cheeks. The bespectacled girl smiled and waved back excitedly.

"New jewelry?" Illana asked in a whisper. "Couldn't help but notice their familiar design. Function or fashion?"

"I hope both," Renée whispered back. "But that remains to be seen."

"Now," Bastien spoke clearly. "I've summoned everyone here today to discuss the future of our endeavor."

"Some of you have already made great strides in learning to weave magic, while some of you are new to it. However, regardless of your level of mastery, all of us must come to an agreement. From my Looking Glass, I've enchanted a fragment. From that, this door. If I am correct, if my talisman has not led me astray, then what waits for each of us beyond this door should be of great benefit to us all."

Marcel jumped in. "What my dear brother is trying to say is, each of us must enter, one at a time, and undergo a trial. A trial that will reach into our very being and read our character, in a sense. Like the Looking Glass, this door will reveal exactly who each of us are. If we are worthy of the power we hold, we should each receive a talisman of our own. If not, well…"

"We can't know for sure," Bastien took over, "but expect the consequences to be dire. This is not something to be taken lightly."

Their words were met with silence. Marcel's smile faded. Bastien spoke again.

"Marcel has agreed to go first, but if any among you desire to take his place, speak now."

"What?" Antoinette cried out. "You can't!"

Marcel said nothing. He stood there, looked her in the eyes, and said not a word. The silence that followed hung over them like a blade ready to fall.

"Say something," Antoinette demanded.

Marcel looked to the door.

"I'm not going to just stand here and watch you put your life at risk! How could you keep this from me?"

"I'll go." Renée raised her hand. She turned to Antoinette. "It's okay. I'll go first."

Renée walked up to Antoinette, put a hand on her shoulder, and looked her in the eyes. Antoinette's were turning red, but her expression softened as Renée spoke with a half-hearted smile. "You should know me well enough by now, Antoinette. If there is a danger, then surely, I'll be the first to find it."

Antoinette turned away. Renée returned to the brothers A'Mysteriouse and asked, "What do I do?"

Bastien nodded, and Marcel shook his head ever so slightly. Renée only nodded in return.

"All you must do is enter. Once the trials are completed, the exit should become visible to you. You should know that once you close that door behind you, there is no return until you've completed the trials."

"I understand." Renée put her shaking hand on the knob and then looked over her shoulder at Illana. Illana nodded back.

Renée took a breath and opened the door. Inside, there was only darkness. She didn't hesitate to enter, shutting the door behind her.

Renée had no way of knowing how long it had been before she came stumbling out. To her, it felt like a day, but the sun above did not seem to have moved much. She looked at the others with wild eyes, heaving breaths, and a relieved smile.

"I made it?"

Marcel was the first to meet her. He kneeled in front of her, grabbed her shoulders, and looked into her eyes. "You did. What happened?"

"I found this." Renée lifted the object she held in her right hand, "A talisman, I would guess."

"HA!," Marcel practically jumped and then waved over his brother. "Bastien, come look! She has a talisman!"

Bastien hurried over to examine the object. It was a stone that appeared to loosely resemble a human heart wrapped tight in tree roots, small enough to rest in the palm of his hand. He lifted his looking glass, fumbling it in his excited fingers. The others had gathered close behind.

"Yes, let's have a look," he mumbled, and within seconds, his eyes lit up. "Remarkable."

"What is it?" Renée asked between settling breaths. "What does it do?"

Bastien let his looking glass fall to his chest and gestured for everyone to back up. "Give her some room, please. Renée"—he turned back to face her—"if you'd kindly step into the grass over there."

Renée looked past the short segment of wall at the edge of the room and walked toward it. She stepped over and onto the grass. The feel of the ground beneath her feet was immediate, and it brought a smile to her tired face. "Oh, I see."

Renée closed her eyes and pressed the small stone heart against her own chest. A pulse emanated from her, and a small ripple of grass rose and fell around her. The next moment, the ground at her feet lifted her up. Slowly, she rose, until she was looking down on everyone else. In front of her, more ground lifted. One after the other, columns of grass, dirt, and stone rose, only to stop just short of the one before it. Soon, there formed a staircase. She opened her eyes and descended. She wasn't tired at all, not in the way weaving made her feel.

"The Stone Heart," Bastien proclaimed. "Control over stone without the need to weave with magic. Use it wisely."

"I will." Renée stifled her excitement as best she could.

"I'll go next," Marcel spoke up. He marched to the door and grabbed the handle. He looked to Antoinette, who was joined by Renée. Renée grabbed her hand as they both watched Marcel embark on his trial.

So Little Time

Nikollette returned to her study just as footsteps stomped through the hall in her direction. They passed as she reached the door, and when she opened it, she saw Barnaby storming off.

"Is there something the matter?" Nikollette called after him, "Is everything alright?"

Barnaby stopped dead in his tracks. His head slumped, and his shoulders slowly rose and fell before he turned to face her. The look on his face said plenty.

"Everything is fine," he sighed and looked at his feet. "The head came off your grandfather's statue. A gust of wind."

"I see," Nikollette responded. Had Barnaby been looking at her, he would have seen the knowing smile on her face. It had gone by the time he looked up and she asked, "Where are the girls?"

"They're still out back, I think."

"Thank you, Mr. Bishop. Sorry to have stopped you."

Barnaby managed a half-hearted smile before heading back toward his bedroom. Nikollette went the other way, eager to tell Ophelia the news.

She found the two girls outside in the field, and sure enough, Grandfather had lost his head.

"Grandfather has certainly seen better days."

The girls jumped at the sudden sound of her voice.

"I'm sorry, Lady Nikollette. I—," Amarine tried to explain.

"He said the wind knocked it loose," Nikollette interrupted Amarine's nervous explanation. She examined the fragments of broken stone and the chunk of her grandfather's face staring back at her from the other end of the field. "It must have been some wind."

"It nearly fell on me," Ophelia offered up before Amarine could say another word. "Barnaby saved me."

"I see." Nikollette smiled at the two girls whose initial confusion, having turned to anxiety, now faded into relief. "Well, it seems I owe that young man a heartfelt thank you. For now, I have good news."

"She can stay," Amarine nearly shouted and then caught herself. "Sorry, Lady Nikollette. Go ahead."

"Thank you." Nikollette flashed a playful look at Amarine. "As I was saying, Ophelia, you may stay, provided you pass the trials and receive a talisman. The trial is in just two weeks, so I suggest we get to work. I'll ask that you join me in my study now so we can go over the finer points of what it is you are about to face." She turned her attention back to Amarine. "And Ms. Ilses, if you would be so kind as to fix us a couple of cups of tea. It would be greatly appreciated."

"Yes, of course." Amarine hurried past Nikollette and into the manor.

Ophelia joined Lady Nikollette in her study. It looked different in the daytime; felt different. Last night, it had seemed a safe harbor in which one might weather a storm. Quite literally, in fact. It was simple, safe, and exactly as it appeared to be. A nice room in a nice home.

However, with the light of day beaming through its tall windows and catching on the dust motes that swirled in the warmth, the study felt cozy. Among it all, there hung an air of mystery, as though it held within each book and each glint of light bouncing off its fixtures and odd knick-knacks, secrets all too eager to be discovered, provided one simply asked the right question.

"With the trials in two weeks, I've come away with the task of preparing you." Nikollette sat down. "So, I've little time to beat around the bush, so to speak."

Ophelia sat in the chair she'd sat in the night before. It didn't feel as comfortable as it had then.

"The Trial of Talismans is not something to be taken lightly, as much as Ms. Ilses might want to make you believe. It can even prove deadly."

Ophelia shifted uncomfortably in her seat. "Deadly?"

"Yes." Nikollette closed her eyes and bowed her head for a moment. Amarine walked in with two cups of tea without knocking.

"Here's the tea," she announced. "Nice and hot."

She set the two cups down on Lady Nikollette's desk, who looked up at her and nodded. "Thank you, Amarine."

"My pleasure." Amarine shuffled out of the room, giving Ophelia a wink along the way. Ophelia wasn't sure how to respond.

Once the door closed, Nikollette continued, "As I was saying, of all who've undergone the trials, they have only proved fatal for one Alice Comstock. Well, as far as we know. You see, she never came out."

"You're saying I could be in there forever?" Ophelia's voice was distant, solemn. She grabbed her tea and took a sip. It was just the right temperature.

"Yes," Nikollette answered. "Though, I do not expect that to be the case, it's best you know that the trial can be difficult, frightening, and quite dangerous at times."

"Was it dangerous for you?"

"It had its moments, but each of our trials is for us alone. No one person will experience the same as another. The trial comes from inside of you."

"And I'm empty," Ophelia said, lowering her head. She looked out the tall windows and into the Deadwoods, again searching her mind for any memory of a life before.

"You aren't empty, dear girl." Nikollette leaned across her desk, "You've simply forgotten who you are. Don't ever confuse the two. Rest assured, you are in there. What I couldn't reveal, I'm certain the trials will. It will find you, and it will judge you. There is no hiding your intentions. There is no masking who you truly are."

Nikollette leaned back in her chair, cup of tea in hand, and looked out the window with Ophelia. Together they sipped their tea and watched the day float along, sitting still within its gentle current. After a few minutes, Ophelia gave her answer.

"I would like to stay. I will attempt the trial."

"As I hoped you would," Lady Nikollette said, adding, "You can leave and go back to getting to know your housemates better, but before you go, there is one more thing."

"What is that?"

"Your full name is Ophelia Ravenward."

"Wait, what? How do you know?" Ophelia looked quite confused.

"I don't. I made it up." Nikollette took another sip of her tea, set it down, and looked at Ophelia. "You see, it felt odd for me to simply give the Eldweavers a first name, so I picked a surname I felt suited you. Raven, for the obvious. Ward, because that is what you have officially become. Really just two facts pressed together rather than a name, but I've never been terribly creative. Hope that is all right."

Ophelia grinned. "I love it."

"Well then, Ms. Ravenward. Off you go."

THE BOY FROM DUSKWATCH

Diedrich Finch appeared at the doorstep of Knightridge Manor in the blink of an eye. He coughed a bit and stumbled. It had been some time since he'd made a trip so far with his coin, and Knightridge was just about as far as one could travel from Spellevue. As usual, the Blackened Bluffs were overcome by gray clouds and a heavy gloom, but the smell of the ocean and the sounds of waves crashing against the rocky shores made him happy. It was the rhythm that had always felt somewhat meditative. He took it in with one deep breath, then let a sigh flow out from behind his smile.

Diedrich looked the black manor up and down and, as the chill ocean wind pressed against him, he looked forward to the warmth it afforded.

He gave the rather modest black door a knock and waited patiently.

When there was nothing in return, he knocked again, calling out, "Lady Knight, it is Eldweaver Finch. Might I have a word?"

Still, nothing. He listened through the crashing waves and the gusts of wind for the sounds of voices or combat. He found neither. He let the thought stir for a while and then snapped his fingers when he'd finally figured it out.

"Duskwatch!"

If they weren't home, they'd be there, training with the Duskwatch Guard. No finer human opponent against which to hone one's non-magical abilities.

Another flip of his coin, and he departed. It was a short trip, a fact for which he was immensely grateful.

Although she was surrounded by the shouting of soldiers, the clattering of blades, and the grunts of combatants, Corina Kight still heard the unmistakable sound of a courier coin from somewhere behind her. She turned her head to the side, catching a glimpse of Eldweaver Finch from the corner of her eye. She returned her focus to Lydia, who was sparring with a young Duskwatch Guardsman in training, Cassian Darrow, wondering what news of danger had arrived to test the mettle of her wards.

The Darrow boy, sixteen years of age she had heard, could have easily been confused for any adult Guardsman. He stood over six feet, towering above Lydia in comparison, and had the build of someone not to be trifled with. Despite Lydia's Blade of Mist, young Darrow held his own, even once having caught Lydia off guard, nearly bringing her to yield. If not for Lydia's talisman and imbued leather armor, Cassian would have disarmed and defeated her ten times over. He was a fine fighter indeed.

Beside Corina were who she assumed to be the boy's parents. His mother cheering him on and his mountain of a father watching in silence, pride glinting through his otherwise stoic expression. Their clothes spoke of wealth, and their son's early acceptance into the guard spoke to power.

"Lady Knight," Corina heard Eldweaver Finch say as he took a spot beside her, "I thought I might find you here."

"Hello, Eldweaver Finch. What seems to be the trouble?" Corina wished Eldweaver Gideon would have been sent instead. Eldweaver Gideon would have made his point already.

"No trouble," Eldweaver Finch said with a pleasant tone. To her, it felt as false as it always had. He continued, "Though it might be a good idea to leave a note, in the event there had been danger. Naturally, that is where I expected you to be."

"Then to what do I owe the pleasure of this visit?" Corina asked. The words tasted bitter as they left her tongue, but she did her best to sweeten them.

"Ah, I see Lydia has met a worthy opponent," Eldweaver Finch observed. Why he insisted on squeezing every last drop from every interaction was beyond her.

"Yes, he is quite the fighter. I must assume the matter is urgent if you went to the trouble of tracking me down?"

"Right, well, let me get right to it."

Please do.

"As you know, there will be a Trial of Talismans held in two weeks' time for Lord Winthrop's potential second ward." He paused, letting the silence stew.

"Yes, I'm aware," Lady Knight spoke through tightened lips. "Is that what you came all this way to tell me, or is there something more relevant to Knightridge Manor you wish to discuss?"

"Quite," he replied. "Lady Nikollette has come to us to request a third ward."

"What?" Corina stopped watching Lydia spar and turned to face Eldweaver Finch completely. "A third is not allowed, but you telling me this can only mean you've already allowed it."

"Yes, you see—"

"No, *you* see. I know *why* you let her have another ward, but the question is, how could you allow your favoritism to be so transparent?"

"No, no, you misunderstand." Eldweaver Fich stammered a little as he spoke. "You see, everyone will have the opportunity to put forward an additional ward."

"And this was decided by her simply asking?"

Eldweaver Finch shook his head. He appeared reluctant to explain, but Corina did not waver. Eldweaver Finch looked around, noticing – as did she – the Darrows stealing glances at the two of them. Finch leaned in close and spoke softly.

"There is a girl," he explained, "who came from the Deadwoods and found herself at Lady Nikollette's door. She has no memory of who she was or how she'd gotten there."

"And?"

"And Lady Nikollette could not see anything through the Looking Glass."

Corina thought it over but found herself unmoved. "I don't see how that matters in the least. Who cares what her little looking glass may or may not see? I fail to see how this requires special treatment for some girl. For all we know, either of them could be lying."

"Yes, well, as you know Eldweaver Gideon has been lobbying for additional Spellweavers for some time, and Lady Nikollette has informed us that, once her wards are ready to leave her manor, she will be giving up magic entirely. The three of us feel that these strange circumstances, coupled with Lady Nikollette's departure, warrant more aid for our cause. She is possibly the most powerful among us, and her loss will leave a hole in our defenses." Eldweaver Finch was serious; Corina could feel as much in the weight of his words.

She turned away from Finch at the sound of Cassian yielding to Lydia. Lydia had finally disarmed him, and he had taken a knee. Both were gasping to catch their breath.

"Well done," Corina said as Lydia extended a hand to help the young man to his feet.

Her brother, Owen, stood opposite the small sparring arena, a smirk across his face. He spoke in a tone to match. "You'd think, after having known us all these years, you'd have memorized all our moves by now, Cass. Or has that growth spurt of yours simply left you a lumbering hulk of your former self?"

His arrogance will be his downfall, Corina thought.

"Ha," Cassian replied. "Big talk from such a small boy. Without those trinkets, I'm sure I could take you both."

Corina watched the three of them sharpen their tongues on one another, reminding her that – as strong and as capable as they may be – they were still only children.

"Excuse me," a woman's voice interrupted Corina's thoughts. It was Cassian's mother, Mrs. Darrow. "I couldn't help but overhear you might be looking for an additional ward to take on as a Spellweaver?"

"No," Corina was quick to reply.

"Yes," Eldweaver Finch replied at the same time.

"You are mistaken," Corina insisted. "To take on a new ward and prepare them for the trials in only two weeks would be irresponsible. Dangerous even." She glared at Eldweaver Finch with her final comment.

"There seems to be a disagreement," Mrs. Darrow continued and then looked only to Eldweaver Finch. "Might I suggest my son, Cassian? He is strong, capable, and a quick study. I believe Spellevue would do well with an asset such as he."

"So too would we consider it a tremendous honor," Eldweaver Finch responded.

Lydia, Owen, and Cassian walked around the small arena to join the discussion.

"What was that?" Owen asked. "Are you to take on another ward?"

"No," Corina answered.

"Well, it is an option," Eldweaver Finch said, "and there will be no such offer again, not for some time."

"You *must* let Cassian try." Owen was adamant and then caught himself under Corina's eye. "Of course, that is your decision, Lady Knight."

"You'll find no finer candidate," Mrs. Darrow added.

"I would be most honored," Cassian finished.

"Would you be willing to risk your life?" Corina asked Cassian and then looked at his parents. "Your son's life?"

"Yes," Cassian and his mother replied in unison.

Corina looked at his father. "And you?"

Mr. Darrow looked her in the eye, unflinching, and Corina only hoped he saw the dire warning in her words reflected in their exchanged glances.

"He will meet any challenge," Mr. Darrow finally answered.

"It is your life to do with what you wish." Corina looked away, took out her coin, and added, "If you pass, it will become my life to command. Understood?"

"Yes," Cassian answered.

"I expect the two of you to train him for the trials. Until then, I will have no part. I will see you all in two weeks." She flipped her coin and appeared in her bedroom, wondering if Cassian possessed a will as strong as his body. If she had made the right choice. If he could be entrusted with magic at all.

More than anything, in that moment, she felt doubt.

THE LORD OF BLOODMOORE

Nestled in a desolate valley among the Ironhide Mountains, Bloodmoore Manor stood alone, the distant ruins of Ironveil Kingdom were the only other sign that anyone had ever lived this far into nothing. With each visit, Illana Fairwind couldn't help but think how far a cry it was from the lush green canopy that surrounded her home, Silverleaf Citadel. The crimson manor sat in stark contrast to the surrounding gray landscape and the pale white mist that often formed in this valley. She could only suppose it was the silence of solitude that Lord Winthrop found appealing. Regardless, she looked forward to seeing him and his ward again.

Before she could knock, Illana was met by Lord Winthrop. He opened the door in one sweeping motion, leaving his long arms outstretched. Practically shouting, he said, "Illana! What a pleasure to see you again. Have you a neverbeast in need of slaying?"

Before she could answer, he followed the question with another. "Ah, but if it was a neverbeast, why send an Eldweaver? Which likely means there is no beast at all but rather news of some great import?"

She looked up at him and smiled. "Once again, Lord Winthrop, you've spared little time in cutting to the heart of the matter." Illana chuckled, an act few were able to draw from her, but Lord Winthrop had a way about him.

"Then come right in." He bowed as she approached, an arm tucked in at his waist and the other pointed into the manor. "I'm sure Mordecai and Constance would be pleased to have company."

"A lack of company in the region?" Illana asked as she walked in.

"No, not..." He stood up quickly and added. "A joke? From Eldweaver Fairwind? This must be some news."

Once Lord Winthrop closed the door, she turned to face him. "While I'm here, you can call me Illana. I insist."

"Then I insist you call me Avery," Lord Winthrop responded. "I do bore of the formalities, and I was never terribly fond of the title 'Lord.'"

"Understood." Illana nodded.

"Come and sit," Avery said, strolling past her and toward the sitting room just beside the foyer.

It was a spacious room, circular in shape, and the large windows provided a generous view of the gray and white nothing that surrounded them. Illana took a seat on a long sofa facing the window, and Avery sat across from her in a high-backed chair, of which both pieces of furniture looked as though they had seen better days.

"Would you like something to drink?" Avery asked.

"No, but thank you," Illana answered, adding, "Shall I wait for Mordecai and Constance, or should I just get right to it?"

"Please, let's jump right in," Avery said with a glint in his eye, leaning slightly forward. "They're out back training, and if they don't come in on their own, we'll meet with them later. Provided you have time to spare, of course."

"As you wish," Illana said and then began her explanation.

She told him all about the girl and her mysterious appearance about whom he seemed quite intrigued. Then there was Lady Nikollette's request. One they had not decided upon lightly. A decision he reservedly agreed with. Finally, she offered him the option of inviting a third ward to take part in the trials, should he have one in mind.

When she was finished, Avery leaned back in his chair and quietly considered her proposal, playing with the curled ends of his mustache as he did.

"So," Illana asked, "have you a candidate in mind?"

"Perhaps." Avery's expression told Illana he understood the full weight of this choice. "A young squire from Stillriver. Charles Cottman."

"Stillriver? I wouldn't take you for one to frequent Stillriver."

"You would be correct. However, I grew up with his mother, in the same little village, before she moved on to grander things. I've known Charles since he was little, and when his father passed, I made it a point to visit him whenever I might find myself able to stomach the opulence of a kingdom." There was a certain disdain in his voice at the end of his comment that made Illana smile. "Regardless," Avery continued, "I wouldn't dare make such an important decision without the input of the others."

The sound of a door opening and closing followed by the swelling of young voices announced the arrival of Constance and Mordecai.

"Perfect timing," Avery noted as the two entered the room.

"Avery," Mordecai called casually as she rounded the corner, "we've finished our—"

He stopped short, and Illana could see that her presence was a surprise to them both. Mordecai started over, straightening his posture and formalizing his tone. "I mean, Lord Wainwright, Constance and I have finished our training."

"It's quite alright." Avery waved off Mordecai's concern for a breach of etiquette. "You can continue to use my first name, regardless of company. As far as I'm concerned, I make my own rules in my own Manor."

Illana smiled and then nodded at them both. She could see their tension melt immediately.

"Is there trouble?" Mordecai asked. "If so, I'm ready."

Illana admired the boy for his tenacity. His shirt was stained with sweat, and there were bits of broken stone trapped in his short hair from what she could only assume to be the remnants of the boulders unlucky enough to be the targets of his combat training. It was clear he had exhausted himself to some degree.

"No trouble," Illana responded and then looked to Avery, adding,

"I'll let him explain."

"Thank you." Avery nodded, then looked to Constance and Mordecai. "Eldweaver Fairwind here has presented us with the opportunity to put forward a third candidate in the upcoming trials. Instantly, Charles Cottman came to mind. His time serving as a squire has afforded him ample understanding of combat tactics, and I believe him to be studious enough to quickly take to magic. Furthermore, I believe he possesses the quality of character needed to complete the trials. However, I would like to ask if the two of you might agree with me. Or not. You'll not hurt my feels either way."

Mordecai and Constance exchanged looks. They seemed uncertain, but Illana noticed something else. She saw, subtle as it might have been, a conversation without words. Soon, their confused looks shifted into knowing smiles. Then, in unison, the two of them turned to Avery and said, "We agree."

"Then that settles it." Avery stood up, so Illana did the same. He extended a hand, which Illana took. As he shook, he remarked, "Looks like I've yet another harrowing trip to the full belly of Stillriver."

"It's not all bad," Illana replied. "They are a fine people."

"Yes, quite true," Avery said as he took his hand back and placed it in the pocket of his vest, tilting his chin up. "And may their white walls remain forever unstained by the harsh realities outside of them, and may their golden adornments remain a polished mirror to reflect their purity and plenty."

Illana laughed then added, "Mind your tongue. King LeGrande, may he find wellness, has given nothing but his full support to

Spellevue. I would hate to find your clever tongue responsible for its loss."

Avery gasped and delicately placed his other hand on his chest. "I would hope you would have more faith in the cleverness of my tongue, dear Eldweaver."

Illana said nothing but smiled at him, then Mordecai and Constance, before taking out her coin and giving it a flick.

Avery always had a way about him.

NOTHING

Victor Gideon had not visited the Deadwoods since the Endless King had first appeared. There had been no reason to. The dried-up surface of dirt crunched beneath his boots, giving way to a soft, muddy underbelly. Every few steps, he found his feet heavy with it. He was forced to stop and scrap his heels against the exposed roots of any nearby tree. He began his exploration from the edge of the woods near the A'Mysteriouse cemetery. Tracing Ophelia's path back to its source would be impossible, but starting at its end seemed like the most sensible place to begin.

After walking for some time, long since Deadwood Manor had fell from his view, he had yet to find a single thing out of the ordinary. It brought both comfort and concern.

The last thing he wanted to do was accuse Nikollette of lying, an act beneath her, but the more he wandered the desolate forest, the less he could think of any other explanation.

He stopped and looked at the lifeless trees, each seemingly identical. With his heel, he chipped away the dried skin of the dead ground until the mud lay bare. Kneeling, he grabbed a stick and traced a series of squares in a row with multiple lines pointing outward on either side of the squares. When he was finished, he stood back up and stepped on it.

The ground trembled ever so slightly. The trees shook, causing what few ravens that might have been perched to scatter. Then the trees slid apart, separating before Victor, forming a vast clearing. When they came to rest, he had an unobstructed view that stretched further than he could effectively see.

With the magic embossed in his leather boots, he stepped into the air. He made it a little more than half the height of a tree before he felt the symbols losing strength. It mattered not. He was high enough, and he could see everything he needed to see.

Either Nikollette had lied or the girl had.

There was nothing.

AID TO EVERGREEN

Ophelia had been given two books to take with her when she left Nikollette's study: *The Foundational Theory of Reality* by Bastien A'Mysteriouse and *The Art of World Weaving* by Marcel A'Mysteriouse. She had little luck deciphering the stale text of *Foundational Theory*, but the way *World Weaving* was written spoke to her. There seemed almost a poetry to the way magic was described. She could hardly put it down, and after a late night of reading, Ophelia found herself more tired in the morning than she would have liked. Especially when Lady Nikollette asked her and Amarine to take a walk to Evergreen to pick up an item for her at Remy's Rarities.

"What do you think it is?" Ophelia asked as they strolled along the empty road.

"Couldn't say," Amarine answered. "Remy has all sorts of things. I used to just hang out in his shop when I lived in town and poked around at everything. Never understood what half of that stuff was. Sominor is a big place with tons of people, and I only really know my little slice. I suppose that's true for everyone though. I guess I could use my coin to hop around, but Lady Nikollette probably wouldn't care for that if I didn't have a good reason. Hey"—she looked at Ophelia—"you look tired. Couldn't sleep?"

"I was up reading. Lady Nikollette gave me a couple books to look over."

"Oh?" Amarine's voice upturned with her eyebrows. "Which ones?"

"*Theory of Reality* and *World Weaving*." Ophelia yawned, then added, "Didn't really understand *The Theory of Reality* though. I put it down after a few pages."

"Oh, yeah. I remember those. Not the best part of spell weaving, but it gets better. Oh." Amarine pointed at the road ahead. "There's Evergreen, just around those trees."

Ophelia looked through the Deadwoods. Sure enough, there it was, nestled among a green forest

Amarine picked up to a jog. "Let's go."

The town was larger than she expected, but Ophelia stuck close as they walked along the dirt paths that cut between the buildings. People waved to Amarine as they went. She waved back and said her hellos, but never stopped. Ophelia was surprised, especially when one of the strangers tried to ask, "How ya been? It's been so long!"

To her credit, Amarine replied very seriously. "Can't talk now, Ms. Harlow. I'm on a quest."

"Well, if you have a moment to spare, I could sure use your help at the home," Mrs. Harlow called after them.

"I'll try," Amarine yelled back without turning around.

"Who's that?" Ophelia couldn't help but ask.

"Oh, Ms. Harlow? She is the headmistress of the home for the unkept. She's nice enough, I suppose."

"So, we are going to help after Remy's, right?" Ophelia felt the question needed to be asked. She'd not known Amarine long, but it felt as though Amarine didn't want to help. The huff that came out of her all but confirmed Ophelia's suspicions.

"Yeah, I guess. I suppose it wouldn't hurt to visit."

"I'm sure it'll be fun."

"I'm sure you're right."

Eventually, they arrived at Remy's Rarities, as made apparent by the large, painted sign fixed above the door.

"Elowen? Is that you?" Amarine nearly shouted upon entering. The young woman at the counter looked up. Her face shifted rapidly through a myriad of expressions. Busy, thoughtful, surprised, excited.

"Amarine!" Elowen shouted as she ran around the counter and met them in the middle of the shop, her arms as wide as her smile. "It's so wonderful to see you again! How's life in the big house? How's magic? Who is this?"

Before she could answer, a deep voice boomed from behind a door in the back.

"Is that Amarine I hear?" the voice asked, as the door opened. Out stepped a short, portly man, who had to turn sideways to slip through the space. Get over here, girl!"

"Remy," Amarine said as she ran over to him, leaving Ophelia to stand alone. "I'm sorry I haven't come by in so long."

"Well, why would you?" Remy's face dropped suddenly. "Running around Sominor with your magic. Living in the A'Mysteriouse manor. No time for dirty, old Evergreen, or fat, old Remy."

"Oh, hush." Amarine swatted at his arm. The three of them shared a laugh.

Ophelia chuckled along. Amarine, Remy, and Elowen turned and looked at her as the laughter died. She felt like her skin might just burst into flames. What was she laughing about? She didn't even know what they were talking about.

"This is Ophelia." Amarine rushed back to her side and hooked an arm under hers. "She's going to be living with us from now on."

"Lovely to meet you, young lady. Please don't let this one get you into trouble. You seem like such a sweet girl." The sincerity in Remy's voice put Ophelia at ease.

She smiled. "I'll try."

"Yeah, she can be pretty persistent," Elowen added.

"Hey, now." Amarine mounted a half-hearted protest; she changed the subject. "Speaking of trouble, where is Finley?"

"Oh, dear." Elowen shook her head.

"That no good boy of mine," Remy explained, shaking his head as he did, "went on a solo trading trip to the *magnificent* Kingdom of Stillwater. Convinced me he could handle it. *Begged* me to let him go. You know what happened?"

"What?" Amarine seemed genuinely concerned.

"He fell in love." Remy threw his hands into the air. "First girl that smiled at him, he up and fell in love. No good boy. He's decided to live there. Get married. Start a family. I know it's hard to tell by my voice, but I'm happy for him and Liora. His bride-to-be is a lovely young lady. I can't be too upset though, because now I've got Elowen. She's determined, smart, and has a good head on her shoulders. Nothing like that foolish boy I call a son. Again, so happy for him."

"Sorry for your loss, but I'm glad Finley is happy," Amarine replied.

"Me too," Elowen added. "Couldn't have happened at a better time. Just got booted from the home since I turned seventeen a few months ago. Remy was kind enough to take me in."

"As hard a worker as I always wanted." Remy beamed with pride, "Speaking of work, it was Elowen here that tracked down Lady Nikollette's order. Hard to find a blue-cap mushroom anymore."

"Yeah," Elowen chimed in, "I picked it up in the hills east of here, at the edge of the forest's deadline the day before we got the order. I was excited to come across such a rare find, even more to find I didn't have to cross the deadline to grab it. The Deadwoods is not someplace I wish to go."

Amarine nudged Ophelia with her elbow, never taking her eyes off Elowen. "How lucky!"

"Tell me about it," she answered with a proud smile.

"Here you go." Remy placed a bundle of cloth on the counter and opened it with gentle hands. Inside was a small mushroom with a blue cap, green gills, and a white stalk. "I'm sure your lady knows better than to eat this, right?"

"I'm sure she does." Amarine examined the small mushroom, then smiled as she took it from Remy and wrapped it up again. "She's got something useful in mind, I'm certain."

She handed their prize to Ophelia, who tucked it into her jacket pocket with care.

"Say, you stopping by the home?" Elowen asked. "I heard they had a hole in their roof. Maybe you could help?"

"Yeah, yeah." Amarine rolled her eyes. "I'll get to it."

"Something wrong?" Elowen asked.

"Ms. Harlow already asked her on our way here," Ophelia added, finally happy to have some clue as to what they were all talking about. Amarine looked at her, scrunching up her nose and tightening her lips.

"Oh," Elowen said, then chuckled. "I see."

"What?" Ophelia's curiosity on the hunt. "What do you see?"

"Nothing!" Amarine tried to stop her, but Elowen just smiled and continued.

"Well, you see, Ms. Harlow always caught Amarine breaking the rules or sneaking out. She seemed to always be walking into the room at just the right time, or maybe Amarine just always seemed to be breaking the rules at the wrong time." Elowen shook her head and snorted. "You were lucky she liked cats."

"Yeah," Amarine replied, acceptance in her voice. "I suppose that was quite lucky."

The room grew silent when Amarine added, "I miss Tabitha." After a moment of uncomfortable silence, Amarine slowly came back to her bubbly self. "Anyway, as much as I hate to cut this reunion short, we really must be going. Gotta stop by the home, then back to the manor. Lady Nikollette needs Ophelia to study. Big event in a couple days. Ophelia is becoming an official Spellweaver!"

"Is that so?" Remy asked. He and Elowen looked at her as if they had known her for years. He continued, "How exciting. I wish you only the best and hope to see you both back here sooner rather than later."

"I second that," Elowen agreed.

"We'll try our best." Amarine smiled, took Ophelia's hand, then led her out the door and back through Evergreen.

The home for the unkept was not as large as Ophelia expected it to be. In fact, it looked a bit smaller than Deadwood Manor. Her next thought was how unfair that seemed to her. There were sure to be more than three children living under that roof. The roof which appeared to have a rather sizable hole on one side of it. It looked as if it were mid-repair.

"Well, that's new," Amarine said as they drew nearer. "Wonder what happened."

"Maybe the storm," Ophelia mused.

"It does look a bit burnt around the edges I suppose," Amarine replied. "Lightning maybe."

"How many kids live there?" Ophelia couldn't help but ask. "Seems small."

"It gets cramped," Amarine answered. "I'm not sure how many live there now, but when Elowen and I lived there, it was ten kids, including us. There were two large rooms, with four boys in one, and six girls in the other. Not the worst place, but I don't miss it. Especially Ms. Harlow. Uhg."

Ophelia could see the furrowed brow forming on Amarine's face.

"I don't know," Ophelia countered, hoping to calm her down. "She seemed nice enough to me."

"Yeah, sure, she's nice *now*," Amarine huffed, "but when I was living there, it was always, *'Amarine, don't do that. Amarine, stop talking so much. Amarine, you know that's against the rules.'* Bah! Rules, rules, rules. Always with the rules, that woman. How is anything new or exciting meant to happen if we all just keep doing the same things?"

Amarine's hands flailed in her frustration. Ophelia couldn't help but let out a giggle. Amarine flashed her an angry look that broke beneath a smile, then joined Ophelia in a laugh.

"Amarine!" Ms. Harlow's voice cut through the laughter, clear over the sound of busy streets. "Amarine, over here!"

Amarine groaned while rolling her eyes at Ophelia, then turned to Ms. Harlow with a bright smile. "Oh, hi!"

"Let me guess, need to patch that hole in the roof?" Amarine asked as they approached.

"That's about the size of it. I wouldn't normally bother you with something so mundane, but the gentleman who was fixing it fell and broke his arm; poor thing. I'm afraid another storm might come rolling in, and that hole opens to the attic, just above the girls' room."

"I see," Amarine spoke seriously while giving the hole a thorough study. She glanced at the road beside the home and asked, "Are those the materials for the repair?"

"Those are them," Ms. Harlow answered with a smile. "Think you could help? I'm not sure what magic can and cannot do."

"Well…" Amarine gave her an uncertain look. "I'm not really supposed to use magic for stuff like that without Lady Nikollette's permission. It's against the rules, you see."

"Oh, I didn't know."

"Of course not. How could you?" Amarine gave Ophelia a quick wink while Ms. Harlow was looking to the roof with concerned eyes. Amarine continued, just as serious as before, "But I'm happy to take the blame on this one. I think Lady Nikollette would approve. Plus, you practically raised me. So, guess now isn't the time for me to stop dancing around the rules, right?"

Ophelia held back her smile as she watched Amarine work at Ms. Harlow, who smiled at Amarine gleefully. "Oh, really? Thank you! If you do get into trouble, please send your lady my way. The blame would be all mine."

"Deal," Amarine said with a nod and marched toward the pile of lumber and tiles.

"Oh, and Amarine," Ms. Harlow called after her. When Amarine turned, Ms. Harlow added, "I didn't *practically* raise you. I did raise you."

Amarine shook her head and continued her march. The unkept children watched from the windows and, one by one, trickled out to get a better look. Ophelia stayed beside Ms. Harlow and watched from a distance. Though she was rather curious to see how Amarine would go about it, the last thing Ophelia wanted was to distract her while weaving a spell.

"Give her some space," Ms. Harlow called out to the children who gathered around. They all backed up. Taking up the rear, a small boy stood on his toes, struggling to get a peek at the action on the other side of the group.

"So, was Amarine as much trouble as I hear?" The question practically begged Ophelia to ask it.

Ms. Harlow turned to Ophelia and chuckled. "I don't know what you've heard, but I would hazard to guess she wasn't nearly that bad. Frustrating, certainly."

"Well, just what Elowen told me."

"Elowen, what a nice young lady," Ms. Harlow commented with a smile. "Whatever Elowen said is likely the objective truth. I'm sure Amarine's version of events would paint me the villain, and mine, her. Elowen, on the other hand, was always well-behaved and even-tempered. I hoped she would have stayed to work at the home, but I suppose she rather wanted something a little more exciting. Remy always has something new and exciting in his peculiar little shop."

"They seem nice, Elowen and Remy. Actually," Ophelia considered, "everyone I've met so far seems really nice."

"Well," Ms. Harlow raised an eyebrow and said, "I suppose you haven't met many people then."

"I have not, actually."

Ophelia could see the puzzled expression on Ms. Harlow's face, and her lips were nearly ready to ask a question when the crowd of children erupted in cheers, followed by the neigh of a not-too-distant horse. Ophelia and Ms. Harlow turned to look, just in time to watch the flash of light fade away and the building materials float toward the roof.

From the corner of her eye, Ophelia saw the small boy backing away from the others, still on the tips of his toes, straining to see Amarine's magic in action. However, it was the fast-approaching shape that peeled Ophelia's gaze away from the home entirely.

A horse was headed toward them, unbridled, and the boy was working his way out into the road to meet it.

In a blur, Ophelia found herself tumbling to the dirt, her arms wrapped around the boy, and the horse racing past. Ms. Harlow was the first to reach them.

"Anthony, are you alright?" Her voice trembled in what was nearly a scream, adding, "You saved him."

Ophelia looked at Anthony and he smiled back. She asked, "Are you alright?"

"Yeah," he said, as though the two were only playing.

She loosened her arms as Ms. Harlow grabbed Anthony by the hand and helped him up. Ophelia stood up after, wiping the dirt from her clothes and giving herself a quick once over. The only damage appeared to be a scrape on the top of her hand. When she looked back up, the attention no longer centered around the enchanted building materials coming together over the hole in the roof, and Ophelia had never felt more uncomfortable.

Murmurs rolled through the crowd, the children mostly, wondering what had happened. Amarine, much to Ophelia's relief, shoved her way through. "Watch out now. Make some room."

When she was finally face to face with Ophelia, Amarine asked her what happened.

"Anthony couldn't see what you were doing. I saw him backing into the road. There was a horse and I just…"

"She saved Anthony," Ms. Harlow finished the story that Ophelia had been struggling to find the words to finish. "Your friend is a hero."

"Thank you," Anthony said before being absorbed into the group of unkept children, who looked him over as if he'd come back from the dead.

"Did she use magic?" one kid asked.

"Are you magic now?" another added.

"I don't know," Anthony answered with a smile.

The rest of the crowd had already dispersed, the excitement having petered out.

"I can't thank you enough," Ms. Harlow said, grabbing Ophelia's hand and shaking it. She turned to Amarine and added, "You as well, Ms. Isles. The roof is as good as new. Please, tell your lady how grateful we all are for the two of you."

"No problem," Amarine said with a confident smile. "All in a day's work for a couple a Spellweavers."

"Well, I'm not—" Ophelia tried to explain.

"You are a hero. Stop being so modest," Amarine interrupted, then turned to Ms. Harlow. "We'll pass along your gratitude. Good to see you again."

"You too," Ms. Harlow replied.

Ophelia and Amarine took their leave.

Once they were out of earshot, Amarine whispered, "You were amazing! You're going to pass your trial for sure! I just know it! Honestly, I knew from the moment I met you. I'm an excellent judge of character." She looked lost in thought for a moment, adding, "Well, I guess Ms. Harlow is nicer than I thought."

Ophelia laughed a little.

"What? Even I make mistakes every now and then," Amarine said with a laugh.

The day before the trials, Ophelia spent her time trying to force her way through *The Foundational Theory of Reality*. Lady Nikollette had instructed her that the book was required reading, and though she didn't expect Ophelia to get through it before the trials, she expected her to try her best. To make the task all the more difficult, just outside her window, she could hear Amarine and Barnaby training.

It felt the more she resisted the urge to spend her day watching them, the more difficult it became to ignore them at all. Soon, where her mind should have been filled with detailed instruction on the inner workings of reality, as told by Bastien A'Mysteriouse, she found only the sound of her housemates enjoying a sunny day and the temptation to join them.

So, she did.

It started as innocently as convincing herself she needed to stretch. During which time the magical wardrobe caught her eye. She was still clothed in a style very close to Lady Nikollette's. It looked nice enough, but it didn't feel like her. She examined herself in the mirror and tried to imagine what she might prefer. She thought about Amarine, in her flowing dresses and light blouses, and of Barnaby in his well-fitted dress attire and long coats. She tried to remember what the people of Evergreen had worn, but those moments had gone by in such a blur that her memories of them were fuzzy, at best.

She scrunched her face and shook her head. None of it was right.

With her eyes closed, Ophelia took a long, slow breath in, then let it out. She tried to picture herself standing out there, in the field, practicing magic. She pictured herself fighting the various monsters decorating Amarine's room. When she had the image, she grabbed the handle of the wardrobe. The entire thing shook and came to an abrupt stop. When she opened the wardrobe, she found her prize.

It was perfect.

She took some time in front of the mirror to admire her new look. A lavender gray blouse with black buttons and black threading, very similar in style to the high-necked lace worn by Lady Nikollette. It was tucked into a knee-length, black skirt. Covering it all was a dark indigo, hooded coat that ran down mid-thigh with pearl-gray buttons. Beneath the skirt, dark gray pants that tucked neatly into black, calf-length boots whose three buckles ran up the outside. She felt comfortable. She felt strong.

She felt like herself.

Couldn't hurt to step out and show Amarine and Barnaby, she convinced herself, peering at them through the window. They were arguing over something. Amarine turned her back on him, then looked up at

Ophelia. She smiled mischievously and waved Ophelia down to join them. Ophelia nodded back excitedly.

She didn't expect to find Lady Nikollette just outside her door.

"Where are you off to," she asked as she looked Ophelia up and down, "in your new outfit?"

"I was just going to step out and show Amarine," Ophelia answered sheepishly, "if that's alright, of course."

Nikollette looked past Ophelia, to the desk where a thick book sat open, nearly in the middle. She looked back at Ophelia, "I suppose that's enough reading for one day. Besides, your heroic deeds in Evergreen should certainly be rewarded. Go enjoy yourself. You've more than earned it." Lady Nikollette stepped aside, gesturing to the empty hall with her hand.

Ophelia smiled, then took off toward the stairs, eager to watch Amarine and Barnaby weave magic.

Excited to show off her new look.

Hopeful for what was soon to come.

TROUBLED ROADS

Morning came to Ophelia like a gentle hand, rousing her from slumber in the early hours of the day. The sun had only just begun to paint the dark skies with its light. She had been dreaming before she woke up. It had become unsettling but not so much as to call it a nightmare. She was in the Deadwoods again, but she wasn't running. She was looking into the hole she'd crawled out of, but it was blurry, vibrating. Other than its white walls, Ophelia had trouble describing it to herself as anything other than a hole. Before she woke, she had turned her attention away from the hole and into the dead trees that surrounded her. Among them stood a man. He was watching her. It made Ophelia's skin crawl.

"I believe we are similar," The man said. Ophelia didn't like the way he said it, but had no reply. He continued, "They'll hate you. It isn't right, but they will. For that, I'm sorry."

"Who are you?" She asked.

"I thought you might recognize me from my portrait." He

answered, then looked upset as he added, "Unless they took it down. I can never quite tell what state the manor is anymore. Dreams are strange like that."

"Dreams?" She asked.

"Yes, I am dreaming," he replied.

Upon waking, she was more than pleased to find herself in bed. Safe.

Shortly after waking, Ophelia turned her thoughts to the trial that lay ahead of her. Excitement made short work of expelling what sleep remained in her, while apprehension made shorter work of turning the excitement into simmering anxiety just beneath her skin. Instead of sitting in bed, worrying about what might be, Ophelia decided to busy herself.

Yesterday, she had placed her dirty clothes into the wardrobe when she had gone to bed. Today, they were gone. The wardrobe worked quickly to produce a new outfit for her. It may not have been the exact same, but it was similar enough and exactly to Ophelia's liking. Once dressed, she gave the wardrobe a gentle pat.

"Excellent job," she whispered. "You've done it again."

She could have sworn she felt it vibrate under her appreciative pat.

The sun had only peaked its face out from the horizon, and still, there were no signs of stirring within the manor. So, Ophelia took a seat at the desk in her room and examined the book that sat upon it.

Just as before, she could feel a connection to the book in more than just the sensation on her palm as she ran her hand across the cover. The leather was worn but still in great shape. A simple triangle was embossed on the cover, with three small triangles pointing inward, embossed at the three points of the larger. Running through was the angular feather design.

The quill, Ophelia thought, *but how did she…*

Her thoughts trailed off as her hand ran across the quill. She closed her eyes and could practically feel its soft texture against her fingertips, as though it were rising out of the cover and into her hand.

Her focus honed in on the feeling. It grew in intensity.

"Ophelia." Nikollette's voice cut through the silence and caused Ophelia to jump in her seat and turn around as Lady Nikollette continued, "You're ready, I see."

"I am."

"What are you doing?"

"I was"—she turned and picked up the book—"just admiring your book. Can you really summon lighting with it?"

"Oh, my Timeless Tome," she clarified as she strode across the room with an effortless elegance. "I can do all sorts of magic, anywhere I can draw a symbol really, but this book is special."

She took the book from Ophelia and turned it over in her hands. A smile floated across her distant eyes, which seemed to be captured in memory. The smile vanished abruptly, but the distance in her eyes remained.

"It doesn't run out of pages, you know." Her voice sounded heavy. "You can draw as many spells as you have the will to, and it will always have room for more."

"Shouldn't you keep it somewhere safe? Closer?"

"No." Nikollette's tone shifted back to normal. "I did not leave it here by chance. It's meant for you. When you pass the trials—"

"If," Ophelia corrected.

"*When* you pass the trials, I imagine such a book would prove rather useful in your training."

"Did Barnaby and Amarine use it, too?"

Lady Nikollette met her question with a soft smile and a subtle nod.

"They tried, but they couldn't manage to summon the quill from its cover. It's a rather finicky book."

"Do you think I can?"

"That remains to be seen, but I certainly hope you give it a try." Lady Nikollette set the book down, walked back to the door, and turned back to face Ophelia. "Come now. Let's eat. You'll need the energy, and we have a half day's journey ahead of us."

"I don't understand. Couldn't we have used the coins?" Ophelia asked as their carriage rolled away from Deadwood Manor Amarine sat beside her. Lady Nikollette sat across from her, with Barnaby across from Amarine. "I know I don't have one, but there must be a faster way to get me to Spellevue."

"We could have," Lady Nikollette replied, "but I'd rather take the scenic route. Getting the lay of the land is always a good use of one's time. Besides, we should arrive with time to spare."

Ophelia nodded, then looked out the window. The carriage continued to roll along. Only the sound of dirt crunching beneath its wheels could be heard. It made her wonder.

"How does it work? The carriage, I mean," Ophelia asked aloud without looking away from her view out the small window beside her. "Magic, I suppose?"

"You suppose correct," Lady Nikollette answered. "Barnaby's handy work."

"Really?" Ophelia turned to him with an inquisitive glance. "You did this? How?"

Barnaby didn't answer right away. His face turned a subtle shade of purple. He pushed his glasses up against his face, took a breath, then answered without looking at Ophelia. "I enchanted it."

Lady Nikollette smiled, sensing his discomfort, and took over, "As I said before, Barnaby is quite skilled at enchanting. That sort of spell weaving requires steadfast focus and unwavering will. Barnaby has the making of possibly the best enchanter I've ever had the pleasure of knowing."

Barnaby squirmed. The purple on his face grew more pronounced.

"That's amazing." Ophelia looked at him and waited for him to turn. He only spared her a sideways glance before returning his gaze to the dead trees passing by. She asked, "Maybe you can teach me one day?"

"Yeah," he mumbled, "maybe."

Amarine leaned in close to Ophelia and whispered, "I swear, he gets better."

They exchanged secretive smiles.

Soon they had come upon Evergreen. The streets were empty.

"I don't like this," Lady Nikollette nearly whispered. "Everyone stay on your guard. Barnaby, stop the carriage.”

They rolled to a gentle stop across the road from Remy’s Rarities. Amarine got out slowly; turning back, she said, “I’m going to check on Remy. He’ll know what’s happening.”

Amarine held her breath and vanished. Ophelia stuck her head out of the carriage and looked around. Barnaby leaned back and closed his eyes. The three of them sat silent for a minute before Barnaby opened his eyes.

“I can hear it,” he spoke softly. “It’s stalking us.”

“What is it?” Ophelia whispered.

“It’s a ghoul!” Amarine shouted as she burst from Remy’s, slamming the door behind her, running toward the carriage.

Ophelia watched it all happen in slow motion from halfway across the road. Small clouds of dirt kicked up with each of Amarine’s hurried steps. A man-like creature with pale-purple skin leaped from a nearby roof and landed on the dirt road. Amarine looked at it. It lunged at her the moment its feet hit the ground.

“Amarine!” Ophelia shouted.

Amarine vanished as the ghoul took a swipe, leaving the creature confused. Barnaby rushed out of the carriage without hesitation. Amarine reappeared beside him.

“Get back in,” he ordered Amarine. He took off his coat and his glasses and growled from somewhere deep within his chest. His black eyes burned with rage.

“I can help,” Amarine contested. Barnaby turned to say something. The ghoul struck him, tackling him to the dirt. The two of them tumbled away.

From across the street, Elowen peered out the window as Barnaby and the ghoul exchanged blows.

"Amarine, Ophelia. Go to Remy's. Keep them inside," Lady Nikollette ordered.

"Right," Amarine nodded and held out her hand, "Grab on, hold your breath, and follow me."

Ophelia did. She watched her troubled world slip away as they ran toward Remy's, weaving between the creatures that roamed through the Neverwas. Ophelia tried not to look.

Inside Remy's, she could see their wispy silhouettes near the front window. When they emerged from the Neverwas, Amarine was quick to pull them away.

"What are you doing?" Amarine scolded. "There's a ghoul out there. Are you crazy?"

"Sorry," Elowen replied. "I've never seen a neverbeast in person or magic."

"Well, it's dangerous. So ju—"

The window shattered, exploding inward. The ghoul snarled and swiped.

Ophelia grabbed Elowen's hand and pulled her way. Remy fell to the floor. The ghoul struggled to find its feet among the shards of glass and broken planks of wood. Amarine worked to help Remy up. Elowen and Ophelia joined her.

Before the ghoul could attack, Barnaby reached through the window, grabbed it by the arm, and hurled it back out onto the street.

The two of them squared off. Ophelia could see Nikollette calmly watching from the carriage.

"You've got to do something," she begged Amarine. "He needs help."

"Right." Amarine looked to Elowen and Remy. "Get something to defend yourselves and get back behind the counter."

"Of course," Remy replied. He and Elowen ran to the back of the store.

"Ophelia."

"Yes?"

"Stay with these two."

"What are you going to do?"

"I don't know yet, but I'll figure something out." Amarine smiled and marched toward the door, flinging it open. The ghoul went hurling through the air past her. Barnaby sauntered up to her, winded and a little worse for wear.

"Nice of you to join me," he said, his breath heavy. "Got any ideas?"

"Just one, but I'm not sure how good it is."

"Well, to be fair, what I'm doing doesn't seem to be working. So, any ideas are welcome," Barnaby conceded, then added, "It's getting back up. Better get to it."

"Sure, stand back." Amarine knelt and Barnaby backed away.

Ophelia watched Amarine run her fingers through the dirt as the ghoul sprinted toward her. She couldn't help but shout. "It's coming! Watch out!"

Amarine placed her palm down as the ghoul flew at her. A column of dust rushed up toward the sky. When it cleared, the ghoul was gone. Ophelia stepped out from behind the counter and took uncertain steps toward Amarine.

"Stay inside." Amarine didn't even look at Ophelia. Her gaze turned upward. "It's coming back down."

She took a few steps back and, sure enough, the ghoul landed on the dirt road with a hard thud and a short bounce. Ophelia heard a loud *crunch*. The ghoul lay motionless.

"You think we got it?" Amarine asked.

"Unlikely," Barnaby answered.

Ophelia joined them. "Looks like you got it."

"Yeah, well, ghouls can heal pretty quick, so I wouldn't be surprised if—" Barnaby stopped talking.

Everything else happened in a blink.

Barnaby shouted, then shoved Amarine into Remy's shop with Ophelia. They landed on the floor. At the same moment, the ghoul popped back up and lunged at Barnaby. He was sent flying down the road.

Inside the shop, Elowen ran past Ophelia and Amarine and shut the door, locking it behind her. The ghoul took a run at it. The door cracked but held. So, it ran toward the shattered window. The four of them scurried back behind the counter.

Lady Nikollette's voice came from across the street. "You don't look terribly tough. I suppose you feel tougher attacking children though."

Ophelia, Amarine, Remy, and Elowen looked on, helpless. The ghoul sneered before turning to face Lady Nikollette.

"Well, come on then," she taunted. Before the ghoul could take a step, Lady Nikollette twirled in the road. Her long skirt spread out around her. Balancing on one foot, she traced a circle in the dirt with the toe of her other.

The ghoul charged at her.

With the circle complete, she spun again, squatting, balanced on her heels. Using both hands, she drew smaller symbols within the border of the circle. By the time she'd finished a single revolution, the ghoul was flying toward her, poised to strike.

Lady Nikollette took a swift step back, forcing herself into a sort of bow. Once clear of the circle, she stomped her foot as she stood up. The ghoul froze in midair above the symbol. A ring of light flashed, then dissipated.

"Cause suffering…" She spoke with a measured calm to the snarling creature. "…expect suffering."

With another swift stomp, the ghoul burst into flame. It was gone in a flash. No ashes, no embers, just a flash of flame followed by nothing.

The people of Evergreen erupted from their homes and shops with jubilant cheers. Ophelia, Amarine, and Barnaby joined Nikollette at the carriage. Barnaby hurried to put his glasses on.

"Thank you." Remy shook Lady Nikollette's hand. "I'm indebted to the A'Mysteriouse name."

"I don't deal in debt," Lady Nikollette responded; she smiled. "But perhaps you can join us at the manor this evening for dinner. You and Elowen. It's been some time since the old house has had company. You can thank us then, if you feel the need."

"We'll be there!"

Lady Nikollette joined the others in the carriage and closed the door. "I'd love to stay and celebrate, but we've got a schedule to keep. Until this evening."

The carriage rolled out of town, toward Spellevue. Amarine closed her eyes and calmed herself. She spoke with a relieved smile. "Well, that was easy."

Barnaby dusted off his clothes and lamented the ripped holes in his vest but seemed to chuckle at Amarine's comment.

Ophelia looked at Lady Nikollette in awe.

"That was incredible," she finally said. "You could have just taken care of that right from the start, couldn't you have?"

"I could have," she answered, "but if I exercised my full ability with every threat of pain or death, how would you ever come to discover the power inside yourself?"

Ophelia smiled, sat back, and let the entire ordeal roll around in her mind. She wondered if she would ever be as powerful as Lady Nikollette, as skilled. The image of the ghoul's demise flashed across her thoughts just as the fire had flashed across its entire form. Her smile slipped away.

"Do we have to kill them?" she asked. "The neverbeasts, that is. Do we *have* to kill them?"

Lady Nikollette met Ophelia's question with a soft smile. "I would encourage you to meet each challenge you face with mercy in your heart. Many neverbeasts are no different from the beasts of our world. Some even find a place among the natural order of things. Others, however, only seek to sow suffering. For those that possess the intelligence to know suffering, yet still seek to cause it? From me, the only mercy they'll meet is a swift end. You, however, are not me. My most sincere hope is that each of you will grow to be better than me. Not just as weavers, but as people."

The weight of her words brought the carriage to silence. They each looked out their windows, watching Sominor roll by as they continued along their journey.

THE DAUNTLESS HEART OF RENÉE ROCHÉ

Marsh Hollow was overjoyed when the Spellweavers returned triumphant. Marcel, Bastien, Diedrich, and Renée were just thrilled to have walked away from the trio of swamp thumpers with their heads intact. Fighting neverbeasts that were made entirely of living vines, in the middle of a soggy swamp, had been a considerably difficult endeavor. If not for their talismans, they knew they would have died. In fact, Diedrich had. More than once. However, the four of them were not about to let the good people of Marsh Hollow know that. All they needed to know was that the four brave Spellweavers had emerged victorious, and their town was safe. The drinks could flow, and the revelries could begin.

They sat together at a large table in the center of the Marsh Hollow tavern, The Swill. Not the best name, but a misnomer to be sure. They were nearly through their second round of Flicker Fizz, and Renée was pleased to find – despite the drinks' intoxicating nature – that sitting next to Marcel had made her feel nothing at all outside of a deep friendship.

"How did it feel?" Renée asked, instantly regretting her lack of tact in the question. "I mean, are you okay? Dying could not have been fun."

"Well…" Dierich's cheeks and nose glistened, rosy, as he answered, looking at the talisman on his finger. "I can't say it was comfortable, but I can say it was at least a quick death. I can't thank you enough for these things, Bastien. Saved our hides out there today."

"Yes, well, I'm just pleased it all worked out," Bastien raised his glass and took another sip of the sparkling blue drink; he set his glass down and added, "Though I'd just as soon give it all up if it meant no more neverbeasts."

"Don't forget, brother. It's the neverbeasts that came first." Marcel had just started his third glass. Renée could see his eyes beginning to sparkle. "But even if they did vanish tomorrow, magic isn't something I'd ever give up. There's beauty in it. Art. And none more gifted with it than our dear Renée!"

Renée lowered her head, hiding away her smile, as the three men lifted their glasses and gave her a cheer. She looked at them and nodded. "I appreciate it, gentlemen, but I wouldn't be here without your instruction."

"Doubtful," Bastien countered.

"Had I not been handed this gift through a dream, I'm certain you would have figured it out on your own."

"While we were struggling to keep these things at bay, you were the only one clever enough to think the problem through. I never imagined a spell could be woven *with* a talisman. A containment circle of stone was quite the sight."

"Well," Renée added. "I had to think of something to give us enough time to plan a way to defeat them. They certainly weren't going to let us just sit there and discuss it."

"I'll drink to that." Dierich raised what little was left in his first glass. Marcel and Bastien joined him. They all took a big sip.

"Another round, my friend? Your drink is empty," Marcel asked.

"No, thank you," Diedrich replied, "One is plenty. Any more and I court embarrassment. You may be able to handle the flicker, but I know my limits, and limits are the key to a functioning society."

"Bah." Marcel tilted his head back and finished his third glass. His eyes had taken on a tint of dark blue, and the flicker of starlight danced among them. "Limits are meant to be pushed. Expanded!"

"Hush," Bastien commanded. The joy in his expression had gone. "Do you feel that?"

"I just finished my third flicker fizz brother. All I feel is happy," Marcel chuckled.

"Quiet." Bastien's gaze was distant. Someplace else entirely. He wrapped his hand around his Looking Glass. In an instant, his mind snapped back to the tavern. To their table. "We need to get to the manor. Now."

He practically jumped from his seat and flipped his coin. Marcel followed, as did Diedrich. Renée pulled some silver from her still-damp coat pocket and placed it on the table. She looked at their server. "We've got to run, but thank you for your hospitality."

She took out her coin, flipped it into the air, and watched the tavern melt away. When the foyer of the manor poured in around her, she witnessed Bastien and Dierich running up the stairs. Distant screams and banging could be heard from the second floor. Ophelia's body lay motionless at her feet.

"Marcel," Renée whispered, turning to find him kneeling beside another body, sobbing.

It was Antoinette's.

"My love," he cried, "wake up. Please."

"Marcel." Renée wasn't sure what to say or what to do. In the heat of battle, facing any manner of monster, thoughts came to her with clarity and swiftness, but this? She found her mind frozen and her heart racing. Her chest tightened.

She put a hand on his shoulder. He tore himself away from her touch.

"This can't be real. It must be an illusion." Marcel's shoulders heaved as he cried, squeezing Antoinette's limp body against his own. "I'm begging you. You can't be dead. Wake up!"

More words poured out between sobs, but Renée couldn't understand them. Then, as suddenly as thunder cracks across a storming sky, his sobbing stopped with a sharp sniffle. He sat upright, loosening his grip.

Renée still could not believe any of it was happening. It was impossible. The weight of it all hit her in that instant. It was what she saw – and felt – in Marcel that grounded her in the reality of what she was seeing. They were dead. Ophelia and Antoinette. Her chosen sisters, gone. Tears began to form in Renée's eyes. She had not felt a loss like this since her brother.

Just as suddenly as he ceased his sobbing, Marcel's face hardened, as did his voice. "Whoever did this will pay."

Shouting from upstairs; a struggle.

"It's coming," Bastien's muffled voice yelled out. "Don't let it get out."

Marcel stood up, gently letting Antoinette back down. Renée could see it in his eyes; the shimmering starlight of flicker fizz had faded, and a calm fury had taken its place.

A ghoul raced down the stairs, claws clattering against the wooden steps and tearing at the paper-lined walls.

Marcel raised his hand, his index finger extended, and traced familiar circular patterns into the air.

Renée was transfixed.

You can't draw in the air, can you?

The ghoul froze, its eyes wide with sheer panic as it struggled, futile in its efforts to break free from the invisible force. Marcel took his time approaching, circling the wretched creature before finally stopping no more than a finger's length from its petrified face.

"You have taken everything from me." Marcel's voice was eerily calm, sending a shiver through Renée. "I shall do my utmost to repay you in kind."

Marcel's fist clenched, and the ghoul appeared as if it were being crushed from every conceivable angle, attempting to scream but utterly incapable.

"Brother." Bastien's voice pierced the tension from atop the stairs, an unconscious Nikollette in his arms and Diedrich behind him. "Finish it."

"I will not," Marcel answered, his gaze steadfast. "This creature will be held accountable for what it has done."

"You know, in your heart, that it wouldn't be right," Bastien implored his brother. "End this swiftly, or I will. No purpose is served from torment, regardless of how justified I may feel it to be as well."

"It stole my world!" Marcel screamed, directing his ire at his own brother. "How can you be so calm?"

He clenched his fist again, and the ghoul's bones audibly cracked. Marcel released his grip. The creature began to mend.

"It stole our world too, brother," Bastien said in a low voice. "We too know your pain."

"You still hold part of yours." Anger seethed from Marcel's words as he spoke. "I have nothing."

Nikollette opened her eyes. "What's happening?"

Bastien set her down, whispering something to her as Diedrich added, "Listen to reason, Marcel."

"You have no right to speak of this!" Marcel shouted at Dierich. "You've lost nothing at all!"

Nikollette stepped behind her father.

Marcel's fist went white from the sudden tightening of his grip, and the ghoul twisted and snapped under the terrible might of his magic.

Renée could just hear the softest whispers of laughter escape Marcel's ever-maddening smile. The burning look in his eyes. She'd never seen that look before; not on him, not on anyone.

Marcel never allowed his gaze to wander from the ghoul's distressed face. Not as its skin tore beneath a broken bone or as it choked out gurgling spurts of air.

He screamed, spittle flying from his raging words, "It will know only suffering, until my dying breath!"

The unmistakable sound of a blade punctuated his threat.

The ghoul's head fell to the floor.

Renée looked up to see Bastien holding his short sword at his side. Marcel looked down in horror, trembling. The ghoul's body fell as the spell released.

"What have you done?" Marcel's voice cracked.

"Brother," Bastien pleaded, tears running down his face. "It is over."

Renée watched helplessly through tear-laden eyes. Marcel dropped to his knees before the decapitated corpse of the ghoul and scooped it up into his arms. A flood of grief poured down his weeping face.

"You had no right to take that from me! This creature's suffering was all I had left! It deserved to suffer!"

"Suffering is never deserved." Bastien sheathed his sword. "To cause it is to be no better than the monsters we suffer."

"Mom." Nikollette cautiously approached, walking wide around her uncle, tears in her eyes. "Mom!"

She ran to her mother, lying at Renée's feet, and cried over her corpse.

"Do something." She looked up at Renée. "You can save her! Magic can save her!"

Renée knelt beside Nikollette and hugged her. Nikollette cried into her chest. "If only I could."

Marcel released the decapitated body of the ghoul, allowing it to fall to the floor in a lifeless thud, then he returned to Antoinette's side. He lifted her and carried her out the door. Before leaving, he turned to his brother. "I'll never forgive you for the mercy you've given and the vengeance you've stolen."

He left without another word.

Bastien returned to spell weaving in a matter of weeks, and Nikollette followed, almost never having left her father's side. Renée found herself fighting alongside Nikollette and Bastien more often.

Renée helped Bastien construct a mausoleum for Ophelia. Everyone attended the burial except for Marcel. She had heard he buried Antoinette near their small estate nestled among the Greenwood. Since then, he'd locked himself away. For four months he remained hidden, refusing to see anyone.

On her way to Marcel's house, Renée was surprised to find Nikollette sitting alone on an old log, idly carving symbols into the fallen segment of timber.

"What are you etching?" Renée asked.

"Protection spells," Nikollette replied, absent. "He doesn't need my protection, but I don't know what else to do."

"I'm sure he'll appreciate it," Renée said.

"Are you going to see him? He won't see me. He won't see anyone."

"I am," Renée answered.

"Your earrings," Nikollette hopped off the log and approached. "Those are containment wards, aren't they?"

"They are," Renée answered, beginning to feel as though she might be on trial.

"I've been wondering for some time why you wore them. It didn't make much sense at first. I asked myself why someone would wear containment spells like that. Then, it dawned on me. You love my uncle, don't you?"

"I do," Renée admitted.

Nikollette nodded, then looked Renée in the eyes. "Then help him. I've lost my mother and my aunt. I can't lose him, too."

"I will," Renée said, hoping she could.

Nikollette turned and headed back toward the manor, and Renée continued toward Marcel's. A great ache wrapped itself around her heart as she approached.

"Marcel," she shouted from outside his front door. "Please let me in. You can't keep yourself locked away. We need you. Everyone needs you."

She was met with silence.

She pounded on the door and shouted again, "Marcel! I know you're in there!"

"Leave me alone," his voice came muffled from behind the door. "Everyone, just leave me alone."

"I will do no such thing." Renée's voice was stern. "If you don't open the door, I'll open it myself. Then, you'll have no door with which to keep the rest of the world at bay."

The door opened and Marcel wobbled in the doorway. His smile was forced; angry. "Come in, then."

She could see it immediately. The flickering was taking him. His eyes sparkled bright against the deep blue that had filled them, and the skin around them had begun to turn as well. New freckles twinkled with starlight beneath the surface.

If she didn't do something, his organs would fail.

He'll die.

He turned lazily and stumbled to a chair in the living room, where he fell hard onto the well-worn cushions. She walked in and shut the door behind her. The small house was a mess, consisting mainly of empty glass bottles.

"Why haven't you come to see me? To see anyone?"

Marcel threw his head back and groaned. "I just want to be alone. It's not terribly complicated."

"It is," she replied. "It's complicated because we miss you. I miss you. Nikollette misses you. Your brother—"

"Don't." Marcel sat up straight. "I want nothing to do with my brother. He stole the only thing I had left. Justice was taken from me."

"Justice was served," Renée said flatly. "The ghoul is dead. Killing yourself isn't going to change anything."

"You don't understand. How could you? You've never loved like we loved."

"I understand more than you know," she answered, "and I won't let you do this to yourself. I'll come back every day, and I'll break down this door if I must."

"You'll do no such thing." Marcel jumped up from his chair and raised his finger. It trembled.

"Are you going to do to me what you did to that ghoul?" she asked, defiant, as she approached him. "I doubt a hand as unsteady as yours could hardly push a feather, let alone contain me. I'll be back for you, Marcel. Feel free to stop me, if you can."

She turned and left him. Left him standing there in tears. Angry, mournful, hopeless tears.

"Why?" he called after her before she could leave. "Why won't you leave me to sorrow?"

Renée didn't turn around. She removed her earrings and placed them in her pocket. "Because I love you, Marcel A'Mysteriouse. Since the moment your hand touched mine."

For a year, Renée visited Marcel. Every single day. And for a year, Marcel begged her to leave him. He stopped drinking flicker fizz, insisting he was fine and she needn't come, but she kept coming. Somedays looking as lovely as she could manage, others looking as though she'd been dragged through the dirt and thrashed about...because she had.

Not a day went by without Renée.

Not a day went by that Marcel's pain didn't appear to grow.

The flicker had long since faded, and it no longer numbed his broken heart. With its absence came clarity. With clarity came anguish. She could see each expression on his face soured by it.

She never stayed long. He wouldn't let her. She would stay just long enough to bring him a proper meal and force a hug upon him. She would ask how he was feeling.

He would answer, "As ever I did that day."

She would nod and reply, "Then I will return again, with hope."

She did.

Every day.

Without fail.

On her last visit, Renée arrived with dinner and a cake.

"What is this for?" Marcel asked coldly as she came through the door with a smile on her face.

"It's your lifeday, Marcel." She set the cake down. "So I made you a cake."

"I don't want your conjured cakes." She could hear something within him burn. "I don't want your company. I want my wife back."

"I told you," Renée said, her smile wavering, "you'll never be rid of me, not as long as either of us are breathing. And I didn't conjure this cake. I made it, with my own hands, in a kitchen. It took me three days to figure it out, but I finally got it right."

Marcel smiled, walked over to her and the cake that sat on the table beside her. He looked at it, then at Renée. Without a word, he put his finger into the icing and drew a series of lines, finger as steady as ever.

"I don't want it," he said before tapping the cake. It slid violently across the table and exploded against the wall beside the front door.

Tears found Renée much faster than she expected.

Anger followed.

"Why do you have to be so stubborn, Marcel? Why won't you let me help you?"

"When will you stop?" He turned his back, stormed across the room, and looked out a window. "You'll find no love here, Renée. My heart is buried. Right out there, beside hers."

"When will I stop?" Renée asked with a tired calm in her voice. "When my body collapses and my heart has ceased its infernal beating. When the mountains come tumbling down and all the light in the sky has faded into darkness. When every star shining in the most distant corners of the void have extinguished under the relentless hands of time, and the very void itself collapses under the boundless dread of its own nothingness. That, Marcel A'Mysteriouse, that is when I will stop loving you."

"Then you are a fool," he answered her without hesitation. A damned fool if I am the one you chose to love."

"Love is not a choice."

"Then love has made broken fools of us both."

He didn't turn back to face her. He didn't say another word. He just stood there. Renée didn't know what else to say, so she swallowed her tears and her pain and said as best she could with a quiver in her voice, "Then I'll return tomorrow. A hopeful fool."

She left.

When she returned the next day, Marcel had gone.

OPHELIA ARRIVES

Approaching Spellevue left Ophelia speechless. Its walls were made of smooth stone that seemed to shimmer in the light of day. It felt somehow old and new all at once. Like a solitary tree, it towered over the surrounding hills, and from it sprouted towers, like branches, that reached up toward the sky. She didn't think it was possible for that much stone to hold itself up with no support, but here it was.

Above the large door, a stained-glass window shimmered. Interconnected geometric shapes danced in the sunlight and seemed to almost radiate magic out into the world. It was as imposing as it was comforting. Above that, a half-dome of swirling stained glass.

A beacon on a hill.

As nervous as Ophelia was for what waited for her inside, she was eager to see what magic and mystery lay hidden within the walls of Spellevue. Once out of the carriage, she looked up at the stained-glass mural in wonder.

"They're the core symbols." Barnaby offered the answer to a question Ophelia hadn't asked.

"Yes, I read about them some," she replied.

He adjusted his glasses and tripped over his own tongue. He continued the explanation anyway. "Y-yes. Well, the lines are forces, triangles to summon, squares to reshape, pentagons for transmutation, hexagons for enchanting, and finally, circles for containment and protection."

"Are there more?"

"More what? Core symbols?"

"Yes. Seven or eight sides? Or does it only go up to six? I saw no mention of others in the books, but I just thought they might have been old books."

"Well observed," Nikollette interjected. "There very well may be more; however, as each symbol becomes more complex, so too does using them. In all my years, I've yet to see anything more complex than hexagonal spells, and I've yet to experience the need."

Ophelia nodded as if she understood. She turned her attention back to the stained glass one last time before entering.

Upon entering, she was greeted by a grand hall whose walls glimmered from the spectrum of light cast by the window above. The floor was made of smooth stone, with intricate patterns etched into its surface that appeared to shift and change as she walked along. The ceiling was a series of interconnected triangles that seemed to stretch on forever, like a never-ending puzzle waiting to be solved.

"The World's Room," Amarine whispered, as they exited the large hall and entered an even larger chamber.

Ophelia was struck by a sense of awe and reverence. It was a circular room that reached high above, with walls that curved inwards and outwards like the ebb and flow of the tides. But it is the starry ceiling that truly took her breath away – thousands of stars hung among an endless cosmos, filling the room with a gentle, twinkling light.

The most prominent feature of the World's Room was the enormous map of Sominor etched into the floor. It took up almost the entire surface and was exquisitely detailed, with every street, every river, and every mountain range accurately depicted. It felt alive. Within each village, town, and city visible on the map, there was a faint light moving within its borders. Surrounding the stone relief of Sominor, was an ocean whose waves seemed to move, if ever so subtly.

"Beautiful, isn't it?" Amarine whispered as they walked.

"Breathtaking," Ophelia answered. So enamored with its magic and beauty, she didn't even notice the group of people entering from the other end of the room to greet them.

"You've arrived," a jubilant voice startled Ophelia back into the moment.

It was a short man, old and chubby, who wore a red robe tied at the waist with a gray sash. His bald head was framed by a semi-circle of white hair, and Ophelia could nearly make out the twinkling stars above reflected on it. His smile was as bright as the day, and his voice as warm as a cup of tea.

"Eldweaver Finch," Lady Nikollette walked ahead of her wards.

"Sorry, we're late. Ran into a ghoul as we passed through Evergreen."

"A ghoul," he seemed surprised. "We didn't see a beacon on the map."

"Well, perhaps we arrived before anyone had a chance to break it."

"Perhaps. Regardless, I believe introductions are in order. This must be Ophelia. The mysterious young lady who emerged from the Deadwoods, unscathed. Quite the feat."

Ophelia could feel the eyes of everyone in the room fall on her. There was no ill intent in Eldweaver Finch's words, but the recounting of her earliest memories served only to make her feel uneasy.

"Hello," she responded, not sure what to say. "Yes, that's right. Nice to meet you all. Thank you for your hospitality."

"Thank Lady A'Mysteriouse," the slightly younger Eldweaver beside Eldweaver Finch responded sternly. He was tall and thin but not frail, with a thick, well-groomed tuft of gray hair that faded as it went up into a deep auburn. His face was rough from age and seemingly carved into a permanent, pale scowl. He wore a black suit beneath a dark gray robe. He continued speaking, though Ophelia wished he wouldn't. He sounded angry, his voice sour.

"You're staying with her for the moment. Your favor with us is entirely dependent on your successful completion of the trials."

"Eldweaver Gideon," Eldweaver Finch nearly snapped, then addressed the room. "I understand your frustration with the unusual situation we all find ourselves in. I'm sure none among us are more frustrated than Ophelia. Such a terrible thing to forget one's past, but the trials should have no issue sorting everything out."

"Now that we've met Ophelia," the older woman in purple leather robes chimed in, her hair wild and white with streaks of gray, like a storm cloud waiting patiently for the proper moment to rain fury on anyone who might dare to cross it. Her expression was calm and cool, almost blank. She had a dark complexion that seemed to hide shades of gray within the cracks and corners. A patch of scars webbed across her left cheek, climbing up from beneath her collar. Her eyes were a dark brown and seemed to pierce through whatever they might happen to glance at, seeing only the truth. She spoke in a measured and even tone. "Perhaps the others might be willing to introduce their potential wards? Lady Knight, you've only the one, like Lady A'Mysteriouse, so let's begin with you."

A woman to the right of the three Eldweavers, standing among three children, stepped forward.

She wore a stern expression, akin to that of Eldweaver Gideon, but instead of sickly and pale, hers was a rich brown that made her green eyes appear as vibrant as a newly sprung field. A long scar ran across her face, from her forehead, and over the bridge of her nose, before stopping beneath her cheek. It was accompanied by many smaller ones, printed on her face like an epic tale fraught with danger. The sides of her head were shaved, and the hair that ran along the center stood up on end. Everything about her screamed fearsome warrior, even her outfit, which was made up of layered leather garments adorned with metal plates and studs.

"Thank you, Eldweaver Fairwind," Her voice was impatient but respectful. "I, Lady Corina Knight, would like to submit Cassian

Darrow. He hails from Duskwatch, off the jagged shores of the Blackened Bluffs. The youngest to join the Duskwatch Guard and stronger than many among their upper ranks."

As Lady Knight spoke, a young man stepped forward. He was tall, taller than his lady. Cassian looked to be the only other person in the room who might have been able to give Barnaby a real challenge. He had broad shoulders and squared features, topped off with messy, windswept, ashen hair. His steely gaze felt as though it might crush her if she tried to hold it. A fight. Ophelia had the distinct impression Cassian was itching for a fight. It showed in the subtle corners of the arrogant smirk he tried to hide away as he sized her up. He said nothing, only nodded.

Once he stepped back in line, beside Lady Knight and two others — a pale boy and girl with golden blonde hair who appeared to be around Ophelia's age — Eldweaver Fairwind thanked them both and continued. "Lord Winthrop, if you would?"

"I'd be delighted," the pasty, tall man, to the left of the Eldweavers answered in a deep, velvety voice that held within a sophisticated eloquence. Crisp, clear, and sharp; not a sound or syllable out of place. He had a curled mustache and thin goatee that Ophelia thought matched his dark, slender features perfectly. His tailored suit looked old but well-kept. He looked like a man with secrets, none inherently bad. Judging by the wards behind him, she got the impression he was a kind, warm man.

"I, Lord Avery Winthrop of Bloodmore Manor, would like to submit Constance Bellevue." A short, red-haired girl with an innocent smile and an emerald, hooded cloak that appeared a size too big hopped forward as if caught by surprise. "She may not look it, but rest assured she is well within her fifteenth year. As small as she may be, you'll find none with a heart so big."

He nodded at her, then motioned to another boy, who stepped forward dutifully. He was clean-cut and fit, with bright blue eyes and light brown hair. His clothes were nice, formal, but not overly so. "And Charles Cotman. A spirited young man from Stillriver Kingdom. A squire to what remains of the king's guard and rather studious. He knows well what it takes to win a battle and better what it means to survive one."

The three of them stepped back in line with another boy. He looked strong, though not as big as Cassian. On his left hand, he wore a polished, steal gauntlet. It seemed flashy and out of place against his stoic expression and his plain clothes: an old white shirt and black pants tucked into loosely-strapped boots. He was looking at the two blonde-haired children standing beside Lady Knight, who looked back at him with little more than disinterest.

"Thank you," Eldweaver Fairwind said as Lord Winthrop stepped back in line with his wards. She then turned to Lady Nikollette and gestured forward. "Lady A'Mysteriouse?"

"Thank you, Eldweaver Fairwind." Lady Nikollette bowed and stepped forward. With a subtle hand, she beckoned Ophelia to join her. "I, Lady Nikollette A'Mysteriouse of Deadwood Manor, would like to submit Ophelia Ravenward. She has come to us from the Deadwoods with no recollection of her past. Humble, eager, and kind,

Ophelia seeks to unravel her past and help secure our future."

Ophelia bowed, then she and Lady Nikollette stepped back. The Eldweavers bowed, and Eldweaver Fairwind finished, "Your submissions for the Talisman Trials and admittance to the service of Sominor have been accepted. We shall gather in the trial room in one hour's time. Thank you."

The formalities that seemed to hold the room dissipated in an instant, and as Lady Nikollette walked toward the Eldweavers, Amarine snatched up Ophelia's hand. "Let's go! I want to show you my favorite place!"

Ophelia smiled as the two of them ran off past Lord Winthrop and his wards. She smiled at them. They smiled back.

Amarine led her across the map of Sominor to a large door. She looked back at Ophelia as she pressed her body against it. It opened slowly, revealing tinted daylight. Together, they slipped through the opening and shut the door. Ophelia was awestruck. A vast garden stretched out in front of her, saturated with life. The air was soft with a peace and tranquility new to her. A sprawling landscape of lush greenery and vibrant flowers, whose winding pathways of stone twisted and turned throughout like vines all their own. Two fountains stood among it all, stone spires jutting up from the organic floor, and the water that trickled from them lent the air a refreshing mist.

The glass. Ophelia found it difficult to look away from the glass ceiling. It was a half-dome that separated the garden from the world outside. It started out, at its edges, with clear, squared panels. As her eyes followed it to the center, the panels morphed into shards of every color that spiraled toward a singular point. Nothing about the half-dome looked rigid or fragile but, rather, another living thing in this new, vibrant world.

"This is where they grow all the herbs, roots, and flowers the Spellkeepers use to conjure up everything they need to assist weavers in battle. Tonics, salves, oils, you know," Amarine explained, walking backward along a stone path and gesturing at the garden absently, "medicine and the like. It is one of my favorite places."

"It's beautiful," Ophelia replied, her mouth ajar, then she realized that this was the same half-dome of glass that sat above the entrance to Spellevue. She said, "Wait, how are we here? We didn't go up any stairs."

"Oh, I forgot to mention, there are no stairs at Spellevue because all the doors are enchanted," Amarine explained.

"I see," Ophelia replied, again taking in the graden.

Amarine continued, "I like to come and walk through it whenever I'm here. I put in my sapphires and just lose myself in music, and beauty, and aroma."

As Ophelia followed Amarine, she let her fingers run gently across the leaves and petals and took in the fragrance; intoxicating.

"I can see why you love it here."

"Yes, it's wonderful. Besides," she said, smiling, "beats being stuck in there with the twins. I'd rather fight that ghoul again!"

"Who are they?"

"Lydia and Owen De'Leon. Their parents run Duskwatch." Amarine pressed her fingers against her chest and bowed. "Governor and Governess De'Leon to you and me," she finished before popping back up. "Honestly though, they are quite talented when it comes to fighting, but their magic leaves room for improvement. Maybe if they spent less time going out of their way to make everyone else feel bad about themselves, they'd be better at it."

"Yes," a man's voice, old and pleasant, said, "but we can't help the nature of others, only how we react to them."

Ophelia turned with a startled jump. Amarine turned slower with a smile. "Eldweaver Finch!"

She ran back to Ophelia as Eldweaver Finch joined them.

"Ophelia, this is Eldweaver Finch. But I'm sure you remember that." Amarine chuckled at her own forgetfulness, "And Eldweaver Finch, it's so nice to see you again. Hope everything has been well. I'm so happy to be back—"

Eldweaver Finch laughed and raised a hand. Amarine stopped talking. "Amarine, my dear, a pleasure to see you again. Ophelia"—he turned to her— "welcome to Spellevue. Are you ready for the trials?"

Ophelia nodded, then shook her head. "I hope so. I'm not sure. I guess I'm nervous."

"That's perfectly all right. We all were. The trials, though, know exactly who has entered. So long as your intentions are pure and your will is strong, you should have nothing to worry about. This, I can assure you."

"Don't forget the talisman," Amarine added excitedly. "I can't wait to see what you get!"

"Yes, well, that is only part of it. A reward, if you will. The purpose is to test your character and ability to weave magic."

Ophelia smiled; she also wondered what her talisman would be. She also wondered what power the Eldweavers must wield. The question came out like a compulsion. "What is your talisman? If you don't mind, of course. I'm sorry, is that rude?"

Eldweaver Finch laughed; his belly jiggled. "No, not at all. I spend plenty of time talking with Amarine. I'm used to blunt statements and tactless questions," he said, glancing at Amarine, who smiled back. "Besides, curiosity is the finest trait a Spellweaver can possess. After all, how can one be expected to alter the very reality in which they find themselves without first being curious as to how they might go about accomplishing such a feat?"

Ophelia relaxed. Eldweaver Finch continued.

"Well, to make a long story shorter than it ought to be, but longer than it need, like all talismans, mine is quite unique. I suppose it's fair to say, it has even changed me quite a bit. For the better, I'd like to imagine."

"How?" Ophelia asked, curious.

"You see, I was a very different person in my younger years. Back when I was merely called Diedrich. Before all these titles and formalities. Younger me would have reveled in the officiality of it all, come to think of it." He chuckled to himself before continuing. "I was a stickler for rules, you see. From the unwritten to those etched into the very stone upon which our society is built. If I had to pick a moment when everything started going so horribly right, I would say it was when I received this."

Eldweaver Finch turned the ring on his right ring finger with his thumb. It was a worn, gray metal with a series of crossed lines that appeared to be hand-etched encircling the outer surface. He continued, "My prize, so to speak, from my time in the trials. My talisman. The Replicant Ring. With it, I can make copies of myself, like so."

Another Finch stepped out from the first, as if stepping through any old door. The second continued their story. "Each as real as the original, and therein lies the problem. Well, I used to think it was a problem."

"That's incredible," Ophelia could hardly believe her eyes. "How could that ever be a problem?"

The first took over. "We can each hear, smell, see, and most notably, feel what the others are experiencing; all at once. It can be a bit confusing from time to time."

"How do you know who is the original?"

The two Finches laughed, then the second answered, "We suppose the ring knows. Otherwise, we are as one. Which brings us to the point. Having more than one of us could be quite useful in any manner of encounter. Suddenly, we were able to do the work of entire teams of weavers. The complexity of our spells grew. We were formidable. However, we grew careless. Arrogant even. This, of course, led to mistakes. When facing off against neverbeasts, mistakes can lead to death. We've been mauled by banter bears, bludgeoned by swamp thumpers, and even eaten alive by an entire nest of the most adorable little knee nibblers anyone has ever seen. The pain was excruciating, to say the least. None more so than the many deaths we suffered during the final battle against the Endless."

"The Endless?" Ophelia asked. "What are those?"

"I'm surprised your lady hasn't told you. Seems quite the oversight to withhold the dangers that come with spell weaving. My story is already long enough. I suggest you ask Lady A'Mysteriouse about the Endless once your trial has concluded."

Ophelia looked concerned but nodded in agreement.

"Their numbers stretched out before us, well, endlessly I suppose. There was scarce time to weave any sort of magic once they came down upon us. We relied mostly on our talismans and our weapons. During the battle, I made more copies of myself than I care to remember." The second Finch said as he walked back into the original.

The original Finch continued, "But I'll never forget the pain each one of us suffered. I didn't talk much after that. Though I was physically unharmed, I walked away with many scars. I decided at some point, I don't know when, that life was too painful – and too painfully short – to fret so much over rules. I've come to understand that much of what makes life worth living can often be found at the edges of disorder. Rules are meant well enough in the moments for which they are written but perhaps not always in the moments we find ourselves."

Eldweaver Finch looked down at his ring. Turning it again, he said, "I only regret that I wasted so much of my life fretting over such things, but I thank my talisman every day for teaching me the value of living."

A silence hung between them, until Eldweaver Finch looked back up at them. "But enough of an old man's life story. I know this garden is beautiful, but might I suggest you two head back in and get to know the others?" He looked to Amarine. "I can't imagine Ophelia has met them, and it may come off as rude the way you stole her away."

Amarine sprang to life, having been captivated by Eldweaver Finch's story, despite likely having heard it before. "Oh, no! You're right!"

"Yes, well, you'll all be spending ever-increasing amounts of time with one another in the years to come, should your trial prove successful. You'd do well to make a few friends early on." He smiled at Ophelia, adding a wink for good measure.

"Let's go." Amarine grabbed Ophelia's hand and took off.

"Wait." Ophelia took her hand back and extended it to Eldweaver Finch. "It was a pleasure meeting you."

He smiled and shook her hand. "Likewise. Now, off you go."

The girls ran out of the garden and back into the World's Room, leaving behind Eldweaver Finch and the faint sound of a sneeze and sniffle.

THE POWERLESS HEART OF RENÉE ROCHÉ

Following the disappearance of Marcel, Renée had tried her best to track him down to no avail. Defeated, she had returned home to her family's manor and the people of Roché Village some months later. Her parents were happy to have her back. She was not happy to be back. Not under these circumstances. It wasn't until her father approached her to discuss giving up magic and focusing on expanding the Roché family, that she remembered why she had been so eager to leave in the first place. Marcel had only been a part of it.

"This is where you belong, dear." Her mother spoke to her like a mother would a disappointed child. "We have a duty to this village, to our name."

Renée hated when her mother talked to her like that.

"I know where I belong, mother," Renée replied, as calm as she could be, "and it is out there. There are more people than just those in

Roché Village that need help."

"I understand, but you needn't throw your life away for that man who took you away from us. What was his name again?"

"Marcel." Renée's temper was wrestling itself free.

"Whatever it was," her mother continued, "he's left you, and I think it is high time you left him—him and everything—behind you. Magic is all well and good, but what you need is family. A family of your own."

Renée stood up, knowing full well that staying any longer would only lead to a fight. Her parents were getting older. Her mother wasn't going to change. There was no sense in a fight.

"I'll not be giving up magic," Renée said, tense, as she walked out of the room. She relaxed, adding, "But I understand very well the importance of family. So, you'll have me back, but only on my terms. I hope you understand."

She walked out before her mother could protest.

She tried to think through where Marcel might have gone, however her time at home and wrapped in thought yielded nothing of value. Worse still, she found herself haunted by guilt. She needed to do something more than sitting and pondering.

Her first stop, she decided, would be Greenwood Manor. None of this had been her fault, but she did leave poor Nikollette without so much as a goodbye. She only hoped her apology would be enough.

It was far from a short trek from Roché to Greenwood Manor, and she certainly could have used her Courier Coin, but walking felt a more fitting trial. Deserved, even.

She arrived three days later to find Nikollette sitting on a headstone in the family cemetery. Well, it would have been more accurate to say Nikollette found her. Renée had been oblivious, strolling up to the door, ready to knock, only to be called to by Nikollette.

"You're back." Her voice came flat. "Why?"

Renée searched for the answer, flustered by the unexpected question. A fair question, to be sure. She walked toward the cemetery and answered, "It didn't feel right, leaving without saying goodbye."

Nikollette hopped off the headstone and met her halfway. "Yet, you did. Come to say goodbye then?"

Renée was surprised by how much Nikollette had grown. Nearly as tall as she was. Though she was only coming up on seventeen, she looked older behind her scowl. Renée desperately wanted to diffuse the tension. "You've grown."

"People grow." Nikollette left no space for Renée's gambit to play out. "You'd been gone for some time. We all lost him, we all loved him, but you're the only one who ran away."

"I'm sorry." Renée's head lowered, a guilty bow heavy with shame. "I hope you can forgive me."

"I'm sure I will." Nikollette seemed to force the words out. "But there are no shortcuts on the path to forgiveness."

Renée smiled as she looked back up at her. "You sound just like your father."

"Good."

"Indeed." Renée let her smile drift away. This wasn't the moment for a smile anyway. "Speaking of your father, is he home? I've come to ask for my return to Spellevue. I should have never left. I would like to teach again; train again. I want to help."

"He's home," Nikollette answered, her eyes locked onto Renée's, "but he's busy talking with my uncle."

Renée found herself breathless, if only for a moment. She couldn't believe what she was hearing. How long had he been back?

"Why didn't you tell me Marcel's back?"

A wry smile snuck through Nikollette's expression. "Why didn't you say goodbye?"

Just then, the front door of the manor burst open. Marcel came marching out, with Bastien close behind.

"You can't, Marcel." Bastien was furious. Renée had never seen him so upset. "You mustn't!"

"I can, and I will." Marcel turned to face him.

"Marcel." Renée's voice came out meek.

Marcel glared at her with the same anger he'd shown his brother. He said nothing but flipped his coin and vanished.

"Bastien." She turned to him, her eyes glistening. "What happened?"

"That fool has lost his mind," Bastien shouted, then stormed inside. Renée and Nikollette ran after him.

"Father, what did he say?"

He stopped in the foyer and turned to face the two ladies. "He has it in his head that he can bring back your aunt and your mother with magic."

"That's not possible, is it?" Renée's concern melted into sincere curiosity. "I mean, dead is dead. Isn't it?"

"I don't know, and I don't care," Bastien countered, "but I will not be part of anything so dangerous as resurrecting the dead. I have mourned my loss, so must he."

He looked at Nikollette, and added gently, "So must we all."

"Do you know where he has gone?" Renée asked.

"Is that why you've come back? To try and save my brother, again?"

"No," Renée tried to explain but was cut off while searching for the words.

"She wishes to make amends," Nikollette said, placing a hand on her father's chest, easing the fire that still burned behind his eyes. "She wishes to return to Spellevue. She's only worried about Uncle Marcel. Just like me. Just like you."

Bastien nodded. "Good. Sominor needs all the help it can get. I know not what magic Marcel is toying with, but I cannot imagine anything good could come from it. We'll do well to have your sharp mind and skilled hands back in our company."

A new magic. Renée wished so desperately to know what it was. *The good we could do with mastery over death.*

"Happy to be back," was what Renée said.

Spellevue had not changed much in Renée's absence. Illana, Dierich, Victor, and Dominic were very much the same people they'd always been. She was welcomed back with open arms. Unknown to anyone else, including Nikollette, Bastien had tasked Renée with a secret mission.

Between encounters with neverbeasts and training sessions, she was to search for Marcel, wherever he may be hiding. So, with each battle fought and won, she would bid farewell to whoever had accompanied her under the guise of visiting her family, and she would scour Sominor in search of the man she loved most dear.

Each time, she came up wanting.

Sometimes, she didn't even try, simply resigning to actually return home to be with her family.

It was after one of her expeditions, some five months after having last seen Marcel, that she returned to Greenwood Manor to report back to Bastien and continue mending her relationship with Nikollette. When she arrived this time, she found the two of them in their family cemetery. They were on the ground, in embrace. Upon approach, she could see why. All the graves had been dug up. Each plot empty.

"What happened?" Renée's hushed voice crept up from behind them. Nikollette jumped. Bastien stood up slowly; he turned to face her.

"He took them," he explained, his voice shaking. "He dug them all up and took their remains."

"Who?" Renée pleaded for answers. "Who could have done this?"

"Marcel." Bastien burst into tears. Nikollette jumped to her feet to console him.

"That's…" Renée couldn't find the words. She settled on, "He wouldn't."

"He did," Nikollette countered. Hers were the eyes of a girl forced to grow up faster than she should have. The eyes of a woman forged in the fires of loss. They looked as true as the words behind them.

Renée shook her head. She backed away. She tried to convince herself this was nothing more than a nightmare. Marcel would never do something so awful. He wasn't capable.

"Renée." Nikollette's sharp voice cut through Renée's delusion. "Help me get my father inside. Then we can figure out what to do."

She nodded but didn't move.

"Renée!"

"Sorry." She finally shook herself free enough to be of use. "Yes, let's get your father inside."

Just as Renée got her arm hooked into Bastien's, a deep tremor rolled through the forest. Ravens took flight, leaves fell like rain, and headstones toppled into the empty graves they stood watch over. The trio turned to face the Greenwoods.

"What was that?" Nikollette asked.

"It came from your uncle's house," Renée answered.

"How do you know?"

"I can feel it." Renée placed her free hand over her talisman. "I need to go to him. I need to stop whatever it is he is doing."

"I know what he is doing." Bastien's tears had run dry, and he hobbled free of the caring grip of the two women beside him, toward the forest. "He's trying to bring them back. He's trying to raise the dead."

Before another word could be uttered, a distant cloud like a billowing mushroom slowly rose from the forest. It loomed over

Marcel's home. Another tremor shook the ground. It started soft, then gradually built with the expanding cloud. Just as Renée was about to lose her footing, it all stopped.

"Do you think it worked?" Nikollette asked. Renée could sense a slight hint of hope in her troubled voice. "Do you think he brought them back?"

"I don't…"

All at once, the cloud collapsed in on itself, slamming down into the forest. Its gray billows rolled violently along the treetops. Within seconds, Renée could see the cloud fast approaching through the thick tree line. Before she could say a word, it rolled over them, knocking them off their feet and back toward the manor. Renée screamed, but she couldn't even feel the sound of her own voice tearing through her throat. The world had become a violent torrent.

As suddenly as it had come upon them, it stopped.

Renée jumped to her feet. The stillness that enveloped her forced her guard up. It was as unsettling as the dark mist that surrounded them. She helped Nikollette and Bastien to their feet. They stood back-to-back, waiting for whatever might come next.

Nothing did. Only silence.

Slowly, the dark mist dissipated. The manor had taken extensive damage. The graveyard had only a few remaining headstones standing, along with Ophelia's mausoleum. Greenwood forest, however, had been reduced to nothing more than a memory marked by dead trees sprouting from a bed of gray dirt.

"What have you done?" Bastien murmured and then shouted into the dead woods in front of them, "WHAT HAVE YOU DONE?"

Marcel was nowhere to be found when Renée, Bastien, and Nikollette ventured out into the dead woods to find him. Even his house no longer stood where Renée knew it had once been. The path to it was etched into every muscle fiber within her legs. Left with only questions, the three of them flipped their coins and entered Spellevue to share the dreadful news. News, they came to find, they knew terribly little about.

"So"—Illana met their tale with a skeptical tone—"you know *something* happened, but you don't know what exactly. Hardly anything we can do about something we know nothing about."

"I'm telling you," Bastien found himself pleading before the very students he had trained to weave magic, as though he were a stranger to them, in desperate need, "he has taken to a dark path, and each step he takes along it will be a footprint seared into our destruction. We may not know what happened in those woods, or what vile corruption he has summoned, but what we saw, what we felt, it was very real. Terrible beyond anything you've ever encountered."

"But you don't know what," Victor countered.

"No," Renée asserted. "We know it was Marcel. And you all know, along with Bastien, that he wrote the book on magic. None among us can begin to approach whatever new power he has written now."

"Regardless," Diedrich argued, "his trespasses that we can account for so far are that of a regular order. Grave robbery? Burning down a forest? These are not laws which us Spellweavers are meant to uphold.

These offenses are the purview of the guard nearest their committing. What do you expect *us* to do?"

"I expect you all to live." A voice came rolling over them like a cold mist.

Every soul present turned to face Marcel who, alongside his wife, stood at the great hall leading out of Spellevue. At first glance, they appeared as the happy couple they had always been, Marcel, strolling toward them with that smile of his, big and bright as the day itself. His eyes glowed a subtle gold, and the air around him seemed to vibrate, warping and bending. It was as if reality itself knew not where to place him, only that he didn't quite belong where he was.

On his arm, Antoinette clung as tight as a foolhardy girl in the throes of young love, but her white, sunken eyes and pale gray skin made clear that she was no longer completely human. Where once she was as vibrant as a ray of light on a cloudy day, a hallow dullness now overcame her, like the unbearably loud hum of complete silence.

"Marcel." Bastien seemed at a loss for words.

"This isn't right." Renée found the words for him. "You *know* this isn't right."

"I'd argue anything else is wrong." Marcel's smile never faltered, and his lips never moved. His voice seemed to come from somewhere behind his smile, not from it. As if hidden deep within whomever this was, they might find the real Marcel, devoured and corrupted, the smile nothing more than the hungry mouth of an endless cave, ready to swallow up anything and anyone who dared come too close.

Nikollette recoiled, hiding behind her father.

Marcel's cold eyes darted right for her. "My darling niece, don't be afraid. So long as I'm here, death cannot find you. It cannot find any of you."

Marcel turned in a circle and laughed. Antoinette, without Marcel, stood perfectly still with her empty smile focused directly on Renée.

"You see," Marcel continued, "I hold dominion over death! No more loss, no more grief. All Sominor may live without fear of what never was. They can dream any dream they like without fear of what waits for them when they wake. Stand with me, and together we can build a Sominor as endless as the oceans that surround it. A Sominor as endless as me."

"And if we refuse," Victor asked, defiant, "will you see us dead?"

"You may as well already be." Marcel laughed.

"You're not my uncle! You're not Marcel! He would never." Nikollette found her voice.

Marcel only laughed. "I am more than your uncle. I'm more than a man. I rule over death. I am a king without end. An Endless King!"

"We will not stand for this," Illana shouted. "Do you hear me? We will *not* stand for this."

"Then kneel." The tone in Marcel's voice lowered to nearly a growl, but his smile never left. He lifted both his hands out in front of him in one smooth, delicate motion and extended his index fingers.

Renée's eyes lit up. She shouted, "He's weaving!"
She stepped in front of the others, arms outstretched. The talisman around her neck began to glow, her heart of stone beating hard and heavy.

As Marcel traced the air, a crack snapped and raced through the stone map of Sominor beneath his feet. In an instant, the floor before Marcel and Antoinette rose up, forming a wall between them.

A moment later, it exploded toward them. Massive pieces rained down, but not a single speck of dust came close to Renée or the others. Her stone heart made sure of it.

Before the dust could settle, Illana fired off a torrent of purple and black flame from her flint. When she stopped, Renée wasn't sure if she hoped he survived, or if the threat had passed.

When the smoke cleared, she had her answer.

Two charred bodies stood there staring back at them. Their burned skin tore with audible cracks as the two of them took a few steps forward. Renée and the others only looked on in horror, until Marcel and Antoinette stood before them, their smiles having never left and their charred skin having fallen away. They looked as just as they had when they arrived.

"What have you done?" Bastien mumbled.

"I made a wish, my dear brother," Marcel answered, "for dominion over death."

"Then burn…" Illana stepped forward and shouted. "…endlessly!"

She struck her obsidian flint again, and once more a river of dark purple flame poured out toward Marcel and his wife. With the flip of a coin and the fading echo of laughter, he was gone in a useless flash of flame.

The World's Room had gone silent, left only with the bewildered faces of the spellweavers that stood within.

"Now, will you do something?" Bastien turned to his students, his friends, and asked.

"Now we have no choice," Diedrich replied.

"We must stop Marcel," Illana added. "He cannot be allowed to live."

Victor added, "We must bring this to an end before it can go any further."

"Listen to yourselves." Renée tried, in vain, to remain calm. "He was one of us. One of the best of us. How can you so quickly come to his execution?"

"He's too dangerous," Victor replied.

"He's lost." Renée's voice burned with grief. "Now is when he needs us. Not to do what is easy, but what is right. Magic did this to him, and magic can undo it."

"Fine," Illana conceded. "You are right, but none of our lives outweigh the lives of the helpless. Do all you can to find a way to cure this curse, and we will do our best to stop it."

Renée looked to Bastien, grabbing him by the shoulders. "You'll help me, won't you? He's your brother."

Bastien sniffled, pulled away, and turned his back on her. "That wasn't my brother. My brother is dead."

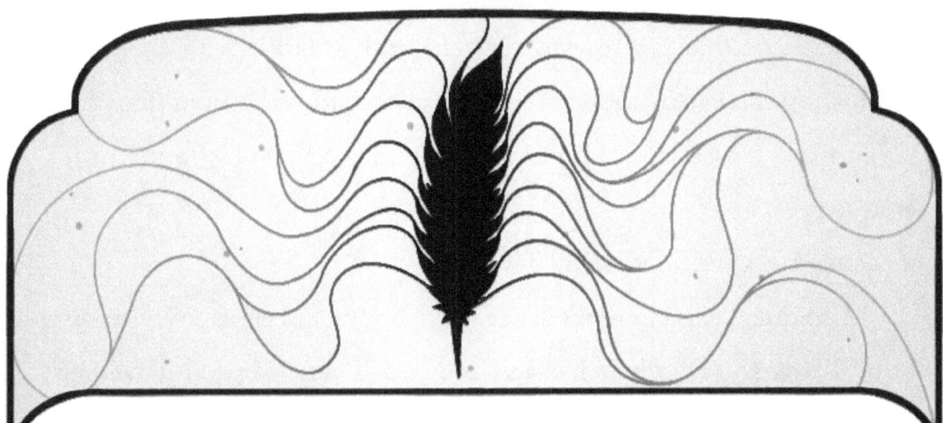

THE TRIALS BEGIN

When Ophelia returned to the World's Room with Amarine, she found four new faces. They wore black and gray, bound together by yellow leather accents that made each of them highly visible and nearly matching. An older gentleman stood near the Eldweavers. He was surprisingly muscular for his age and was bald with a thick, gray beard. Ophelia looked away quickly once his gaze fell upon her.

Speaking with the lords and ladies was a young man. He appeared cordial as he conversed with the seasoned Spellweavers. They seemed to like him quite well. He was tall and slender, with darker features and stark black hair styled short and tidy. Standing at his side was a girl, likely a few years older than Ophelia, her face partially obscured behind her long hair, only half of which was pulled back behind her ear. She nodded along with the conversation the young man was engaged in.

The one who stood out the most was a girl who appeared to be

Ophelia's age that ran toward Ophelia and Amarine with an excited expression. Her hair bounced in tight curls with each bounding step. Even from across the room, Ophelia could see a twinkle in her nearly purple eyes.

Amarine waved. "Rosalin! There you are!"

"Amarine," Rosalin replied, her voice bright and clear. "Where were you? I was so sad when I didn't see you. I was worried it was just Barnaby."

Ophelia looked at Barnaby as Rosalin and Amarine hugged. He glanced over at them with a sour face.

"Rosalin, I'd like you to meet Ophelia. Ophelia, meet my friend, Rosalin."

Ophelia turned back to Amarine, then looked to Rosalin. Rosalin stood there smiling, with her hand held out. Ophelia shook it.

"Hi. Best friend actually, or has that changed?"

Amarine laughed and shook her head. "No, it hasn't. Meet my best friend, Rosalin."

"It's nice to meet you. Are you a Spellweaver, too?" Ophelia asked.

"Oh, no," Rosalin chuckled. "I wish. No, I didn't get a talisman from my trial. Kind of sad, but I was happy to meet Amarine and know she received one shortly after my attempt. I'm a Spellkeeper. Free room and board, nice people, and plenty to do. Plus, I get to be around magic. Are you excited for your trial?"

"More nervous than anything. I'm told it's dangerous."

"It can be, sure, but as far as I know, in all these years, only one person never came out."

"So, I've been told." Ophelia bowed her head.

"No one really talks about it, because it's so unlikely," Rosalin interrupted before Amarine could get a word in. "Don't worry though. As Amarine's best friend, I believe her to be an excellent judge of character. If she believes in you, so do I."

"Yeah, I'm sorry I didn't mention it, but I was certain you'd be fine." Amarine assured, "You may not remember anything about yourself, but I know you're a good person. Don't doubt yourself. Once doubt takes hold, it's difficult to shake it free."

"You sounded like Lady Nikolette just then," Ophelia joked. They all shared a laugh.

"Oh!" Rosalin nearly jumped. "You should meet Constance and Charles! They're also going through the trials."

Rosalin turned and waved her arms in their direction until the boy with the gauntlet noticed. He nudged Constance, and she looked over at the girls. Charles turned around as well. Rosalin waved them over. Ophelia grew more nervous.

"Mordecai," Amarine said to the boy in the gauntlet. "I feel like I haven't seen you in months!"

He smiled. "Because you haven't. How have you been, Amarine?"

"Oh, you know, itching to get out in the field."

"From what I hear, you just have. A ghoul? How did that go?"

"Oh, well," Amarine said with a smile and shook her head, "If not for Lady Nikollette, I'm not sure Barnaby and I would have come out on top."

"I wouldn't sell yourself short. Looks like you both came out unscathed. Not an easy task against such a neverbeast."

"Thank you." Amarine turned her attention to Constance and Charles. "And you! It's been ages!"

"It has," Constance replied. Her voice was nearly as small as she was.

"Hard to believe you're fifteen," Amarine said, adding, "You don't look a day over twelve."

Amarine and Mordecai laughed, and Constance joined, if only sarcastically.

"Laugh all you like," Constance said, "but one day, I bet I'll be taller than you. You'll see."

"I look forward to it." Amarine gave her a hug. When she let go, Amarine looked at the other boy, Charles.

"And this is Charles, is it? It's a pleasure to meet you. You're from Stillriver? How long have you lived there? Do you know the king?"

"Nice to meet you, too. Please, call me Charlie. I am. Always. And I've met him, but I wouldn't say I *know* him. I think that answers all the questions, right?" Charlie looked up as if searching his own mind. He mouthed Amarine's questions silently and counted on his hand. "Yes, I think so. Unless you have any more, of course. I'm happy to answer."

Amarine apologized. "I'm sorry, I get excited meeting people."

"No need to apologize," Charlie assured her, then looked at Ophelia. "And this is Ophelia? I've heard tell of your daring escape from the Deadwoods. Quite the tale."

Ophelia's cheeks turned the slightest pink as she answered, "Yes, well, not really. Loads of running and loads of ravens. Not much to tell."

"Don't forget the undead buck," Barnaby added. "That was a bit more than not much."

Rosalin's eyes lit up. "I've only read about the Deadwoods. Is it true everything in the woods is undead? They say it's something in the trees that brings the dead back to life, though I've never seen it myself." She sounded disappointed, which struck Ophelia as odd given the serious threat that the undead buck had posed.

"You aren't missing much. Trust me," Ophelia answered. Her sudden grim tone seemed to dampen the mood. She added with a smile, "I'm just happy to have made it out alive and to have found Lady Nikollette, Amarine, and Barnaby."

"Yep." Amarine wrapped an arm around Ophelia. "I'd say you are just about the luckiest person there ever was to have found us. Despite what anyone else might tell you, Deadwood Manor is the best."

"Keep dreaming," Mordecai responded, "and maybe it will actually come true." The group burst out into laughter.

"A nightmare, more like." A cold voice cut through the moment like the freezing rain that had poured over Ophelia in the Deadwoods. She looked to see Owen with Lydia at his side, and Cassian towering behind them both.

"No one asked you, Owen," Amarine replied, "so mind your own, and leave us be."

"Hey, you don't have to get so upset," Owen smirked as he spoke, "It was a joke. Mordecai is allowed to make a joke, but I can't? Seems rude. Right, Lydia?"

"Very," the blonde girl beside him answered with the same smirk Owen wore. "My brother was just trying to be part of the conversation. We're all on the same team here."

"Funny," Mordecai said as he took a step toward Owen and Lydia. He looked down at them and continued, "You don't ever seem to act like it."

Cassian stepped forward, squaring off with Mordecai. "So far as I've seen, I could say the same to you. Why do they insist on giving such power to the weak?"

From across the room, Eldweaver Fairwind announced, "The trials will begin shortly. Please join with your lord or lady and make your way to the Trial Chamber, ready to meet whatever fate might have in store."

The Trial Chamber stood out to Ophelia compared to what she'd seen of Spellevue so far. The hexagonal room was made up of smooth stone slabs. Along the walls, shorter slabs stuck out that Ophelia assumed were meant to be seats. The dark gray stone that made up the room's interior was dull and featureless, save for the glowing inlay on the floor. Nested hexagonal patterns sat slightly askew from one another, forming a sort of spiral that forced one's attention directly to the center. There, one would find a door.

It was a simple door that would have been completely innocuous if not for the fact that it was made entirely of glass—except for a round iron knob—and seemed to lead to nowhere at all.

"The Looking Glass Door." Eldweaver Finch gestured toward it as he, Fairwind, and Gideon stood in front of it. "Our most sincere respect to each of those brave enough to venture through the trials that await. Your quest to help secure Sominor begins here, but may it not end here."

In the otherwise silent room, Ophelia could hear Charlie gulp at the comment. She felt her own throat tighten.

"Constance Bellevue," Finch continued, "you were the only one meant to undergo today's trials, so you shall be the first. Are you ready?"

Constance stepped forward. The innocent look on her face seemed to age suddenly as she answered, "I am."

"Then step forward and enter." The Eldweavers stepped aside with Finch's final command.

Constance approached with a growing severity in her expression. When she reached the door, she looked back at Mordecai. He nodded; she returned the gesture. Only an endless darkness greeted her when she opened the door. Without looking back, she stepped in and closed it behind her. Much to Ophelia's surprise, the glass shattered and fell to the floor. The doorknob, however, remained where it was.

One hour and twenty minutes. That's how long Ophelia was forced to sit in silence on one of the uncomfortable stone slabs. Ten minutes into the trial, she had quietly asked Lady Nikollette how long the trials lasted.

"A few hours, usually. Once, an entire day. The quickest was Owen at nearly forty-five minutes," had been her response.

When the shards of glass began to reassemble themselves into a door, she was awe-struck, relieved, but also worried.

Constance came tumbling from the door and fell to her knees. Her green cloak wrapped around her like a shell that heaved up and down with each labored breath. Mordecai ran to her before most in the room had even gotten to their feet. He kneeled at her side.

"Constance, are you okay?"

Constance looked up from beneath her green hood. It fell away, revealing an exhausted smile hiding behind her wild, red hair. "Yeah, I'm great."

She stood up with Mordecai's help, revealing an object in her hand. She looked up at him and spoke softly. "I've got a talisman." She then turned to the rest of the room and held it out for all to see. "A talisman!" she declared with pride.

Everyone formed a loose circle around Constance, and Lady Nikollette stepped forward. She lifted her looking glass up to her eye and studied it. It was a small, heart-shaped, object made of brass wire and gears. It reminded Ophelia of the inside of a large clock she'd noticed while roaming the halls of Deadwood Manor. No one spoke but waited for Lady Nikollette to finish her assessment. When she was done, she let her Looking Glass fall back down to her chest, then turned to face the group and announced, "To use this talisman, I feel it would be best that we all go to the arena."

The Eldweavers didn't argue but simply ushered everyone through the halls of Spellevue.

After passing through only two doors and a winding hall between them, they entered a large room that Ophelia could not imagine having fit anywhere within Spellevue. Not given the walk they had taken, nor the proportions of Spellevue from the outside. It was a large expanse of terrain contained within an oblong dome. It consisted of a small mountain, a forest, two rivers that connected at a lake in the middle, and rolling hills of grass. It was like a miniature Sominor within Sominor. She couldn't believe her eyes.

Nikollette asked everyone, save for Constance, to remain atop one of the grassy hills. She led the young girl over to some nearby boulders and drew a few sigils into the ground. The rocks lifted from the dirt, then fell back down in a loose pile of rubble.

"A clockwork heart!" Lady Nikollette shouted and proceeded to say something inaudible to Constance.

Constance became visibly excited. She worked the talisman over in her hands, one holding it, while the other appeared to turn something. When she was through, she tossed the talisman into the pile of rocks. In seconds, the rocks jiggled, coalesced and took the vague form of a giant stone man. It turned its head toward Constance and kneeled at her feet with a bow. Constance jumped, clapped, then patted it on the head. It stood back up. Nikollette, Constance, and the stone golem then strolled back to the group.

"It can control stone?" Eldweaver Finch asked. He sounded concerned.

"Yes," Lady Nikollette answered, "but not like you think. It can control any inanimate object. Winding up the gears in the heart allows it to, for a time, give life to the lifeless and serve at Constance's disposal. A golem of her own design to fight or provide aid as she chooses. Much like Eldweaver Gideon's horn."

"For how long?" Eldweaver Gideon asked.

"That depends on how much she winds it or when she chooses to dismiss it. When the gears stop turning, the heart stops beating. If she so chooses, she can simply put it to rest."

Lady Nikollette nodded to Constance. Constance nodded back, then looked at her stone golem and said, "Thank you. That will be all."

The golem bowed and the stone tumbled back to the ground in a neat pile. The clockwork heart floated out of the rubble and back into Constance's hands.

"Quite useful," Eldweaver Fairwind remarked.

"Powerful," Eldweaver Finch added.

"Well done," Lord Winthrop said. "A heart as big as yours deserves no less."

"Let us return to the Trial Chamber," Eldweaver Finch announced. "We will continue along with Bloodmoore Manor and young Charles Cottman."

Ophelia looked at Charlie. The smile he had worn while watching Constance and her talisman melted away in an instant. She could see his hands trembling. He was quick to hide them in his pockets.

THE PERILS OF PRIDE

Charlie appeared much less confident entering the door than Constance had. That much would have been clear to anyone paying attention. For a moment, as Charlie stood before the door with his hand resting on the knob, Ophelia wondered if he might not go through with it at all. She wondered if turning back now was even an option. She wondered what Constance had experienced inside.

When Charlie had finally entered and the door shattered again, Ophelia found herself once more surrounded by the dead silence and sheer boredom that came with waiting. After an hour, the Eldweavers dismissed everyone for half, or until the door re-assembled. Ophelia could not have been more relieved. She, Amarine, and Barnaby made their way back to the arena with Constance and Mordecai.

"What was it like?" Ophelia asked. "Were you scared?"

"Well…" Constance considered the question for a moment. "I was told to keep it to myself. That each Spellweaver's journey is their own, and I can see why now. I will say this, though. It had its fair share of harrowing moments."

"Okay." Ophelia was a little disheartened. "I at least hope my talisman is as wonderful as yours or Amarine's."

"Hey," Amarine cut in as they all entered the arena, "I wonder if your golem is a sort of neverbeast. Can you create another? I'll go into the Neverwas and see what it looks like."

"Okay." Constance smiled. "Let's find out."

Constance was about to use the same pile of rocks but was stopped by Mordecai. "Let's see what else it can do. Barnaby, care to give me a hand?"

"Huh?" Barnaby asked as though he had been someplace else entirely.

"Help me break up some trees to add to the rocks. I want to see what Constance's talisman can do."

"Right," Barnaby agreed.

They marched to the nearest trees, leaving the girls at the pile of stones.

"Is Mordecai as strong as Barnaby?" Ophelia couldn't help but wonder aloud.

"Oh, no," Amarine answered. "But he won't be using his own hands on those trees. His talisman is powerful enough to break a tree or two."

"What is it?"

"The Grave Keeper's Gauntlet," Constance answered. "Watch."

Ophelia looked on from a distance as Barnaby let his hands wail against a tree. Chunks of wood went flying. At the tree beside him,

Mordecai held out his left hand. The gauntlet shined at the wrist, and Mordecai's hand was replaced but a large, crab-like appendage.

"Whoa." Ophelia found herself at a loss for words.

"Any neverbeast Mordecai defeats," Constance explained, "he can summon their appendage and any ability that comes with it, from the gauntlet."

"It's pretty useful," Amarine added. "One of my favorites, actually. Probably because I consider myself a neverbeast expert to a certain degree. I haven't seen as much as I'd like in person though, and nothing terribly dangerous. So, it's just nice to get to see them in real life anytime I get the chance. Well, one's hand anyway. But I'm rambling, aren't I?"

Constance and Ophelia shared a glance, a smile, and a stifled giggle.

"Perhaps a little," Ophelia said.

Amarine nodded. "Yeah, yeah. Sorry."

The boys dragged their haul over to the pile of stones and dropped two trees worth of wood onto it. Mordecai's clawed hand retracted into the gauntlet, and his real hand came back. His brow glistened with sweat. He commented, "Those trees are heavy."

"Eh." Barnaby shrugged. Not the slightest indication that he'd just cut down a tree by hand and carried it across a hill on his shoulders. "I've lifted heavier."

"Rub it in," Mordecai joked. He turned to Constance. "Well then, let's see it."

"Right." Constance held out her talisman. She wound the gears of her Clockwork Heart three times, then tossed it into the pile.

The heap of wood and stone trembled before rolling up and taking the shape of a golem once again. It had a stone body with wooden arms that had roots for fingers. Atop, where the head would have been, a tuft of leaves flowed with its movements, like wild, green hair. This one was twice as big as the last but noticeably slower.

"Looks clumsy," a snide comment came from the arena entrance. "Probably takes after its master."

Owen, Lydia, and Cassian stood watching.

"Big, sure," Cassian added, "but hardly useful in a real fight at those speeds."

"Still more useful than being able to see a couple seconds into the future!" Amarine shouted back.

"I mean, how absolutely useless," Amarine and Owen said in unison. Amarine scowled and turned her head in a huff.

The three unwanted attendees made their way through the arena until they were standing before Ophelia and the others.

Owen said, "I doubt I would even need my talisman to defeat any of you. Each more predictable than the last. Pathetic."

"I'd have to agree with my brother," Lydia added, with a cold disinterest in her tone. "Each of you lacks any sort of battle sense. For instance…"

With one swift motion, Lydia drew a short sword from the sheath on her hip and threw it at the lumbering golem. It flew through the wood and stone, touching nothing until a metallic *ping* came from within the golem's chest. The Clockwork Heart went flying in the air, and the golem crumbled to the ground.

Lydia smirked as her short sword reappeared in her hand, forming from a fine mist. She slid it right back into its sheath. The Clockwork Heart floated back to Constance.

"They are as useless as you've described them," Cassian said with a laugh. "If they made it through the trials, I should have no problem at all."

"Yes," Owen added. "There is no excuse for such ineptitude, except for the Daughter of Deadwood here, seeing as how she was practically born yesterday."

"That's not my name," Ophelia practically growled.

"You don't like it? Has a ring to it, don't you think, Daughter of Deadwood?"

"That's not her name." She heard Barnaby say from behind her, followed immediately by a grunt and a swift gust of air that sent her hair whipping into her face. Owen stepped to his right as a large boulder shot through the air before crashing into the wall behind them, where it exploded into rubble.

"Hey, now," Owen said with hardly a care. "Had I not seen that coming from a mile away, it would have taken my head clean off." He laughed. "How pitiful."

"Yes," Barnaby responded, "a real pity."

Ophelia noticed Mordecai's gauntlet glow from the corner of her eye. Something slithered out of it. Amarine and Barnaby took fighting stances at her side. Constance held up her heart, ready to wind it up. Ophelia's heart raced.

Cassian, Owen, and Lydia only smiled.

"The door is re-assembling now," Magister Irons announced from the arena entrance. "Stop whatever squabbling you're in the middle of and return to the chamber at once."

They arrived in time to see the final shard of glass slide into place at the center of the door. The knob turned quick and was released just as fast. A thin line of darkness appeared as the door slowly drifted open. For what Ophelia felt was too long a time, there was nothing inside but darkness.

A hand appeared, bloodied.

What followed was a badly beaten Charlie. Gashes on his arm, blood running down them, a cut along his cheek, and a swollen eye made him difficult to recognize.

"I made it?" The words choked out between sobs and tears. He rolled over onto his back, his broken body sprawled out on the floor.

The Eldweavers, along with Magister Irons, circled him. Irons kneeled and asked, "Boy, can you walk?"

"I don't know. I'm just so tired."

"Don't sleep." Irons grabbed his head. "Stay awake, son."

Barnaby stood up and marched toward them without having been summoned. He said nothing as he forced his way between the Eldweavers and Magister Irons. From beneath his shirt, he produced a jagged emerald fastened to a chain. He gripped it in one hand and put his other on Charlie's chest.

Ophelia watched Charlie's wounds heal. His cuts closed, the swelling bruises shrunk and their colors faded, and his tired eyes filled with renewed life.

Barnaby wasn't as fortunate.

"Barnaby," the sound escaped Ophelia. Barnaby's body ripped, and bled, and became bruised in the exact places Charlie had been. Lady Nikollette placed a steadying hand on Ophelia's arm.

"It's okay," she said softly.

Ophelia watched as Barnaby doubled over in pain. He made no sound, but his expression screamed of it. Charlie stood and watched along with the silent room, all eyes on Barnaby. Eldweaver Finch's gaze averted and his head lowered.

Within a minute, the wounds that plagued Barnaby healed themselves. He stood. Charlie jumped up and wrapped his arms around Barnaby.

"Thank you," he said.

"It's no trouble," Barnaby offered, half-hearted, before wriggling free and trudging back to his seat, where he sat back down beside Amarine.

Charlie looked to Lord Wainwright and held his empty hands out, as if to offer up an apology.

"I didn't find a talisman," he said as he lowered his head.

Stifled laughs rose and fell from the twins and Cassian.

"Fret not, young man," Magister Iron's voice boomed. "I, Magister Irons, for your tenacity and steadfast bravery, hereby formally offer you, Charles Cottman, a position among the Spellkeepers. Should you accept, you agree to safeguard all knowledge and reagents needed by Spellweavers to secure the future of Sominor. You take the duty to aid them in their battles and treat their wounds. You devote your life to this cause at any cost. Do you accept?"

Charlie looked to the rest of the room for answers. Ophelia thought it unfair to press him with such an offer so abruptly, especially after such a deadly trial. Lord Wainwright smiled, closed his eyes, and nodded. Charlie smiled back. He turned to Magister Irons, the confusion in his eyes replaced with determination.

"I accept," he said. A gentle applause filled the room.

"May I present, our newest Spellkeeper, Charles Cottman." Magister Irons grabbed one of Charlie's hands and hoisted it into the air. Lady Nikollette and Lord Wainwright stood and applauded. Ophelia and the other wards followed. The wards of Knightridge Manor, along with Lady Knight, remained seated.

Once the applause ended, Charlie took a seat beside the other Spellkeepers. His grin was ear-to-ear as they patted him on the back and shook his hand.

"Cassian Darrow." Eldweaver Finch proceeded with the ceremony. "The trial waits for you next. Are you ready to face it?"

Cassian stood up and marched toward the door. The snide expression and tone had gone, the rude young man replaced by a dutiful soldier. "I am."

Without hesitation, he opened the door, stepped in, and slammed it shut behind himself. When the door shattered this time, Ophelia felt it appropriate.

Once again, after an hour, Eldweaver Finch dismissed everyone to be summoned when the door reassembled. This time, the Spellkeepers joined the others. Lady Nikollette encouraged Ophelia to get something to eat while she could, as her trials would be next.

The Spellkeepers guided the others to the dining hall while they waited. Owen and Lydia opted to stay and await Cassian's return. Ophelia was grateful. The eldest Spellkeeper, Armando – or Mondo, as he preferred to be called – offered to prepare something for everyone to eat while they waited.

The dining hall was surprising to Ophelia. While the rest of Spellevue seemed to have some hidden magic around every corner, the dining hall seemed as unremarkable as the kitchen at Deadwood Manor.

The kitchen in the Dining Hall sat behind a wooden door, and there was an open section of wall through which she could watch Mando cook. She sat between Barnaby and Amarine at one of four long tables arranged two-by-two. Constance and Mordecai sat beside Amarine. Charlie, Rosalin, and the other Spellkeeper, Vasha, sat across from them. The other three tables sat empty. Candelabras hung from the ceiling and lit themselves as they entered. They seemed to be the only thing magical about the room. There was an inviting feel to it that made Ophelia feel welcome, a place one might find themselves missing if away for too long. The smell of something delicious washed over Ophelia. Her stomach growled.

"Hungry, Ophelia?" Vasha asked.

"I'm sorry." Ophelia blushed. "I can't believe you heard that."

"It's perfectly fine," Vasha replied. "Nothing to be embarrassed about. My stomach has been begging me to feed it since you all arrived. I found myself so wrapped up in the garden since I woke up, then preparing for your arrival, that I forgot to eat breakfast. I'm positively starving. Don't worry. Mondo is an amazing cook."

"Chef," Mondo called out from the kitchen. He came through the kitchen door back-first, turning to reveal a large pot in his hands. "There's a difference."

"Sorry." Vasha looked at him and replied, "You're an amazing chef, Mondo."

"Thank you." He set the pot down at the end of the table, where a stack of bowls sat beside a pile of spoons. One at a time, he filled the bowls and passed them down.

"No, thank *you*," Vasha countered.

"Yes, thank you, Mondo," Ophelia added as she looked down at the stew in front of her. "It looks delicious. What is it?"

"It's nothing much. A chicken stew with a couple secret ingredients and a pinch of Moonblossom to ease a troubled mind."

"Oh, my favorite." Vasha looked at Ophelia. "We don't get to have it often because Magister Irons is sensitive to Moonblossom. It puts him right to sleep."

"Yeah," Mondo added. "I remember the first time I made it for him. I had no idea. He nearly drowned in his stew!"

Vasha and Mondo laughed. Rosalin let out a slight chuckle between bites.

"Go ahead," Mondo encouraged. "Give it a taste. Everyone will be finished before you get a chance to even take a bite."

Ophelia looked to Amarine, who had just scooped a spoonful into her mouth, but still managed to add, "Id dawicious."

Ophelia giggled.

A bit of stew dripped down Amarine's cheek. She swallowed quick and wiped her face.

"It's delicious," she clarified. "Come on. No telling when your trial will start. Eat up."

Two bites. That's all Ophelia was able to eat before the dining hall door burst open.

"The door is re-assembling." Lord Wainwright this time. "Spoons down. Let's go."

Ophelia shoveled another spoonful into her mouth as she got up from her seat. She tried to savor each morsel as they hurried back to the chamber.

This time, when they returned, the door had already re-assembled itself. They sat, waiting in complete silence. Ophelia felt her entire body relax. She felt like she could just close her eyes and let the soothing silence carry her to sleep.

Moonblossom, she thought. *Must be the Moonblossom.*

The waiting continued for some time, until the Eldweavers gathered in whispers beside the door. When they finished, Eldweaver Gideon stepped forward.

"Cassian Darrow has failed the trials."

Lady Knight said nothing. She folded her arms and shot a sideways look at the twins. Ophelia noticed Lady Knight didn't seem concerned or worried in the same way that was clear on the faces of her wards, the Eldweavers, or Lady Nikollette and Lord Wainwright. It was as though she had been slighted in some way. It was anger.

Sitting beside her, Lydia's usually sharp expression softened as she lowered her head, and Owen's eyes glistened while his face struggled to remain unaffected.

"If anyone would like, we can take a moment to grieve this loss," Eldweaver Fairwind offered up.

"Just get on with it," Lady Knight grunted.

Eldweaver Fairwind looked to the De'Leon twins. Owen and Lydia looked at each other, then nodded reluctantly to Eldweaver Fairwind.

Eldweaver Fairwind then turned her gaze to Ophelia, her head titled ever so slightly. Ophelia simply nodded back, pushing through the fear that she too might not make it out alive.

"Then let us continue," Eldweaver Fairwind said to Eldweaver Gideon.

"Ophelia Ravenward," he said, "the trial waits for you. Will you face it?"

Ophelia swallowed any fear that might have been building and stood up.

"I will."

THE ENDLESS HEART OF RENÉE ROCHÉ

Renée returned home to her parents and the good people of Roché Village. She would not rest until she found a way to save Marcel. If he could sort out the magic needed to make him the horror he'd become, then certainly she could sort out the magic needed to bring him back. While part of her understood their reactions – all they had known was putting down threats – it was Bastien's reaction that hurt the most.

"There is no cure for death," Bastien had explained.

"He is not dead," she had countered.

No matter how she positioned herself or her argument, her words seemed only to fall upon deaf ears. She felt as though she stood before strangers in a sanctuary of Marcel's own design. One she had helped build. Regardless of how it all played out, Renée at least hoped young Nikollette would make it through with her heart still intact.

Her parents were excited to hear that she would be staying with them. Her mother even more so when Renée admitted it would likely be for some time. She saw the age in their faces, a weariness she'd not noticed before. She took over caring for the manor, and helping the people of Roché Village, so that her parents might rest. Unknown to her parents, with her talisman, she had also conjured up a hidden space beneath the manor, in which she could expand her knowledge of magic without disruption or cause for worry.

Renée thought it best to return to the place it had all started. To Marcel's home deep in the dead woods. If ever there was an answer to this dark riddle, she reasoned it must lie within that wretched land.

She arrived just up the road from what she had heard was now referred to as Deadwood Manor. The blown-out windows had been fixed, and the side of the manor that had taken the brunt of the damage looked brand new. If not for the dead woods that surrounded it, one would never guess anything had happened at all.

The ground was brittle at its surface, but beneath was soft and sticky. The black mud clung to her boots in heaps. She had only made it halfway to Marcel's home when a rustling among the trees caught her attention.

A rabbit bounded out from behind a fell log. Renée greeted it.

"Hello, little rabbit. I'm afraid you'll find no food in these woods."

The rabbit turned. Molting fur clung to dead skin in clumps. Ribs pierced its rotten flesh. Half its face was nothing more than a skull.

A twitch of its ear and tilt of its head. With no warning, it sped toward Renée. She kneeled, her finger stuck in the dirt. The whistle of an arrow, followed by a soft thud, brought the rabbit to stand still before Renée could draw a single line. The arrow stuck in the poor creature's only remaining eye. The rabbit thrashed about, violently trying to reach Renée. It acted as though an arrow hadn't just gone straight through its tiny head.

"Burning them is best." Nikollette's voice was unmistakable, though older, sadder. "They are difficult to destroy otherwise."

Renée stood back up and looked to the woods on her right. Nikollette came trudging toward the rabbit, bow in hand. When she reached it, she slung the bow over her shoulder, then pulled out her Timeless Tome. She scrawled a simple spell and placed it on the rabbit.

"You can rest now," she whispered. Embers crawled across the rabbit, which crumbled into a pile of ash. Nikollette pulled her arrow from the dirt and slid it back into the quiver on her back.

"They don't die?" Renée asked.

"They already have," Nikollette answered, still staring deep into the ash. "The gloom brings them back. Brings them back hungry."

"The gloom?"

"From the deadwood trees." Nikollette marched past Renée and pulled out a small knife. She stabbed it into a nearby tree and pulled it out. A gray liquid oozed from the bark like sap. "Whatever Uncle Marcel has done seems to have poisoned the woods. Left him as dead and empty as that rabbit." She looked Renée in the eye. Renée had never seen this hatred in Nikollette, this anger.

"Perhaps this gloom can cure him?"

"You still want to save him?" Nikollette's mood turned from cold, to sour. "Haven't you heard what he's done?"

She had not. She dared not ask. She shook her head.

"He's been turning people into whatever he is. Whatever Aunt Antoinette has become. Puppets, Renée. He's turning them into mindless puppets."

"He wouldn't."

"He is."

"No." Renée couldn't believe it, wouldn't. "He's still in there. He's still Marcel. He's still your uncle."

"My uncle is dead."

She sounded just like her father. It had only been one month, but to Renée, it was beginning to feel like a lifetime.

"Come with me, Nikollette. Help me end this madness."

"I am helping. I am fighting to clean up the mess our family has caused. I refuse to cower behind the walls of my manor. I will stand and face whatever terror the Endless King might bring."

Renée felt wounded. She wasn't cowering; she was fighting, too. Fighting the best way she knew how.

"If you don't want to join us, Renée, then perhaps you should go. Leave. You're quite skilled in leaving."

Renée pulled a small vial from her pocket and removed the cork. She scooped some gloom off the tree, sealed it tight, and tucked it back into her pocket. When her hand came back out, she was holding her coin. "I hope to see you again, once this is all over."

Nikollette turned her back. With the *ping* and ring of a flipped coin, Renée had gone.

Months raced by like passing thoughts. Renée buried herself in her work, unconcerned with the world above her. She kept her discoveries well-cataloged in a tome at the heart of her ever-expanding workshop. Since beginning, she had discovered many new magics.

She found ways to manipulate light and shadow, making these otherwise intangible elements very real and quite dangerous. Neither of these magics brought her any closer to a cure.

Then she found a magic hidden away in her own blood. At first, she was delighted. She thought that surely magic born of blood might hold the key to resurrection, that it must have held curative properties of some kind. She mixed samples of blood with the gloom she'd taken. Many deadly spells resulted from blood magic alone, but when mixed with the gloom, the results were far too chaotic for her to ever hope to control.

No matter what she tried, she could not find a way to reverse it. She wasn't even sure how to replicate it to begin with.

One day Renée's parents came to warn her their village and castle were no longer safe. They and the people of Roché Village were starting to flee across Sominor to Stillriver Kingdom. The Endless King and his horde were coming.

No, this isn't possible. The thought practically begged to be made real.

Her parents said they were leaving in two days' time and wished for her to join them.

Marcel arrived in one.

She heard their screams, even from deep within her workshop.

When she rushed up to find them, they had already turned. Marcel stood behind them, still smiling, Antoinette at his side.

From behind his smile, his voice bled out from somewhere inside. "Renée, my dear Renée. It has been so long and yet merely a blink. You look as lovely as ever."

"Marcel." Renée could scarcely find the words. She stood paralyzed. Tears formed and rolled down her face as he approached her.

"Fear not, my dear. When death is gone, so too goes fear."

She watched as he ran his fingernail along his own arm, drawing the gray liquid that had become his blood. His fingers painted with it, he brought his hand up to her cheek and caressed it gently. She felt a shiver run through her, a wretched comfort. When she closed her eyes, she could imagine them, together, before all of this. His gentle touch.

Marcel's nail cut her cheek.

The tears came more easily, and Renée's silent sorrow turned to sobbing.

The sobbing turned to choking.

The choking turned to laughter.

As if nothing had changed, before Renée stood the man she'd fallen so helplessly in love with. He was as handsome as he had ever been. Not a hair out of place.

"Do you see?" Marcel asked. "This is life without death."

"It's beautiful," Renée answered.

"It is," her parents said from behind Marcel.

"Ha," he chuckled. "Let us share this gift and finally bring peace to Sominor!"

His horde — Renée now saw it for the friendly crowd it was — cheered and filed out of the manor in an orderly fashion. When Marcel left, she followed. He stopped her.

"You must stay Renée," he told her. "Stay here. Stay safe."

"But I can help you. I've learned so much."

"I know you can, but if we lose…" he trailed off.

She looked into his eyes, unsure of what to say.

"If we lose, we'll need you to bring us back," Antoinette finished, smiling. "Renée, you are the only one capable of bringing us back."

"When we win, Renée, I promise to return to you. We can all be together when the day is won."

"Then I'll stay," Renée finally conceded. "Until you summon me, I'll stay right here."

She stood there, in the spot she'd promised to stay, and waited for Marcel with a smile on her face. The days crawled by until, finally, she felt him cry out for her. Then he was gone.

Her heart broke again.

Tears rolled down her smiling face.

Years had gone by.

Renée had not moved.

Nor had she slept nor eaten.

She only cried and smiled.

Marcel had been right. With death no longer her concern, it was difficult for her to be anything but happy. There was a peace within her that no heartache could dim. Still, beneath it, the heartache remained, as undying as she had since become.

"Renée." A voice swam through her mind like a thought. "I'm sorry I could not come back for you, Renée."

"It's okay." Renée's joyful voice broke the silence that had since weighed down the vacant halls of her childhood home. "I can come to you. Tell me how you died, and I will join you."

"I have not died, my dear Renée. I have been trapped. Trapped in an endless slumber."

"If I can hear you, I can save you. Tell me where you are."

"I am in a dream. I am a dream."

"I will do anything you ask of me, Marcel. Tell me how to wake you."

There was no answer. Renée finally moved. Her joints cracked, but there was no pain. Never pain. Not anymore. She searched the manor, calling for him. "Marcel, can you hear me? Tell me what to do."

Nothing.

There was no way of knowing where he was trapped or how.

The Neverwas, Renée thought. Aloud, she said, "I will find you, Marcel. I will rescue you. I will open a door, and I will tear you from your slumber. I love you, Marcel."

"And I you, Renée," the faint voice of a dream drifted through her.

Time passed over Renée with little consequence. Her work was all there was left. Her workshop expanded, chamber after chamber filled with botched experiments and enchanted failures. She was unaware how long it had been or how much of her own blood she'd spilled. All she really knew was, after each failed spell, or hex, or creature conjured completely on accident, she felt no closer to bringing her Marcel back.

"If only I could sleep," Renée lamented. "If only I could dream. Then, I could find you in slumber. How can I set you free if I can't even reach you?"

The only other living thing within earshot was a lump of misshapen skin that slept on her desk, its single eye closed, drool dripping from its toothless mouth, and its boneless mass rising and falling in a peaceful rhythm.

"Can you see him? Can you see Marcel?" She sighed. "Why am I asking you? I still don't even know what you are or how I conjured you into existence. I'm not even entirely sure what it is you are meant to do. Sleep, I suppose."

She watched the blob sleep, envious, and thought, *if only you knew what I was saying. If only you dreamt as we dreamt.*

She sat up suddenly, like lighting had struck her chair, run up her spine, and brought her brain to life.

"Dreams!" she shouted. The blob on her desk screamed, undulated, and clumsily rolled off. It hit the floor with a yelp and worked lumps of muscle under itself, wobbling as it rolled away from the excited Renée.

"If I am to reach into slumber, if I am to pull Marcel out, then I must open a door."

There would be no rest until it was done.

THE TRIAL OF OPHELIA

The doorknob was warm. She had expected it to be cold. It hummed gently beneath her timid fingers. The moment she touched it, she could hear it sing. Her reflection, the only one she had seen in the door since she'd first laid eyes on it, looked back at her with worry. She swung the door open and faced the darkness. With it came a force – tender, beckoning her into its embrace.

When she stepped in and closed the door, a light shone down from above her. She was in a hole. She had been there before. Her skin prickled with an irritating pain. All along her body gray threads connected her to the surrounding walls.

Panic was swift to find her.

The threads grew in thickness and pulled her in all directions. Ophelia screamed. She twisted and turned, desperate to tear herself free, each movement becoming more pointless as the threads pulled tighter. Just as she was about to give up, just as she felt her body might be pulled apart, the threads snapped under the force of their own greedy tension. For a second, she was weightless, then she fell. Her arms frantically searched for something to hold onto.

Roots.

No, bones.

For the second time in her life, Ophelia found herself climbing out of a hole.

She emerged in the Deadwoods, exactly as she had expected to. However, this time it wasn't raining. The moon hung above her in the clear night sky, and an unkindness of ravens circled it. They didn't seem to pay her any mind. For that much she was grateful. As it had before, the hole from which she emerged had vanished.

Ahead of her, a flash of lightning appeared, followed by a crash of thunder appeared from the cloudless sky. The ravens broke from their formation at her startled scream and cawed loudly. Ophelia covered her ears until they had gone.

A growing flame among the trees caught her eyes. It was a vibrant purple, whose light cast looming shadows that gnarled and clawed along the dead ground toward her. Like the dark talons of some hungry beast.

She felt small.

At the center of the flame, a figure emerged. She felt its eyes fall upon her. A heaviness pressed upon her heart, as if something were trying to twist it to their own whims. She felt helpless as the compulsion to call out stole away with her voice.

"Hello?" The word eked out, nearly inaudible.

"Hello," a voice whispered back from right beside her. At that moment, the purple flames snuffed out and clouds filled the sky. The darkness returned.

Or had it always been there?

The figure grew, bubbling and warping, limbs twitching and changing, until it towered over the Deadwoods in the form of a raven. The raven leaned in close, stopping a finger's length from Ophelia's face. A cold gust of air poured over her.

"What—" was all Ophelia could utter before the raven's beak split open. An unseen force wrapped around her heart and pulled her into the raven's dark maw.

The wind blew past her, and she fell face-first into a void. It felt as empty as her past anytime she had attempted to seek it out. Without warning, she found the ground at her feet. She was running through the Deadwoods again.

Cold rain bit at her skin, the muddy ground sank underfoot, and she was overcome with the idea that an undead buck was hot on her heels. When she glanced back, there was nothing but empty woods. Her knees slammed into something hard, sending her toppling into a puddle.

She shot back up, wiping the dirty water from her eyes. Pain shot through her body in bolts. A headstone stuck out of the mud behind her.

Ophelia couldn't help but wonder how a headstone had come to find itself in the middle of the Deadwoods. Something was chiseled into the stone, beneath the mud covering it. She reached out a hand and wiped the mud free and read the word.

Mercy.

Before she could form a single thought about what it might have meant, another headstone burst out of the mud beside her. She screamed.

Putrid flesh swung from a skeletal hand that shot out from the ground beneath it. With it came the horrid scent of rot. It reached for Ophelia, gripping the toe of her boot. She kicked the dead hand free and jumped up, tearing off through the Deadwoods as swift as her feet could carry her, as hard as her breath would allow.

Along her path, more headstones unearthed themselves, screaming for her attention; blocking her path, and forcing her to turn. She didn't slow. She kept running, full speed, past the headstones and the dead hands of those they watched over, through the dead branches and around the trees, until her chest burned with bitter cold air. This time, however, there were no ravens to guide her, only fear.

She ran until she came tearing out into a clearing. More headstones surrounded her. The rain stopped, as did she, and a stillness crept in with the pale light of the moon. Beneath each headstone, an empty hole. No coffins, no bodies, just air and dirt.

"You are with us," voices whispered from below. "And we, with you."

Ophelia's mind screamed for her to look away, but her heart lured her forward. The grave seemed to invite her in, made her feel as though everything would be just fine if she chose to lay down. That this place was safe.

"We can guide you."

"We can save you."

"You'll be with us forever."

"Daughter of Deadwood," the voice of the raven whispered to her.

She turned to find nothing. When she turned back toward the cemetery, the graves had vanished. Instead, only a single step in front of her, there stood Deadwood Manor. The ground hung at an unnerving distance below her. Old statues looked up at her. This wasn't the window to the study. Inside this window, just beneath it, sat a cushioned bench.

Ophelia pressed her face up to the window and pounded on it. A young girl, who looked remarkably like Lady Nikollette, jumped in her seat. On her desk, the girl penned furiously at the pages of a book.

"Hey," Ophelia screamed, "let me in!"

The girl didn't so much as glance at her. Instead, she tore the page free and tossed it over her shoulder. It fell to the floor with the weight of a stone. A second window appeared behind the first. Ophelia didn't understand. She pounded on the window again. Once more, the girl jumped, scrawled something, ripped it free, and tossed it to the floor.

Two more windows. The girl was further away and more obscured through the four panes of glass. The more Ophelia pounded and yelled, the faster the girl seemed to write, and the more windows stood between them. They appeared at such a rapid pace; Ophelia couldn't keep count. Before too long, she found herself pounding on a dark tunnel of endless glass.

It shattered.

Ophelia fell through.

It was a short fall, and she recognized instantly the room in which she landed, even with her lying on the floor and looking up at the ceiling, hexagonal and unmistakable. She was in the Trial Chamber. She was back at Spellevue.

"I made it?" she asked, then laughed. "I made it!"

She sat up. At her feet, strewn about the floor in a shimmering mess, shards of glass sparkled. The doorknob still hung in the air.

"What's going on?"

Ophelia jumped to her feet and turned to the others. They were all sitting there, unmoved, their skin pale and their faces sunken.

"No." Ophelia shook her head. "No, this isn't real."

A sound echoed through the open door leading to the empty hall. Someplace in the distant corridors of Spellevue. Someone was still there. Still alive.

"Hello?" Ophelia worked her way through the labyrinthine passages of Spellevue, following the sound to its source. Each door seemed to fold Spellevue back in on itself. She walked at first, but as the sound grew, so did her pace.

Before long, she was running as fast as her legs would carry her. Her shoulder ached from slamming through door after door, and her spirit sank deeper when she was met with nothing more than another corridor, each increasingly similar to the one before it. Ophelia had nearly given up until she turned a corner. The corridor opened to rows of pillars that led to a large, round door. Etched into the metal was a fractal of interconnected rings that appeared to move like intersecting ripples on water. A figure stood before it, slamming its fists onto the surface.

"What happened?" Ophelia asked. Her voice came out meek.

The figure paused mid-swing and slowly turned its head with a low growl. The light from the fire burning within the pillars flashed in the creature's eyes. Ophelia recognized its face. How could she not? She had stood nearly within arm's reach as it snarled at her through a broken window. She had watched it mend broken bones and jump back to its feet after falling from such tremendous heights. She had watched it burn to cinder under the skilled hands of Lady Nikollette.

"You're dead," she told it, as if she could convince it to not exist. "I saw you die."

The ghoul smiled.

"I remember you," it growled. "You looked delicious."

Ophelia took a step back.

"Don't go. I'm hungry."

Ophelia turned and ran. The halls twisted in spirals and rolled in hills. Each open door slammed as she came near. The warm breath of the ghoul caressed the back of her neck in a chilling rhythm.

"You can't run forever," its ragged voice whispered into her ear. She could practically feel its lips against her face. Her skin crawled.

It's right, she thought. *One way or another, this is going to end. I have to do something.*

A pain pounded at Ophelia's right hip, followed closely by the left side of her neck. Each step brought another wave of pain. Each wave intensified. A book bounced at her hip, held by a strap that ran across her chest.

I know this book, but I don't know magic.

Ophelia grabbed the book and held it as she continued to run. Echoing laughter came at her from every direction. The stone floors of Spellevue crumbled a little more with each corridor.

I must try.

She held the book in one hand and held her other hand over the image of the quill. She had no clue how to summon it. Her legs on auto-pilot, she cleared her mind.

Intent. Will. Action.

The texture of the feather shifted up under her hand. She ran her fingers over it until they closed around the hollow bone that ran through it.

"Got it," she whispered, then stopped, turned, flipped open the book. She found herself alone in a dark room in front of a glass door, the quill in her hand nothing more than an ordinary raven's feather.

Her chest, heaving from exhaustion, felt like it might explode when a burst of laughter escaped. She had never been so happy to see a door in all her life.

Ophelia regarded the feather in her hand with much curiosity. Black, with glints of purples and blues. She wondered what powers it held and marveled at the idea that something so light, so common, so small could carry any weight at all. Her fingers ran along it, from the base all the way to the tip.

Soft.

Ophelia looked at the door. Her reflection smiled back.

The glass door swung open to reveal Spellevue on the other side, like a sole painting hanging in an entirely black room. She was concerned when she wasn't met with any familiar faces. Her first step through was one filled with caution. The rest of her followed, emerging like a long-slumbered and world-wary animal at the start of spring.

The benches were empty.

This isn't happening.

She turned to see if the door was still in pieces. It wasn't.

"Is anyone there?" She didn't yell this time. Instead, it was a near whisper.

"Ophelia." A girl's voice struggled to speak from outside the room.

Ophelia rushed out to find it. Just outside, Vasha lay on the ground with a swollen face. Down the hall, Rosalin lay, a small pool of blood beneath her.

"What happened? Where is everyone?"

"Gone," was all Vasha could manage to say before she lost consciousness.

"Vasha." Ophelia panicked. She tried to wake her, but it was no use. Carefully, Ophelia leaned over and put an ear to Vasha's chest. Her heart was still beating.

When she sat back up, another beating sound came dancing down the hall. It was a sound she knew.

It was the sound of something pounding its fist against a large, metal door.

A Beacon is Lit

Barely a breath had passed since Ophelia had stepped through the Looking Glass Door; its shattered fragments on the floor. At that precise moment, Lady Nikollette's eyes caught sight of the amulet adorning Magister Iron's neck, pulsating with an unwelcome glow. The timing felt exquisitely ill-fated, and yet he appeared oblivious to the phenomenon. Lady Nikollette cleared her throat, causing the room to pivot their attention toward her. She extended her finger, singling out Magister Iron.

"It would seem as though a beacon has been lit," she informed him.

He looked down and grabbed the amulet. "A keen eye as always," he said before turning to Mondo. "Mondo, why don't you go and check the map? Pay a visit, and return to us with your findings. We'll dispatch accordingly."

Mondo nodded and ran out of the room.

"Unfortunate timing," Eldweaver Finch remarked.

"I was thinking the exact same," Nikollette agreed. She had never much believed in coincidence. Not when magic was in play.

In a matter of minutes, Mondo reappeared, his expression urgent. Startled whispers filled the air as he relayed the news: the beacon had been lit by the governor of Springhill, a quaint settlement that had emerged from the ashes of Roché Village in the aftermath of the Endless War. A breathtaking hue of vibrant purple painted the evening sky, coming from the desolate Roché Manor. An unsettling revelation followed—the disappearance of two individuals, a mystery that had sent a rippling unease throughout the inhabitants of Springhill.

"That's impossible," Eldweaver Finch remarked. "That manor has been empty for years. Victor and I searched it after the war. The Roché family perished. What force could have taken up residence in those abandoned halls?"

"He's right," Eldweaver Gideon confirmed. "And Locals know well to stay clear. It couldn't be her, could it?"

"Who else knows magic but her and us?" Eldweaver Finch asked.

"It is unwise to jump to conclusions," Eldweaver Fairwind spoke, trying to calm the two men. "No one is saying Reneé has returned. We shall go and investigate. Ophelia has only just begun her trials. Likely she will not be finished for at least, what was it?" She looked at Owen.

"I'm sorry?" He seemed surprised.

"Your time. How long did it take you?"

"Oh, forty-five minutes, ma'am."

"She'll be in there for at least forty-five minutes, I would imagine. That should give us ample time."

"And if Reneé is alive?" Nikollette asked, calmly rising to her feet. "She would be formidable, even for you. Pardon my saying, it may even require us all."

"I hate to admit," Eldweaver Gideon said, his tone grave, "but Lady Nikollette is right. She always was one step ahead of us, and if she's been hidden away, left to her own devices, there's no telling what magic she might wield."

"We can't rightly take everyone," Eldweaver Finch said in disbelief. "It would leave Spellevue vulnerable. It would leave Ophelia vulnerable."

"I'll stay," Magister Irons offered. "Vasha, Rosalin, Charles, and myself. Mondo is more than capable to aid you all, and the four of us can manage Spellevue in the meantime."

"Perhaps the young Spellweavers should remain?" Lord Wainwright asked.

"We will do no such thing," Lady Knight protested. "Let your wards grow weak. Owen and Lydia are always at the ready to serve."

"Perhaps it would not be such a bad idea if we all go together," Eldweaver Fairwind suggested. "The three of us and our noble lord and ladies should be enough to handle anything that awaits us at that manor. I feel it would do well to teach and inspire all our young Spellweavers to observe their seniors fighting together, should it come to that."

Silence hung in the chamber as Nikollette and the others considered the choice that lay before them.

"You know where I stand." Lady Knight stood tall.

Lord Wainwright looked to his wards. Mordecai and Constance nodded to him with a fierce determination on each of their faces. "Count us in as well. We'll never deny the call."

"Well." Nikollette sat for a moment and closed her eyes. She already knew what Amarine and Barnaby would say. They were not ones to seek out conflict, nor were they apt to back down. "I suppose whatever happens is meant to happen."

They each pulled out their coins, apart from Constance.

"I haven't got a coin," she said sheepishly.

"Right." Magister Irons reached into a pouch on his belt and produced one. "This is meant for you. We normally present these once the ceremony has ended. Simply imagine where you want to go and flip it."

"I know," Constance answered.

"Well," Magister Irons gave her a smile as he spoke, "I suppose you also know where Springhill is?"

"I do."

"Off you go then."

Nikollette listened to their coins ring one by one. Once they'd all gone, she told Magister Irons, "If she comes out before we return, do not bring her to us. Promise you'll keep her here."

"I promise," Magister Irons answered.

She flipped her own coin.

When she arrived, it was Constance who first caught her attention. The poor girl lay sprawled on the ground, gasping for air, her strength depleted. Mordecai hurried to her side.

"I did warn you," he chuckled lightly, his concern tinged with amusement. "Just focus on catching your breath. It gets easier, I swear it."

Nikollette joined them. "A formidable journey for your inaugural flip," she remarked. "You performed admirably. It's commendable that you managed to remain conscious after such a distance."

Constance mustered a faint, pallid smile.

The next thing Nikollette couldn't help but notice was the conspicuous absence of the purple glow. According to Mondo's report, the entire town should have had a purple glow cast upon it. Yet there shone only the waning light of dusk which painted the landscape with its subdued hues.

Last, she noticed the Eldweavers as they approached the governor with purposeful strides. If memory served her right, his name was Wendall Briarman. With a heightened sense of intrigue, she quickened her pace to join their gathering, her curiosity burning as brightly as ever. He was desperately trying to convince the Eldweavers that they'd not come in vain.

"I'm telling you, the entire hill was glowing just seconds before you arrived." The governor sounded frightened. "He saw it." Pointing to Mondo.

"Yes, I did," Mondo answered. "It looked to be coming from the manor."

"You are certain of this?" Eldweaver Gideon asked. "Absolutely certain?"

"Yes," Mondo and the Governor answered together.

"And the missing? Who were they? Would they have any reason to go into the manor?" Nikollette asked.

"Samuel and his daughter, Charlotte. Two days ago, they ventured into the mountains to find gems. Charlotte collects them. They might have passed near the manor, as there is a walkable mountain pass nearby, but they wouldn't have gone in. No one goes in. Samuel said they were going to journey out, set up camp, stay the night, then come home. They were a day late. I thought nothing of it. Then, this light started flickering at the manor. It just kept getting brighter. That's when I broke the beacon. I know it's for emergencies, but I felt like this is an emergency."

"Well," Eldweaver Finch considered, "supposing the manor was glowing, then yes, it is an emergency. Tell me, have you seen any neverbeasts around in the past weeks?"

"No, none. Nothing unusual. If we had, I would have summoned you sooner. Springhill has been nothing but peaceful for years. Honestly, it's been a governor's dream. Aside from the occasional mischievous youth, there's not much excitement to be found here."

"Glow or not," Eldweaver Fairwind added, "we owe it to the governor, and Mondo, to take them at their word and investigate. Be it nothing or otherwise."

"Thank you." Governor Briarman bowed slightly with a worried smile. "I speak for all of Springhill when I say it would ease all our minds greatly."

The moment the governor was finished, it was as if someone had lit a fire of purple flame. Their shadows grew long as the distant glow saturated the surrounding lands. Everyone in Springhill stopped what they were doing and turned to the source.

"There!" Governor Briarman shouted. "There it is! It's even brighter!"

"I see," Eldweaver Finch replied. "That settles it then."

Eldweaver Gideon took out his coin, as did the others.

"Hold on," Eldweaver Fairwind commanded. "We don't know what awaits us at that manor. Perhaps it's best we walk. The last thing I want is for a trap to materialize around me."

"Right," Eldweaver Gideon replied. "Let's get moving, then."

Nikollette walked along, flanked by Amarine and Barnaby, as their party traversed the distance in silence. As they left Springhill, the grass gave way to sparse, black stone where once stood Roché Village. The skeletal remnants of the long-abandoned homes lined the way.

With each passing moment and each determined step, the light ahead grew more radiant. Soon, the grass had gone completely, and only the loose gravel crunched beneath their feet. As they drew nearer, the brilliance became blinding, causing everyone to shield their eyes. Then, in a radiant burst, it erupted into a dazzling spectacle. The ground quaked beneath them, unleashing powerful vibrations. Constance, struggling to maintain her balance, nearly succumbed to the overwhelming force.

The light gradually faded, casting a soft veil of purple haze. A melodic hum delicately permeated the atmosphere. It made Nikollette's skin crawl.

Their pace slowed as they approached the manor, their steps heavy with trepidation. The Ironhide Mountains behind Roché Manor were still as imposing as ever. The foreboding atmosphere justified the unease that had so gripped the people of Springhill. Death, a pervasive presence, loomed in Nikollette's heart, flooding her senses. A dreadful anticipation took hold as she feared the worst for the missing villagers.

With each pulsating beat of purple light, the manor's windows seemed to throb, casting their disconcerting glow in steady pulses. The manor doors hung open, beaming the brightest. A silhouette, unmistakably that of a woman, stood before it. It captured Nikollette's attention in an instant. The name slipped past her lips, an unintended whisper compelled by some unknown impulse: "Reneé."

In response, the figure turned, calling back to her, "Nikollette, you've brought them all?"

"Reneé," Eldweaver Gideon's voice rang out, alarmed, "what have you done?"

"Lower your voice, Victor," Reneé retorted, her gaze fixated on Nikollette. "Can't you see? They slumber."

On either side of the manor doors, suspended from chains, hung a man and a young lady, their bodies restrained and seemingly lifeless.

"I've merely fulfilled my promise," Reneé added, her voice unsettling in its conviction. "I've discovered how to save Marcel. He'll be overjoyed to find you all awaiting his arrival."

From within the pulsating light, a figure materialized.

THE LOVELESS HEART OF RENÉE ROCHÉ

Dreams. How many times had she wished for a way to save Marcel from the eternal dream in which he'd been cursed to languish? Renée wondered how she could have been so blind all these years. The power to create something out of nothing, to weave a new reality where the old had once stood defiant and provide sanctuary from a world fraught with fear, and disease, and death. The source of all things which she had devoted her life to mastering. The magic of dreams.

"But how?" She asked herself, "How am I to reach in and pull him free? If beasts can leave, then so too must a man."

Tome upon tome, hidden deep within the expansive caverns of her workshop – once humble, now vast with hidden knowledge and unknowable danger – Renée poured through all that she had discovered. A mania set in, and the world melted away, until there was nothing left but herself and the scribbled ink on worn parchment that contained the entirety of her decades-long efforts.

For days, maybe weeks, she read back through her works. And for all her time and effort? Nothing.

She sat, defeated, in the deepest room of her workshop, her desk littered with old books, the cool glow of conjured stars above her. She regarded them fondly. She missed Spellevue almost as much as she ached for Marcel.

"Soon," she reminded herself. "Soon you'll have them all back. Don't give up now."

The squishy ball of living flesh she kept at her side breathed with its mouth agape, understanding nothing.

"Isn't that right?"

It blinked. A spit bubble formed around its lips. Renée popped it, absent in thought.

"But how can I enter a dream without sleeping?"

The question gnawed at her like a newborn knee-nibbler. She sat with it for days on end, letting it fester, hoping it might grow. Time measured in the sleep cycles of the amorphous flesh sack beside her. When she could no longer look at the creature she had conjured, as hideous as it was useless, a thought came to her.

Go for a walk.

She thought that perhaps stepping away was precisely what she needed.

Wandering through her workshop was like rediscovering a life she had forgotten. How long had it been since she'd visited the manor?

How long had she been so driven to continue forward that she had lost sight of the journey that had brought her so far? Each room in her workshop was a dedicated study in magic, unearthed through relentless determination or inspired enchantment.

The first, her most recent failure before Marcel had shown her life without death, had been dedicated to the magic of flesh and blood. She had spilled so much at the time, but now it felt so trivial a thing. The creature she had inadvertently conjured slumbered on her desk most days. She still had no idea as to what its purpose might be.

Next, she entered a room shrouded still in a preternatural darkness. The gloom she had recovered from the deadwood trees proved useful in unlocking the secret of light and shadow. The latter being the more powerful of the two. She remembered having left the cloud where it was to deter any would-be interlopers. It was easy to get lost in, but her muscles remembered the way through.

Finally, her first attempt at saving Marcel – though he didn't need saving – was lined with puppets. They stood watching, layered in dust, and unmoving aside from their eyes. She'd managed to bring them to life in a semi-sentient state, but she could not manage to do the same with once-living flesh. Even now, standing guard as they'd been told, they awaited further command.

All of it, worthless.

Though her endless smile never left her face, behind it, sorrow. It poked away at the veneer of happiness.

She realized she had begun to forget his face.

The stairs leading back to the manor were winding. The stone wall ran cold beneath her fingers. Moss grew between the bricks. When she came to the top, she was met with a wall.

"A wall," Renée spoke dreamily, her hands running over it in search of something her mind had let slip away with time. More aware, she said, "A door."

Renée wrapped her hand around her talisman. The wall rumbled and the stones parted; carpets of moss fell free and landed in piles before her. A wave of dusty air rushed to fill the space, and a trickle of orange light came through, landing just at her feet.

Light; she hadn't seen the light of day in many years. She remembered it being warm – comforting even – but when she reached her hand into it, she felt nothing.

A tear formed and rolled down her smiling face.

When she came to the nearest window, Renée searched for Roché Village. It was gone. An empty hill peppered with ruins stood in its place, but in the distance there appeared to be a new village. She wondered what it was called. She hoped, one day, to visit. She would, once Marcel was back. They'd travel Sominor, and together she and Marcel would save everyone.

"Come on then," she heard a voice from somewhere in the distance say. "It's a day's trip, father, and we've only just started. If you keep moving at this pace, we'll be forced to set up camp before we even get to the gulch. I don't know about you, but I'd rather not have to spend the night near Roché Manor."

"Yes, I know." Another voice, older. "These old legs certainly aren't what they used to be. You know, when you were a little girl, even when you walked fast, you were much slower."

"And when I was a little girl, I remember you having been much faster."

"You remember correctly."

First to appear over a distant hill was a young girl. She looked happy. Her jovial bounce was one of youth. Not even the large backpack and satchel could wear her down. Less energetic, there came the man. Hunched over in his ascent, it made his backpack look as though it held stones enough to build a cottage. He was older, but the resemblance between them was clear enough for Renée to know.

"Family," she whispered. She missed hers. She wished to have spent more time with them. Marcel would bring them back.

"Do you need me to give *you* a ride on *my* back?" the girl asked her father with a giggle. "Because there is no way we are sleeping here."

"Just let me get up this hill, will you? I'll be faster once the ground levels out."

"Sleep." Renée's mind was captured once again by the concept. "I miss it."

An unassuming thought, passing like any other, until it became ensnared on its way.

They can sleep. A new thought had grabbed hold of the other, and she wasn't entirely certain if it had been her own or the voice of Marcel that had conceived it. *If they can sleep, they can dream.*

The front door. It was the door he had left her through; she thought it only fitting it be the one through which he returned. Every link of each chain had been meticulously engraved with sigils tied to the flesh and blood. The same markings she had scratched into her own hands. Through them, she could feel the two travlers drift through slumber.

She stood between them, in front of the manor doors, her eyes closed as she journeyed through the darkness with her slumbering emissaries. Like horses, she took their reins and bid them to take her into dreams; into a world that never was and never would be.

Specs of light fluttered in and out of nothing. Next came a blurry haze of shifting shapes and patterns. The chaos of it overwhelmed her senses, and she struggled to maintain her grip. She could feel it press against her, pushing her back, as though she were nothing but an interloper in a sacred kingdom. Screaming at her to understand; the realm of dreams was no place for the woken. She paid it little head and pressed onward until the fabric of the chaos tore apart, swirling out into a world much like her own but so very different.

"Marcel." Renée's voice echoed through the whirling dream world. "Marcel, can you hear me?"

"Renée," his distant voice called back.

"I'm here. I'm at the manor."

"You have found me." The sound of his voice was closer. "As I never doubted you would."

"Where are you?"

"Right here."

Renée turned around. There he stood. As handsome as she remembered. Each detail of his face came crawling back up from the deep recesses of her mind, like grass at the first rain after a long drought. Her smile stretched, and laughter bubbled up from within. It quickly turned to tears.

"Don't cry," Marcel wrapped his arms around her. "It is nearly done."

"I've missed you," Renée said through muffled cries. "I've missed you dearly."

"And I you," he said, running his hand gently through her hair.

"We can stay here," Renée suggested. "We can just stay here forever."

"You know I can't. My family. Our friends. We can't leave them to die."

Renée pulled away and looked him in the eyes. She found longing, caring, and purpose. She would do anything he needed her to, because she loved him.

"I know. I'm just so tired."

"I understand. You haven't slept in so long. I promise, once we are finished, and all of Sominor is saved, life will be a dream all its own. More wonderous and beautiful than anyone could possibly imagine. I've seen it. My gift. It would be selfish not to share."

He was right. He was always right.

"Then let us begin." Taking a step back, she closed her eyes and held her hands out in front of her. She closed them into fists. A light came forcefully from between her fingers, but she refused to open them. Her arms shook when she tried to pull her hands apart. For the first time in years, the smile left her face, and pain took its place.

Her fists parted, if only a little.

She continued to pull. Screams built up in her chest until they exploded out of her. A sweat formed on her brow.

Her fists trembled and parted a little more.

The force between her hands continued to resist. The pounding of her endless heart beat hard behind her eyes and in her head. Pain, a forgotten sensation, filled her. Then, she felt Marcel's hand on her own.

Together, they pulled her hands apart until they were at her side, and she stood chest-to-chest with Marcel. When she opened her eyes, she heard a whisper from behind her.

It called her name. She recognized the voice. It sounded older, but for her it was unmistakable. This reunion, it could not have been more perfectly timed if it had been planned.

The Endless King stood at the precipice of nightmare, just behind Renée. Nikollette stepped out in front of Barnaby and Amarine, as did the others and their wards. Leading them, the Eldweavers took a defiant stance.

"Renée," Eldweaver Fairwind spoke plainly, "this must stop. So many lives lost. Do not put Sominor through that suffering again. Do not bring that pain of so much death back to us."

"Death?" Renée answered. "I'm as alive as ever I was. The only one of us who appears any closer to death is you, my old friend. Time has been unkind, but not to me. With all the magic at our disposal, Sominor seems to have changed very little. We can end the fear, the death. There can be an endless paradise."

Nikollette watched the Endless King. He watched her.

"Wake up, Renée," Eldweaver Gideon commanded. "You're already dead, as is he."

"I've only ever been alive, Victor. I am far from dead."

"Why are you all just standing around?" Owen shouted. He was furious, "She's unguarded. I can see it plain as day. Stop her, now!"

"Hush, boy," Lady Knight scolded. "Know your place."

All eyes fell on Owen. He refused to shrink.

"Would you like to be the first?" Renée asked. "Come to me; I'll not move."

Owen smiled, shifted his feet – activating a sigil embossed into his leather boots – and took off through the air toward Renée and the Endless King with his dagger in hand. She didn't move, not so much as a flinch, but Nikollette saw it. Renée's shadow. It reached out for Owen's, catching him in midair by his silhouette. He hung there, paralyzed, confused, and helpless. Renée still had not moved.

"This magic," Eldweaver Finch shouted. "This is a perversion. A corruption of all you've been taught."

"You mean, all I taught you?" Renée dropped Owen, her shadow returning to rest where the light deemed it should. "I don't want to hurt any of you. We are here to help. Isn't that right, Marcel?"

The Endless King remained still, smiling at the gathered Spellweavers, new and old alike. He said nothing. It was then that Nikollette noticed he had made no attempt to step through the portal and out of the Neverwas. It didn't take her long to understand why.

"He lied to you, Renée," she said with compassion. "You've done all this for him, and he lied to you."

Renée looked at her, the Endless King, then her again. Nikollette continued, "If he has truly returned, then I ask that he come to me, his dear niece, his only remaining family, and allow me to embrace him. To welcome his endless gift."

Renée looked to the Endless King once more. He did not move, only laughed through his unwavering smile.

"Marcel?" Renée sounded confused, wounded.

He did not answer.

"You haven't built a door, Renée," Nikollette explained. "You've built a window. He can't leave the Neverwas, because he isn't in the Neverwas. He slumbers still in Spellevue, and this is merely his dream. Can't you see it?"

The smile on Renée's face melted, for the first time in decades, as she looked to the Endless King, "Is this true, Marcel?"

He said nothing.

"Marcel, tell me, is this true?"

Only a smile.

Renée reached out for the portal. Her hand stopped at its surface. She shook her head. "No, this isn't right. I was in there. I was with you." She pounded her fists against the portal.

"You weren't," Nikollette answered, having noticed the slowed breathing of the father and daughter chained to the wall. "You were only in their dreams. It wasn't real. He isn't real. He is a projection."

"Youy lying!" Renée shouted, not bothering to turn away from Marcel.

Nikollette said, "You know I'm not. Reach in and take his hand. Bring him here and I will surrender myself to him."

"No!" Renée wailed. Beneath her, the ground rose and fell, sending a ripple out in all directions. It nearly toppled Nikollette over.

"Why do you refuse to see?" Nikollette asked, "He's had you conjure nothing, and two innocent lives paid for it."

"Quiet!" Renée screamed, turning suddenly. A shower of stone rushed toward them.

Were it not for a crimson wall rising from the ground, the stones would have surely proven fatal. Nikollette glanced over at Avery. Blood ran from his palms, and the ruby talisman around his neck shimmered with an eerie red. The wall fell, and so too did Avery. He took a knee, pale and unsteady, as his wards tended to him.

"I can't believe it! I won't!" Renée shouted, turning back to Marcel. "How could you do this to me?"

His laughter rolled over them and echoed through the mountains. Renée yelled, stopping the laughing echoes cold. Silence held them.

"The real question is why," Nikollette mused, her eyes locked onto Renée. "He would have known this could never work."

Renée fell to her knees. Her body lurched forward, and she caught herself with her hands. She sobbed quietly on all fours. Her Stoneheart hung from her neck, swaying in the sporadic mountain winds.

"To what end would it serve him?" Eldweaver Fairwind asked Nikollette. "This accomplishes nothing."

"Nothing." Renée seized on the word. "All for nothing."

She started to laugh. A chuckle at first, one that turned into a maddening cackle. Her shadow grew, reaching out in all directions. The Stone-heart swaying around her neck came to an abrupt stop.

All at once, the setting sun went black and night fell upon them. Renée screamed. The moon and the stars snuffed out, one by one, as Renée's shadow swelled. Nikollette could hardly see the others among the dark miasma.

"Spellevue!" Nikollette shouted. "He brought us all out here, away from Spellevue!"

The Stone-heart around Renée's neck became the only light Nikollette could see. The ground violently shook, and the mountains behind the castle cracked and growled.

"We must return to Spellevue," Eldweaver Fairwind cried. "Everyone, go! Now!"

Nikollette turned to Barnaby and Amarine. Barnaby flipped his coin and vanished. Amarine dropped hers. It bounced into the darkness, Renée's jilted screams nearly deafening. Nikollette and Amarine searched for her coin. A loud crack broke through the screams, coming from the mountain. A roaring rumbling followed. Amarine found her coin, and Nikollette made sure she flipped it.

She turned to Renée one last time, and before she slipped away with the flip of her coin, she looked on as Ironhide Mountain came tumbling down over Roché Manor.

Nikollette reappeared in Springhill. The purple light had gone, and the darkness had dissipated. The mountain peak that once sat behind Roché Manor, was gone. It sat in a pile atop the ruined manor.

"What happened?" Governor Briarman asked from behind her. She turned to face him, her heart breaking.

"They're gone. I'm sorry. I must go, but I'll return to explain everything."

"Are the rest of us safe?"

"You are."

Nikollette flipped her coin again.

Spellevue found her as dark-purple flames flickered out.

Ophelia met her gaze, wild-eyed and weary, before the poor girl collapsed to the floor.

DANGER FROM WITHIN

Ophelia didn't want to believe she was out of the trials. Desperately, her mind worked to convince herself that none of this was real. Her new friends weren't missing, they weren't lying in the cooridoor behind her, clinging dearly to the last vestiges of life within them. That couldn't be real. It was the trial. A nightmare loop of adversity conjured out of her head to test her mettle.

But why does this feel different? Why does this feel real?

"Nikollette, Amarine, Barnaby?" Ophelia whispered as she crept toward the banging sound. "Are you there?"

Banging came back as the only reply.

The magic and wonder that had entranced her upon arrival had been unceremoniously stripped from Spellevue, replaced by nothing more than mounting anxiety and the desire to flee. Despite those feelings, Ophelia pressed on. She might not have had any recollection of her life before the Deadwoods, but she was determined to hold on to those who had made what few memories she now possessed worth keeping. If the danger from her trial had somehow found a way into the real world, she was responsible for it, wasn't she? Was that even possible?

The halls of Spellevue were no longer like they had been in the trials. They didn't twist or turn, didn't rise or fall, and they certainly didn't stretch on and on in an endless maze. There also seemed to be remarkably fewer doors.

Eventually, she found herself faced with a wide corridor, one with a high ceiling, flanked on either side with pillars whose torches flicked from within them, leading her to the door. Just as it had before, standing before it was a ghoul, pounding away at the immovable slab of metal. She didn't need to see its face to know that it was a different ghoul than the one she'd encountered in Evergreen.

This one was bigger.

Stronger.

Even though she hadn't made a sound when she entered, the ghoul stopped what it was doing, its hand slowly falling to its side. Its head twitched up and down, and Ophelia could just hear short, sharp breaths being taken in. The ghoul turned its head, sniffing at the air. Ophelia trembled, and she could have sworn her racing heart stopped beating the second it made eye contact with her. A smile formed on its face.

An eerie symphony of primal echoes rose into a deep, guttural growl as its smile opened. Its black gaze hardened as the growl transformed into a dissonant screech, ripping through the air. It tore at Ophelia's ears. She flinched, and it stopped cold. The ghoul burst forth with jagged claws outstretched, its twisted face contorted into a grotesque mask of sadistic pleasure.

Ophelia ran.

Back through each door, slamming them shut behind her, each buying her another few steps distance.

"Help," she screamed to the hollow halls of Spellevue. "Anyone!"

She closed in on the trial chamber and decided to take a turn. The last thing she wanted was to lead it back to Vasha and Rosalin. If they were still alive, surely the ghoul would be happy to finish the job.

"Ophelia," a familiar voice called out ahead of her. She turned right to find Charlie's head poking out from a room. He waved her in. "Hurry."

She could hear the ghoul bursting through the door in the hall behind her, and she sprinted toward Charlie as quick as she could. He stepped aside as she approached and shut the door the second she had passed. She came up hard against a wall, stopping herself with her hands before slamming into it face first. They were in a small room. A closet she could only guess.

Charlie was quick to work a broomstick into the handle of the door. Outside, she could hear the ghoul turn the corner and slow to a stop not too far from the closet.

"Where you go?" The ghoul sounded as if it were choking on the words. They came out in coughing grunts. Its voice sounded unnaturally human. Like it was imitating multiple voices, all at once. It continued down the hall, stalking. Ophelia could hear it sniffing again. She and Charlie backed up as far from the door as they could, the sliver of light beneath it obscured by shadow.

Ophelia didn't know what to do, but she held her feather tight, stood in front of Charlie, and waited. The ghoul sniffed at the door, then gave the handle a few hard tugs.

The broom held.

Well done, broom.

Silence followed. It lingered there in the closet with them and held their breath for them. Ophelia didn't know what it was her talisman could do, but she hoped it was working, wished it so. She thought that if it had been a Clockwork Heart, she could summon a golem of brooms and blankets to fight the ghoul. Or, had it even been a quill and a book, perhaps she could weave magic and put a swift end to the terrible neverbeast. It was neither of those things; it was a feather. Though it was less than helpful against the likes of a ghoul, she was relieved all the same when the ghoul finally took its leave, taking the silence with it and setting their breath free.

What good is a feather, she wondered, *if I can't even use it to write?*

"I think it's safe," Charlie whispered. "Let's go get Magister Irons. He will be able to help."

"Where is everyone?" Ophelia hoped they were okay. She needed to know.

"There was a beacon, just after you entered the trial. I don't know exactly what it was, but they mentioned Renée. Does that name mean anything to you?"

"No," Ophelia answered. "Magister Irons didn't say?"

"He did not. Told me there would be time enough to go over things during my training. We went to his office once the others left. He wanted to go over his expectations and I—"

"Charlie," Ophelia stopped him. "Let's go find him."

"Right."

Charlie took the utmost care in removing the broom and cracking the door. He led Ophelia to Magister Irons' office, where they found him face down at his desk, a candle burning and a half-drunken tea cup beside him.

"Magister Irons." Charlie tried to keep his voice down as he rushed over.

"Is he…?"

Charlie held a hand in front of Magister Iron's face and waited a moment. "No, he's asleep," Charlie sounded confused, then angry. "How could he sleep through all that screaming? Wake up, you old fool." He shoved Magister Irons, but the Irons did not wake.

"A spell, maybe?" Ophelia still knew very little about this world, but it was the only thing that made sense.

"Maybe, but who? All the Spellweavers are gone, and as far as I'm aware, neverbeasts can't use magic."

Magic. An idea stirred within Ophelia.

"I need to find something to write with," she said, "and some parchment to write on."

"You can't be serious," Charlie countered, incredulously. "You've only just completed your trial, and you don't even know what your talisman does. Have you woven magic before? Do you know how? You'll die facing that thing. It won't wait for you to figure it out. You know that, don't you?"

"I do." Ophelia searched the drawers of the desk as Charlie protested. "But we have no idea when everyone will come back, and neither of us knows how to reach them. Vasha? Rosalin? They were still alive when I found them. Unconscious, but alive. If that thing finds them again, or Magister Irons for that matter, then it might just finish them off."

Ophelia found a loose sheet of paper and a fountain pen. She turned to Charlie, determined. "I may have never woven magic, but I came out of that trial with this feather. This is what I'm meant to do. I'm going to do it. You stay here; barricade the door. Don't come out until someone comes to get you."

"You mean, until you come to get me?" She could see the fear in his eyes when he asked.

She smiled. "When I come to get you."

She left and shut the door behind her. The sound of chairs hitting the other side of the door followed shortly.

She wandered the halls, the raven's feather in her pocket and the pen and paper in her hands. Each gentle step she took echoed across the stone as she worked her way back toward the round door. When she mustered up the courage, she called out for the ghoul.

"I'm here, all alone!"

A familiar sound rolled through the halls. Instead of a growl, it grew to what sounded very much like laughter.

"He-hello?" Suddenly, Ophelia wasn't so certain of her plan. Any remnants of her certainty vanished at the sound of footsteps racing toward her. She took off in the opposite direction.

"No!" she shouted, "Stay away!"

She ran toward the World's Room with the ghoul gaining at every turn. The slapping of its bare feet and the subtle click of its clawed toes made her wonder how such a creature could still look so human, how Barnaby was so unlike this monster.

Hands bouncing with her stride, Ophelia tried her best to weave a spell. She thought about which would be easiest and most effective. She settled on a repulsion spell. She remembered it. Three lines. One in the center, two more at its sides, slightly offset to form a chevron-type pattern. The lines were messy, and the quill nearly punctured the paper she struggled to hold over her palm.

That'll have to do, she thought, tearing the spell free. The ghoul was closing in. She took a moment to apply her will and intent, then threw the scrap of paper behind her.

She looked back to find the ghoul only slightly annoyed by the invisible force, perhaps slowing it down only half a step. She thought some more and settled on a descension spell. This time, she slowed a little to steady her hand. It was simple. The same, but upside down and with a horizontal line running through the bottom.

The sound of the ghoul's clawed toes gained on her quickly.

She tore it free and tossed it down.

This time, she could hear it stumble. When she rounded the next corner, she stole a glance. It was fumbling over itself, trying to get back on its feet.

The World's Room opened around Ophelia, and she ran across the map of Sominor, trying her best to think of something that might stop the ghoul completely, or at least long enough. She felt weak. Not like she had felt after running from that buck, but like she hadn't slept at all the night before.

The buck.

Ophelia thought about the spell Lady Nikollette had used. The image slowly formed in her mind. She forced the memory to the surface with as much clarity as she could. It had been a triangle, with three jagged lines cutting through it.

What direction do the jagged lines point? Does it matter?

Bastien's book had waxed on about the importance of precision in weaving magic into the world, while Marcel's had spoken more about the will and intent behind the art of weaving. At the moment, Ophelia wished she had bothered to clarify this discrepancy with Nikollette.

The laughing growl of the ghoul echoed around her, signaling its entrance into the room. She turned to face it.

It circled her, a sinister smile never dropping from its wretched face. Ophelia took in each breath as if it would be her last. With each lunging movement the ghoul made toward her, a short, involuntary scream escaped and she took a step back. The creature seemed to be enjoying Ophelia's terror. Until it didn't.

She didn't know what it had seen, but it ceased its pacing abruptly and ran directly toward her, tearing across the scaled-down map like some terrible giant set loose upon the land.

The map.

Ophelia kneeled where she stood. She lay the paper on the floor and let the ink from her quill flow free. No time to fret over the details. She drew what she could see in her mind. With each stroke, the hungry breath of the ghoul drew nearer.

An inverted triangle, a jagged line at its center and two more on either side, their jagged points facing inward. Pouring herself into each innocuous line.

The ghoul was upon her as the quill finished working. Ophelia slid the paper toward it and tried to scoot as far from it as she could. She wondered if such a spell could work indoors. There were no clouds in the artificial sky above her. The answer came faster than she thought it would.

The hair on her arms, and legs, and back of her neck all stood on end. A blinding flash of light appeared at nearly the exact same moment, followed by a loud crack. As Ophelia was hurled away from the ghoul, she felt heat envelop her and an electric buzz permeate her senses.

She landed at the edge of Sominor, gasping for air with lungs seized by the dazzling chaos of the moment. She righted herself with shaking muscles. Her breath came back in a fit of coughing. There was nothing in her ears except the reverberant ring of thunder. Looking through blurred vision, Ophelia searched for the ghoul, hoping it had met the same fate as the undead buck.

It had not.

Smoldering on the map, where the lightning had come crashing down, the ghoul lay twitching and blackened. She stood to get a better look and her mind swam, sending her stumbling in search of her balance. Past the ghoul, the muffled voice of Eldweaver Fairwind came as the old woman appeared from thin air. One by one, the others blinked into existence beside the Eldweaver. Ophelia looked at them and spoke. She couldn't hear her own voice, but hoped the word "ghoul" made it out.

Not a second after she'd finished speaking, the ghoul sat up. The burns that had been seared into its snarling face by the lightning, crawled their way back toward the source of the strike, and the ghoul roared furiously at Ophelia. Getting to its feet looked painfully difficult, but before it could stand, it was swallowed whole by a wall of dark purple fire.

The heat washed over Ophelia, and she turned away. The roar of the flames and the wailing of the ghoul rose into her ears as her hearing reluctantly returned.

When the flames had gone, so too had the ghoul. Only a small pile of ash remained, swirling in a whirl of heat, the only evidence it had ever existed at all.

Ophelia looked at the group of Spellweavers, happy to see them alive and well. The meager smile she had managed dropped when she could not find Lady Nikollette among them.

The others rushed to her side. Mondo was first. "Are you alright?" he asked, examining her.

"I'm fine," Ophelia managed to say; the room started to spin. "Vasha, Rosalin, Irons. They're hurt."

"Barnaby." Mondo looked at him. "Do you think you could tend to them? Ophelia doesn't appear to be injured, just disoriented."

"Yes." Barnaby looked at Ophelia. "Where are they?"

"The trials," Ophelia answered, then spotted Lady Nikollette, appearing where the others had a moment ago. They exchanged glances as Ophelia felt the strength drain from her body.

The world went black.

THE RAVEN'S FEATHER

Faces. Worried expressions on each of them. That was what greeted Ophelia when the world came fading back into view. Her head ached terribly, and she felt as though someone had punched her in the chest. Dull vibrations rippled out to her fingertips. Smoke whirled in front of her with the scent of herbs. The last thing she could remember was running from a ghoul. She sat up, startled.

"The ghoul! There's a ghoul!" she nearly shouted between panicked breaths.

"It's gone." Mondo held her. He snuffed out the burning leaves of vibrance he held in his other hand.

"It's okay," Vasha assured her. Rosalin nodded by her side.

Ophelia sat up. Lady Nikollette's red eyes fell upon her, with a smile just beneath them.

"Do you remember what happened?" Eldweaver Fairwind asked.

"I…" Ophelia searched her mind for the missing moments that had landed her on the floor in pain. Worry dug away at the empty space, desperate to uncover the hidden truths she knew to be in there. Little by little, she found them in the order they occurred. "I remember coming out of the trials. No one was there. Vasha and Rosalin were in the hall; they had been hurt. I found a ghoul pounding on a large, round, metal door with three circular sigils contained within one larger one." As she explained, she noticed the Eldweavers exchanging silent glances, "And it chased me when it saw me. I ran, but Charlie saved me. We hid in a closet."

She grabbed her head. A fresh jolt of pain pummeled at the backs of her eyes.

"Take your time, dear," Lady Nikollette assured her. "It's going to be okay."

Ophelia stood up. The pressure in her head and chest rose with her, then subsided. She looked around and noticed the burnt section of Sominor just past the others, on the floor. They all parted as she moved toward it. Images flashed through her mind. She turned toward the hall she'd run out of, the ghoul just behind her.

"I was with Charlie in Magister Irons' office. He was asleep but we couldn't wake him. So, I grabbed a pen and some parchment, thinking I could do something to stop the ghoul. I remembered a few spells from the books I had read. I tried a couple, but nothing worked. So, I lured it here where there was more room. Then I remembered the sigil you drew." She pointed to Lady Nikollette. "When I had enough space, I drew the sigil and the lightning. It—"

"You lie," Owen shouted from across the room. "You could not have woven such a powerful spell."

Ophelia scowled, her eyes locked with his, "I drew the sigil and wove the lightning. I can still feel the electricity." She turned to look at Lady Nikollette. "Did I defeat it?"

"No," Eldweaver Fairwind interjected. "I did, but had you the proper weaver's training, I've no doubt your spell would have had the precision and power needed to fell such a neverbeast."

"We don't even know if she even has a talisman," bemoaned Owen in an accusatory manner.

Like the self-lighting sconces in the entrance hall of Spellevue, Ophelia remembered her talisman in a sudden flash. Ophelia reached into her pocket and produced the raven feather.

"I do." She smiled back at Owen. "I came out with this."

"I wonder what it does," Amarine jumped in. "Maybe the power of flight? That would be useful. I also hope you'd be kind enough to take me on a flight."

"You've got a talisman, haven't you?" Barnaby grunted from across the room. He winced and held a hand to his head. Behind him stood Magister Irons, along with Rosalin and Vasha. "Also, I caught this one asleep on the job."

"Irons," Eldweaver Gideon scolded. "How could you fall asleep when entrusted with the security of Spellevue? Explain yourself."

"My apologies, Eldweaver," Irons bowed his head while he approached. "It would seem as though someone, or something, had spiked my tea with Moonblossom."

"He's right," Barnaby confirmed. "I could smell it before I even entered the room."

"Odd," Eldweaver Finch commented. "I have no reason to doubt you, and I do not, but a ghoul making tea seems a rather peculiar thing. Nevertheless, I'm happy to see you well."

"Something warranting further discussion at another time I hope," Eldweaver Gideon added.

"At your pleasure," Irons replied.

"So." Owen jabbed at Ophelia with his razor tongue. "A feather? Doesn't look terribly useful. Do you suppose that's why it was given to you?"

Ophelia took one angry step toward him. A storm of furious thoughts beat over her mind, too fast and too chaotic for her to settle on one. The words she wished to say, the things she wished to do. She felt, in that moment, that Owen deserved every one of them.

Owen Stumbled back on his heels, as if taken by surprise. Had Lydia not steadied him, he would have landed on his butt. When he'd gathered himself, his face turned bright red.

"You've gone mad! Is anyone going to do anything about that?"

Everyone else looked on in befuddlement. Even Ophelia's raging anger vanished in an instant.

"Do what about what?" Lord Winthrop asked.

"She tried to do me like she did that ghoul."

Constance giggled, and Amarine stifled a laugh. Only Lydia, Lady Knight, and the Eldweavers showed no amusement at the situation.

"She didn't move," Lord Winthrop clarified. He turned to Ophelia, "Did you?"

Ophelia shook her head.

"Perhaps I should have a look at that feather," Lady Nikollette suggested.

Ophelia held it up. "Of course."

Lady Nikollette looked at it just as she had the Clockwork Heart, only longer, with a perplexed expression on her face. She let her looking glass fall but said nothing for a moment before looking to the Eldweavers.

"Its purpose?" Eldweaver Fairwind inquired.

"I'm not certain," Lady Nikollette answered. "I couldn't see anything except for an ordinary feather."

"Ha!" Owen burst out. "I knew it!"

Ophelia turned a wrathful gaze at Owen again. This time, he was quick to strike. Only, nothing met his hand except air.

"How are you doing that?" he demanded.

"I'm not doing anything," Ophelia shot back.

"I see," Lady Nikollette said, drawing curious glances. "Amarine," she continued, "would you be so kind as to take Ophelia into the Neverwas?"

"I suppose that wouldn't be a problem," Amarine replied with a bright smile and sauntered over to Ophelia, locking arms. She asked, "Are you ready?"

Ophelia nodded.

Both she and Amarine took large breaths, and the next moment Amarine vanished. Ophelia could see her in the Neverwas, but she could also still see the others. Like two images laid one over the other. The group in Sominor examined Ophelia with great curiosity, so she could only guess that they could still see her. Amarine did her best to guide Ophelia through the Neverwas, but Ophelia couldn't move. It was as though she had been locked in place, stuck between the two worlds. Eventually, Amarine gave up, letting go of Ophelia and the breath she had been holding.

"Just as I thought," Lady Nikollette announced.

"I don't get it," Ophelia responded.

"Yeah," Amarine joined. "Why couldn't I take her through? I did it before without a problem."

The second the words left her mouth, Amarine clasped her hand over it and looked to the Eldweavers. They did not look pleased.

"We'll discuss that later," Eldweaver Fairwind said. "For now, Lady Nikollette, do you care to explain?"

"Yes," Lady Nikollette answered, "As we all know"—she looked at Ophelia—"or are just finding out, ravens have a natural immunity to magic. They are unaffected by the magic woven by us, as well as the magic woven by talismans, and even any supernatural abilities possessed by neverbeasts. Ophelia, would you mind looking at Owen again?"

She really would rather not. "Okay."

The second she laid eyes on him, her expression soured.

"Owen's talisman, the Eye of Fate, allows him to see moments ahead in time. To divine what intentions rest within actions before they are even acted upon. Lady Knight, keep a hold on your ward. Ophelia, would you imagine all the ways you'd like to repay Owen for the terribly rude behavior he's exhibited toward you?"

"Gladly," Ophelia answered with a mischievous smile.

Owen swiped wildly at the air, even attempting to lunge toward Ophelia, unable to do so beneath his Lady's grip.

"You can stop now." Lady Nikollette's gentle hand tapped Ophelia's shoulder. "The Raven's Feather, it protects its user from magic. Not completely, but enough. Just as Amarine's Neverpaw could not take Ophelia through the Neverwas, Owen's Eye of Fate cannot differentiate between Ophelia's true intent or the intrusive thoughts we all have at any moment of any day."

"So," Barnaby asked with a rather serious look, "if Ophelia were to become injured, could I not heal her?"

"I suspect it might be best to remove the feather from her person first. However, more importantly, I think we should all take a moment to congratulate Ophelia, not only for surviving the trials and defending Spellevue, but for the incredible feat she has accomplished which no one has yet made mention of."

Ophelia had no clue what Lady Nikollette was talking about, and when she looked around the room, it seemed only Eldweaver Finch had an inkling. Lady Nikollette allowed the silence to stew; glances were exchanged with whispered questions.

Lady Nikollette placed a hand on Ophelia's shoulder and looked her in the eye. "I, of course, am talking about the record pace at which Ophelia managed to complete the trials."

More whispers, more glances. Shouting broke through.

"That can't be true," Owen argued. "It can't be possible."

"I'm afraid it is, my dear boy. You see, we hadn't been gone for more than half an hour at most, and our dear Ophelia had been out of the trial for some time, contending with a ghoul."

"She's right," Eldweaver Finch confirmed. "Owen, you would do well to learn humility. You have been bested."

"That's not fair," Owen shouted. "She cheated."

Applause drowned out Owen's protestations, and Amarine embraced Ophelia so tight that she could no longer draw breath.

"You can't cheat the trials," Mordecai argued. "She was just faster than you. Get over it."

"It isn't fair because her head is empty!"

Lady Knight sent a hand across Owen's face without hesitation.

"Mind your tongue," she commanded. "Pettiness is weakness."

A hush fell over the room.

Eldweaver Gideon spoke, "Does anyone else not find it the least bit concerning the talisman she was granted? How can you all ignore such a thing?"

"Eldweaver Gideon," Eldweaver Fairwind interjected, "do not spea—"

"I'll say what I please," Eldweaver Gideon interrupted. "I have earned as much. Since the Endless King, no other has received a raven talisman. Then, Renée returns to bring him back? How could you all be so blind."

"It means nothing, and you should know as much," Eldweaver Finch argued. "Coincidence at most."

"We do not deal in such hollow things as coincidence. You know this as well as I do. The Raven's Feather. The Deadwoods. This is a path I warned we be wary of walking, yet here we tread, heedless."

"Yet you agreed to let her in," Eldweaver Finch calmly added.

"I'm sorry," Ophelia joined in, meager voiced, "I didn't mean to cause any trouble."

"You've caused none." Lady Nikollette looked older to Ophelia. Her age, once artfully hidden in her kind eyes and knowing smile, was revealed all at once in her anger. "Nothing at all."

"I knew it," Owen shouted. "The Daughter of Deadwood, nothing but trouble. Cassian would still be alive if it weren't for you."

"Boy!" Lady Knight shouted.

"I swear," Ophelia said, "I don't want to make anyone upset. I don't even know what you're talking about. Who is the Endless King? Who is Renée?"

Everyone stopped and looked at Lady Nikollette. Some faces puzzled, others upset.

"How could you not tell her?" Lady Knight asked. "Have you so little faith in your wards? Maybe Owen is right. Perhaps Cassian should be the one standing here."

The man in her dreams was right. Ophelia wanted so desperately for him to be lying. What else was Lady Nikollette keeping from her?

"There is time enough to tell her," Lady Nikollette answered, brushing off the accusation masked as a question. She looked at Ophelia. "The past is vast and growing with each day. With the little time I had to prepare you for today, the days gone, I felt, could wait."

"It is not something we need to concern ourselves with now." Eldweaver Fairwind brought the discussion to its end, even if some wished to keep it alive. "We have only the future to look to. The past has been settled. Today is cause for celebration for those who completed the trial and mourning for those who have not. Any concerns to the contrary can be discussed in private."

"Eldweaver Fairwind is right," Eldweaver Finch added.

Eldweaver Gideon marched off. Lady Knight and her wards flipped their coins and vanished.

"Don't listen to them." Amarine smiled as she usually did. "Owen is just jealous that you finished the trials faster than he did, and you basically beat a ghoul by yourself. Not to mention, you've already got more friends than him."

"I'm mostly worried about Eldweaver Gideon. He doesn't seem to like me much."

"Rest assured," Lady Nikollette interjected, "Victor Gideon is a doomsayer. Always has been, always will be. The thing that will likely frustrate you most is that one day, as it goes for all doomsayers, he'll eventually be right about something. But that isn't something you need to worry about now."

"Your lady is right." Lord Wainwright joined the conversation with Constance and Mordecai at his side. "People have always had a way of seeking out meaning in nothing more than circumstance." Lord Wainwright furrowed his brow and deepened his voice, doing his best to impersonate Eldweaver Gideon. "Not a mention of Constance's Clockwork Heart. Since Renée, no other has received a heart-shaped talisman. Then Renée returns to bring him back? How could you all be so blind?"

Eldweaver Finch chimed in. "We'd all do well to pay respects to an Eldweaver, even when they make a fool of themselves."

Ophelia bowed her head. "And Cassian? It's my fault he was in the trials at all."

"No," Lady Nikollette replied. "It was my doing that brought him here."

"No," Eldweaver Finch corrected, "Lady Knight turned down the offer for a third ward. She thought it irresponsible to train someone for the trials in such a short time. Mr. and Mrs. Darrow pushed for this. Cassian made his choice. No one has done anything to cause this. Try, as difficult as it may be, to enjoy your victory. You've more than earned it." Before taking his leave alongside Eldweaver Fairwind, he added, "And all of you, mind your tongues, as you would your surroundings. Both can just as easily bring you peril."

Once the Eldweavers had gone, Magister Irons approached Ophelia. She felt small standing before him.

"For you," he said, extending his hand. His fingers parted to reveal a hexagonal, golden coin in his palm. She took it from him and looked it over. He added, gesturing to the Spellkeepers, "We are indebted to you. We cannot thank you enough."

On one side, the outline of Sominor. On the other, each of the core shapes. A circle at the top edge, a vertical line opposite the circle. A triangle and square to the left, and a hexagon and pentagon to the right. All arranged in a ring around the edge of the coin. It was thick but lighter than she had expected.

"Start small," Constance warned. "Nearly passed out my first time."

Mordecai and Wainwright laughed. Lady Nikollette suppressed her laughter and added, "We'll be taking our carriage home. Plenty of time to learn tomorrow."

"Good plan," Lord Wainwright said with a nod before looking at Ophelia again. "Take care, Ophelia. It was a pleasure meeting you, and I hope our paths cross again soon."

"Likewise," Ophelia responded. She took turns bidding everyone else farewell and took her leave with Lady Nikollette.

PAST, PRESENT, FUTURE

Returning to Deadwood Manor, for Ophelia at least, was a relief. With the trials behind her, she was practically full to bursting with excitement for the many magical things she would surely learn in the days to come, but having already been singled out by Owen and Eldweaver Gideon was far from the ideal start she had hoped for. Despite Amarine's clear joy at Ophelia's addition to the team and her persistent assurances that no one really liked Knight Ridge Manor or Eldweaver Gideon, Ophelia couldn't shake the feeling she had done something wrong. That, just maybe, she didn't belong.

Lingering aches still sat in her head and chest, and though Barnaby had offered to heal them for her, she couldn't bear the thought of causing him pain. It didn't matter to her how fast he could heal; the pain was her burden to bear. She was intent on seeing it through.

"It's fine," she said. "I'll be alright, thank you."

He didn't bring it up again.

Silence was their fifth passenger, at least until they had passed through Evergreen and come up against the Deadwoods.

Amarine said, "I'm sorry, but I can't stand it any longer. Can we just talk about how you nearly single-handedly took down that ghoul?"

"Yeah," Barnaby answered without allowing his gaze to drift away from his window. Ophelia saw a smirk creep into his expression. "I was shocked."

Amarine giggled. "Electrifying, what you did today."

Laughter bubbled. Lady Nikollette added, "Indeed. You *conducted* yourself brilliantly."

The three of them winced.

"No?"

They shook their heads, then burst into laughter. Lady Nikollette chuckled, and added, "All jokes aside. We are all very proud of you, Ophelia."

"Most certainly," Amarine agreed.

"Yes, well done," Barnaby added.

Once the door to the manor was visible, Ophelia could see two people standing there, and she recognized them right away. Remy and Elowen waved to them as they rounded the final curve of the road. The carriage pulled up to the door, stopping next to Remy's wagon. Beside the two sat a large, covered cauldron.

"Have you been waiting long?" Lady Nikollette asked.

"No," Remy replied with a laugh; his belly jiggled and his cheeks glistened in the moonlight. "Just knocked, in fact. This isn't some enchanted door, is it? I haven't summoned you all from some important task, have I?"

"Oh, goodness no." Lady Nikollette walked past him to the front door. She turned the knob and gently pushed it open. "Just an ordinary door, I'm afraid. Come in, won't you?"

"Don't mind if we do." Remy smiled, lifted the iron cauldron with a grunt, and waddled into the manor with Elowen close behind. Ophelia, Amarine, and Barnaby followed.

"And what is that wonderful aroma?" Lady Nikollette asked.

"Stew," Remy shouted, heading toward the kitchen. "I'll let Barnaby tell you what's in it. I'll even let him carry it for me, if he would be so kind."

Barnaby smiled, took the heavy cauldron, and spoke loud enough for everyone to hear him as he walked into the kitchen, "Pheasant, onion, blacktops, salt, pepper, red sage, long-root, wine, and a touch of flicker fizz?"

"Oh, didn't think you'd catch that last one." Remy said, "Most of it cooks out, but I think it adds something subtle to the flavor."

"It really does," Elowen confirmed.

Ophelia followed as everyone took a seat at the kitchen table. Remy lit the fire beneath his cauldron, opened the lid, then gave the mix a stir before putting the lid back on.

"About half an hour, I figure," he said before joining everyone else. He looked right at Ophelia. "Let's hear it then."

"I'm sorry?"

"The trial," he said. "Did you pass?"

"Oh, yes." Ophelia held up her feather.

"With flying colors," Lady Nikollette added.

"She did it faster than anyone ever has," Amarine bragged, wrapping an arm around Ophelia's shoulders. "Then she fought a ghoul! Cast a spell, just like that!" she finished, snapping her fingers.

"Another ghoul?" Elowen asked, shrinking in her seat a little. "Weren't you scared?"

"I was," Ophelia said, "To be honest, I nearly killed myself in the process. Foolish more than anything."

"Nonsense!" Amarine declared. "She's being modest. Why, I don't think I wove my first bit of magic until a whole month after passing my trials."

Ophelia's face turned pink, and she lowered her head slightly.

"Say, Ophelia," Elowen cut into Amarine's shower of praise, changing the subject much to Ophelia's delight, "I wondered if you were interested in playing 'Don't Feed the Beast'? I was hoping we could all play. I brought it with me."

Elowen pulled a small box from the satchel that was still hung over her shoulder. It looked to be carved with the face of a monster, and she placed it on the table as Remy shifted excitedly in his seat.

"Oh," Ophelia answered, "I suppose so."

"My favorite," Remy answered excitedly before Elowen could. "I imagine we could squeeze in a few rounds before dinner's ready."

"I haven't played since I was a girl," Lady Nikollette added with a distant gaze before shaking free the memory she'd fallen into, "but that was with magic, though I can't imagine it's much different with cards."

"It's the exact same," Amarine confirmed; her smile beamed at Ophelia. "You'll love it."

"I'll try, but I can't imagine I'll be very good." Ophelia shrugged.

"No skill required," Barnaby explained. "Just luck. Not my favorite type of game, but it is a fun one."

"How do I play?"

Elowen quickly explained the game. It was simple enough for Ophelia to easily follow. They played three quick games while they waited for the stew to come to a boil, Remy stirring the cauldron between rounds. Barnaby won the first game, Ophelia the second, and Remy the third. The kitchen was filled with shouts and jeers as sheep changed hands with each roll of the dice. When the stew was ready and dished out in bowls, a satisfied silence washed over the kitchen. Ophelia was hungrier than she realized, and the stew was better than she could have hoped. She wasn't sure if it was just the hunger, but this stew was even better than Mondo's. She said as much, without even thinking.

"Don't tell Mondo," Amarine shot back immediately. Stew spilled from her mouth as the words escaped. The room roared with laughter.

"Don't talk with your mouth full, Amarine," Lady Nikollette reminded with a smile. "It's unbecoming."

When dinner was finished, Ophelia played more "Don't Feed the Beast" with everyone except for Lady Nikollette and Remy. They took their leave to the living room to talk. The rest of the evening was filled with laughter in one room and warm conversation in the other. Ophelia thought it pleasantly peculiar how a strange place could feel like home in such a short amount of time. She knew that it was the people in the place to blame for such a magic.

When the evening reached its inevitable end, Ophelia found herself wishing it could carry on into the morning, and further still. To be caught endlessly in the feeling of warmth and welcome, in joy and laughter. With her belly full of delicious stew and her mind content to forget everything that she ever once worried about, Ophelia bid Elowen and Remy a restful night and a pleasant tomorrow.

Lady Nikollette asked Amarine and Barnaby if they would be so kind as to clean up the kitchen and asked Ophelia to meet her in her study. When Ophelia asked if she should be helping with the kitchen, Lady Nikollette assured her the others could manage one night without her. A point to which both Amarine and Barnaby agreed. Lady Nikollette disappeared, and Ophelia stuck around with Amarine and Barnaby for a few moments longer. They shared knowing looks, stifled laughter, and excited hopes for the days that lay ahead.

When Ophelia entered, Lady Nikollette was seated at her desk with the Timeless Tome in front of her. With an exchange of soft smiles, Ophelia sat in the seat across from Lady Nikollette.

"Big day," Lady Nikollette offered.

"Quite," Ophelia replied.

"How does it feel to hold the record for the fastest time to complete the trials?"

"I'm not sure. I don't think it really feels like anything. I was just so happy to have come out at all, and with a talisman no less."

Lady Nikollette nodded.

"Yes, that is certainly the attitude of a weaver with a bright future.

The time to complete a thing is not so important when measured against the outcome, and all that follows."

"How long did it take you?"

"It took me no less than eight hours, if you believe that."

"I don't," Ophelia said with a laugh, shaking her head. "Not for one second."

"Well, it's true. And I trust you won't go telling Amarine. If she knows, everyone is apt to find out."

They shared another laugh that rolled to a stop.

"Might I have a look at your talisman?"

Ophelia hurriedly pulled it from her pocket and held it out. Lady Nikollette took it, then picked up a strand of leather from her desk. She wrapped it around the shaft, then slid beads down and over it.

"Lead, though soft and easily scratched, is quite unmoving in it's resolve." The bead was a dull gray and rough with wear. The next bead was a grayish white; it held a shine to it. "Silver, valuable and pure, cunning and elegant." The final bead was a shimmering yellow. "Lastly, gold."

Lady Nikollette said nothing more but tied the leather strap at the end of the feather then the end of itself. She held out the Raven Feather necklace, dangling from her fingers.

Ophelia took it and slipped it over her head. It had a new feel to it, a weight, and she ran her fingers over the beads before asking, "What's the gold for?"

Lady Nikollette smiled. "Because it suits you."

Ophelia smiled back.

"Speaking of suiting you, this Timeless Tome." Lady Nikollette ran her hands over the cover.

"Yes, I held it in my tria—"

Lady Nikollette put her hand up suddenly. "You mustn't share your trials with another. It is yours alone and might reveal something to be used against you by another."

"I trust you though."

"It isn't a matter of trust when magic is in play. What I wanted to talk to you about was my talisman."

"The Looking Glass?"

"No." Lady Nikollette touched it with her hand. "This was my father's. Mine now, but not mine per se." She placed both hands on the Timeless Tome and slid it toward Ophelia. "This was my talisman. As promised, I'm now giving it to you."

"I…" Ophelia couldn't find the words.

"Don't look surprised. I told you I would give it to you when you passed the trials. You have, so I am."

"I didn't know it was your talisman, though. I can't take it from you."

"You aren't taking it; I'm giving it and you are receiving it. Now, let's see if you can't summon the quill."

"Right now?"

"Yes, go on. Take your time. Imagine it, then make it so."

Ophelia straightened her posture and inched closer to the desk. Her hand hovered over the cover, and she closed her eyes. Breath came rolling in and out of her lungs, easing the nervous beat of her heart. At first, she felt nothing at all, and as time crawled forward, her nerves crept back through her.

A deep breath.

The trials.

Haunting memories came trickling in. The forest, the figure, the ghoul.

The ghoul.

She fixed her mind to the ghoul. Ophelia let its memory chase her through the corners of her mind. Her breath quickened, as did her heart. She needed to stop it. She needed help. She needed to do something.

"Excellent." Lady Nikollette's intrusive voice startled her free from the memories. When she opened her eyes, in her hand was the quill. "I knew you could do it."

Ophelia took in a breath and let out a sigh. "But it took so long. How do you do it so quickly?"

"As anyone does anything well," she replied, matter-of-factly. "With practice."

When Ophelia released the quill, it drifted back into the book's cover, nothing more than an embossed symbol among embossed symbols.

"Use it well. As a talisman, it will allow you to weave without expending hardly any will at all. It's not as fast as other talismans, but it is quite versatile. Now that we've gotten that out of the way, you have questions that are in dire need of answers, haven't you?"

"I do."

"Yes, I could see it painted across your face the whole ride back. Ask them."

"What is wrong with a raven talisman? What is wrong with my having come from the Deadwoods? What is wrong with me?"

"Oh, dear." Nikollette's eyes softened with sympathy. "Nothing is wrong with you. I need you to hear that and, more importantly, know it. Understood?"

Ophelia nodded, uncertain of her answer.

"As for the Deadwoods and the raven talisman, it is not a story I like to tell, but you deserve to know why uncertain eyes have fallen upon you."

Lady Nikollette leaned back and began to speak. "The Endless King wasn't always the Endless King. Before that, he was named Marcel. Marcel A'Mysteriouse. My uncle's talisman was the Raven's Crown. It was made of raven's bones, with a skull at its center. It allowed him to shape-shift into the form of a raven. Bigger than this manor, in fact. He would even take me for flights on his back."

Nikollette swallowed as though something had caught itself in her throat. She cleared it, tears forming in her eyes. "When my aunt died, my uncle lost himself. No one knew exactly what he'd done, but in his desperation he toyed with magic unknown.

"It consumed him and spit out the Endless King, who'd brought with him his dead wife. A creature neither dead nor alive, nor undead for that matter. Unalive, perhaps? He walked Sominor in a quest, he claimed, to end death. He turned soul after soul into what he had become. Unkillable. While the Endless living still retained themselves beneath their affliction, the Endless dead were nothing more than mindless monsters."

Lady Nikollette paused to wipe the tears from her cheeks.

"Are you okay?" Ophelia asked.

"I'm fine; I just need a moment." She took a deep breath, then continued. "There was a war, and it wiped nearly every kingdom from this land. It ended outside of Stillriver. My father struck the final blow, and once the Endless King had fallen, his horde fell as easily as any man. Still, we came to find, he was not dead.

"Behind the door, where you found the ghoul, lies the slumbering heart of the Endless King. Locked away forever. The whole of Sominor could crumble into the endless ocean, and that vault would remain. Its contents, safe.

"While you were in the trials, we were summoned to face a threat. A Spellweaver by the name of Reneé Roché. She was desperately in love with my uncle. Where we all decided to fight the Endless King, she sought to heal him. In the end, she was turned as well. Unknown to anyone, it seems she's been working to wake him from his slumber all these years. To finish what he'd begun. Now she lies dead, beneath a mountain, from her own doing.

"So, when wary eyes gaze upon you, know it is not you they are wary of, but rather their own fears. If *you* know what you are, or who you are, then it shouldn't matter what another being is or believes themselves to be; let alone, what they believe you to be. Do not let them lead you to question who you are. You are more than the sum of their fears. You are Ophelia, you are a Spellweaver, and you are adored."

By the time she had finished speaking, Lady Nikollette's eyes were red with tears, and Ophelia fared little better.

"Did you have any more questions?"

Ophelia didn't. Well, she did, but wasn't sure what they were just yet. Instead, she asked simply, "Why didn't you tell me your uncle was the Endless King? I wouldn't have thought any less of you."

Lady Nikollette slid a drawer on her desk open and pulled out a framed portrait; much smaller than the others hanging in the halls. For a moment she looked at it with a forlorn smile, then turned it around for Ophelia to see.

His silver eyes were unmistakable.

"I didn't tell you because my uncle *wasn't* the Endless King, as much as the lords, and ladies, and Eldweavers might like to claim. My Uncle *is* the Endless King. He was a great and talented man whose capacity for spell weaving was matched only by the deep love he had for those around him. It was grief that divided him, only to weave the darkest parts of his humanity into the darkest magics he could conjure. With a single choice, my uncle ceased being who he once was and became something else entirely."

"I think I understand." Ophelia wiped her tears. "I'm sorry all the same."

"Thank you, but it is not necessary." Lady Nikollette's voice turned upward. "As my father always said, 'What is, is meant to be. What isn't, never was. What was, has had its time and met its end.' It is in that I encourage you to look forward, just as I do, and make yourself ready for everything you've yet to face. Between you, Amarine, and Barnaby, I'm certain there is no challenge you cannot overcome."

"Can I tell you something?" Ophelia asked sheepishly.

"Anything," Lady Nikollette replied.

"I've seen your uncle before," Ophelia said. Lady Nikollette's kind smile melted, and a worried look took its place.

"Where?" Lady Nikollette asked. Her voice meek and trembling. Slowly, she put the portrait back in the drawer of her desk. Ophelia sensed that Lady Nikollette was holding back a great many strong feelings.

"I met him in my dreams."

"And what did he say to you?"

"He said you would keep things from me. That he would never lie." She looked down at her hands, ashamed for having kept it, adding, "He said I was familiar. He said that they would hate me. He said that death was near." Ophelia looked back up at Lady Nikollette, "Did I know him? Am I going to die?"

"He is right," Lady Nikollette said. An admission that brought fresh tears from Ophelia, "He doesn't lie, but an opinion isn't a lie to the person voicing it. I do keep things to myself. Many things. I keep them because they are a burden, or because they haven't found the right moment to be shared. You know me very little, but I appreciate the trust you've lent me, and the others. Please know that I will never betray that trust, even if I do keep things to myself. That being said, should you ever ask, I will answer and keep nothing from you."

Ophelia nodded, wiping the tears away.

"And never forget," Lady Nikollette smiled, "You are nothing like him, so he couldn't possibly know you."

Lady Nikollette stood up and walked around her desk. She stood in front of Ophelia and held out a hand.

"I hope you can trust me, because I trust you. I trust you all to do what is right over what is easy. If, for you, that means walking away, then know that I'll always be here should you wish to find me again."

"Okay," Ophelia nodded again, as she took Lady Nikollette's hand. She stood and looked her in the eyes, adding, "I trust you."

"Good. Now, dear girl, go get some rest. Your training starts tomorrow, and you've plenty to learn."

"Okay," Ophelia answered, the light back in her eyes and excitement pulsing through her body. "I'll be ready."

She left, book in hand and feather hanging from her neck, wondering how she could be expected to sleep knowing magic awaited her when the sun next rose.

THE WHISPERS OF SALVATION

At the heart of Sominor, deep within the slumbering corners of Spellevue, tucked away among the shadow and silence, whispered voices conspired. Just two. They spoke of plans failed and plans to be laid. They spoke of their Endless King and his endless slumber.

"I told him the ghoul would not be able to penetrate the door. They're simply not strong enough."

"Yes, but anything larger would not have been able to slip into Spellevue undetected. Even still, nothing could break that seal."

"I'm beginning to wonder if our King knows what he is doing. We warned him, yet he insisted."

"And now everyone is aware that he is working to return. To finish saving Sominor."

"They will resist."

"They always have. Just as we once did."

"Supposing he wanted them to know?"

"Perhaps, but what good is that?"

"We can't know until we speak with him again."

"When we do, we must remind him, three Eldweavers are needed to open that door."

"I have to believe he already knows this, and I'm worried he is keeping something from us."

"He has slept for too long. Perhaps he has forgotten the world he's left behind. Perhaps he's unaware of how much the world has changed."

"If he was, he can be no longer. He saw us all at Roché Manor. Hopefully enough to show him what opposition we now face."

"Yes, this was never easy, but each passing year makes the task all the more difficult."

"Perhaps we can recruit others."

"But who?"

"The Darrows, in Duskwatch. I'm sure they would do anything to get their Cassian back. I'm told the DeLeons employ a sleepwalker, who might be of some use."

"And what of the girl?"

"What of her?"

"The feather, the Deadwoods. Surely there is meaning there yet to be divined."

"Yes, we should keep close watch over her."

"Over all of Deadwood Manor."

"One by one, they'll line up to thank him for his gift."

"One by one."

The empty halls fell silent once more, and the voices slipped back into the shadows from which they'd come seeping. Spellevue, and all its inhabitants, slept peacefully that night, blissfully unaware of the blight festering within.

Preview Chapter from

OPHELIA RAVENWARD
THE TASTE OF TEARS

Allen Isom

FOR YOUR LOSS

All three of the Eldweavers traveled to Duskwatch together. The task set before them was one of tremendous regret. Though Illana Fairwind knew that what the trials had decided was for the best, that knowledge did nothing to ease her sadness. This had only been the second loss that had come from the trials and, though she felt in her gut Cassian had not possessed the character to become a Spellweaver, she never would have guessed they would lose him entirely. That pain was only magnified by the grieving parents that stood before her. How she wished to cry with his mother, to show the depth of her condolences, but tears were a thing Illana found difficult to come by. They always had been.

For Mrs. Darrow, they were found in abundance.

"What use is all your magic if you couldn't even keep my son safe in your own tower?" The fire in Mrs. Darrow's words was as searing as the very flames Illana commanded.

"It is a risk all take knowingly when accepting the weight of the trials," Eldweaver Finch responded, leaving little room for anyone else to chime in. Illana was grateful.

"Knowingly?" Mrs. Darrow's voice faltered, cracking under the weight of her despair, then caught itself in a screaming anger. "A child! He was Fifteen! You have no place asking a child to risk their life! None!"

When Mrs. Darrow lunged at Diedrich, her fists balled up and ready to strike, Mr. Darrow, stone-faced in his contempt, held her back before she could take a step. Likely, Illana thought, knowing his wife's next move even before she did.

"Let go of me," she hollered, her defiance breaking down into sobbing tears. "They killed my baby. Our son is dead. You stand there silent, and our son is dead." She turned to him, letting her fists finish what they had set out to do on his barrel of a chest. "You do nothing, and our son is dead."

It broke Illana's heart to watch, to hear spoken the guilt she had felt the moment it had become evident Cassian would not be coming out of the trials.

Mr. Darrow let his wife pound away on him, each desperate strike weaker than the one before it. When Mrs. Darrow had exhausted herself, Mr. Darrow just held her, her cries muffled by the thick of his fur-lined coat.

"I will handle this," he whispered to his wife, his words nearly too faint to hear. "Go, lay down. Our son's death will be answered for. I promise."

Not a single Eldweaver spoke a word as Mrs. Darrow gave the three of them a hateful glare before going back inside. Once she had slammed shut the door, Illana expected Mr. Darrow to speak, but he did not. The four of them stood in silence with Mr. Darrow's gaze never leaving Diedrich's. The distant sound of guards marching and training and whispers of the ocean breeze floated among them. If ever there were a song for Duskwatch, this would be its melody.

Victor, to Illana's surprise, was the first to open his mouth. Mr. Darrow turned his attention to Victor before a single sound could escape.

"One question," Mr. Darrow said, his voice hard and cold. "Can you save my son?"

"I'm afraid that is impossible," Victor responded.

"Then spare me," Mr. Darrow said before turning to go back into his manor.

"One last thing," Illana said, producing a glass orb no larger than an apple, inside of which a swirling glow of white and gray mist danced. "Take this beacon. Same as the DeLeons have. Should ever you or Mrs. Darrow find yourselves in need, simply break it and Spellevue will be at your service. It is the least we can offer."

Mr. Darrow froze for a moment, then turned back to face Illana. He approached her cooly and plucked the beacon from her hand. He turned it over, pondering the strange orb for a moment.

"The least," he said before looking up at each of the Eldweavers. "Could you not be bothered to offer the most? May as well be nothing."

He dropped the beacon, letting it shatter on the gray stone porch upon which they stood. Mondo appeared a long, silent minute later.

"What seems to be the trouble? Should I retrieve the other Spellweavers?" He was, as always, reservedly eager and dutifully willing to help.

"No," Illana replied. "It's nothing. If there are no objections, I believe we are done here and our presence is no longer required."

Mr. Darrow said nothing. Victor huffed before flipping his coin and vanishing.

"Sorry for your loss," Diedrich said with a bow before vanishing as well. Mondo followed close behind.

"I can't begin to imagine the depth of your loss. However, beacon or not, Spellevue is willing to do whatever is within our power, should you need us." Illana offered.

In their final stare, Illana saw a tear escape Mr. Darrow's hardened expression.

Her heart broke again as she flipped her coin.

Mr. Darrow retreated into his manor. Inside, his wife stood beside the coat rack, crying, their son's favorite coat clenched in her fists. Between sobs, she drew in deep breaths of what smell might still linger within its well-worn fibers. He approached slowly and placed a comforting hand on her back. The moment his large hand touched her, she pulled her face away from the coat and stared off into a distant memory.

"I know it's been months since he last wore it. Like him, the cold season has passed." Her words trembled. "But I can still smell him. I can remember when I purchased this coat for him. It was to be his first-day training with the Duskwatch guard. He was so excited. He looked so grown up. I could tell he was going to be as big and as strong as you."

"Bigger and stronger, I imagined," Mr. Darrow added.

Mrs. Darrow turned to face him. "One winter. One winter is all he'd worn it for. What I wouldn't give to see him wear it for one winter more."

Mr. Darrow wrapped his arms around her and spoke softly. "Could I do that for you, I'd move mountains." He added after a short pause, a forlorn smile on his face, "But we both know he would have been too big for that coat in a year's time."

A hollow laughter escaped their trembling lips. Laughter turned to tears. As they wept, Mr. Darrow lifted Cassian's coat from the rack and wrapped it around his wife. The taste of salt and the scent of love held them both as the world around them moved along as if nothing of value had been lost.

ABOUT THE AUTHOR

I hate writing these things. I guess I could just copy and paste from other books, but that feels lazy. Also, I don't really like "selling" myself as an author. So, it took me a good while to figure out what to put at the end of this book. I don't want it to be too short, nor do I want it to drag on and on and on and on. Then it hit me! I have six of these books! I can write a nice story about myself across the entire series! A mini biography of sorts. Here we go.

It all started when I was a kid (I think). The first two movies I remember loving were The Labyrinth and Ghostbusters. When I was a bit older, I would sneak downstairs to watch horror movies while everyone was asleep. The first such movie I can remember was Hellraiser. That was a bit more than I bargained for…